Ian Watson was born i[...]
English at Balliol Colle[...]
fiction stories were stim[...]
lecturer in Japan. In 19[...]
short story, was publish[...]
since then his stories hav[...]
and anthologies. They h[...]
form in five collections, *The Very Slow Time Machi[...]
Sunstroke*, *Slow Birds*, *Evil Water* and *Salvage Rites*.

Ian Watson's first novel, *The Embedding*, was publis[...]
in 1973 and received enormous critical acclaim. His
second novel, *The Jonah Kit*, became a British Science
Fiction Award winner as well as confirming his position in
the front rank of contemporary writers. He has been
features editor of the journal *Foundation* since 1975 and
a full-time writer since 1976. His most recent novels
include *The Book of the River* (1984), *Queenmagic,
Kingmagic* (1986) and *Whores of Babylon* (1988).

By the same author

IAN WATSON

The Fire Worm

GRAFTON BOOKS
A Division of the Collins Publishing Group

LONDON GLASGOW
TORONTO SYDNEY AUCKLAND

Grafton Books
A Division of the Collins Publishing Group
8 Grafton Street, London W1X 3LA

Published by Grafton Books 1990

First published in Great Britain by
Victor Gollancz Ltd 1988

Copyright © Ian Watson 1988

Jingling Geordie's Hole first appeared
in *Interzone* © Ian Watson 1986

ISBN 0-586-20763-5

Printed and bound in Great Britain by
Collins, Glasgow

Set in Times

Whisht! lads, haad yor gobs,
An' Aa'll tell ye aall an aaful story,
Whisht! lads, haad yor gobs,
An' Aa'll tell ye 'boot the worm.

1

I kept a careful eye on Tony Smith while he read through the pages which Jack, my other half, had typed. Sometimes Tony shivered, sometimes he looked sick.

Jack had entitled the account *Jingling Geordie's Hole*, but I'd been careful not to let him add anything else. Here was the story which Tony had spoken into the cassette recorder under hypnosis the week before: the narrative of his previous life.

Tony's real name wasn't Smith, by the way. Surname concealed for the sake of confidentiality. And I too had more than one identity.

On the one hand I was John Cunningham, psychiatrist, specializing in what is known as 'past-life ·therapy' or 'reincarnation therapy'. My other persona was Jack Cannon, author of horror novels, my secret pseudonym.

Until I met Tony, I had always kept my two identities quite separate. This wasn't difficult. Patients being treated by past-life therapy didn't – oughtn't to – produce horror motifs. They drew up the brain's warehouse of memory (of cinema, TV, or books long forgotten by the conscious mind) to invent another life in the remote or recent past. This previous life would expose and explore the problems of their real life now. Thus they were into 'historical' fiction, not horror.

Let's let Jack interview me . . .

JACK: 'So how does PLT work? This Past-Life Therapy of yours?'

JOHN: 'A psychological blockage brings a patient to my

consulting room. An anguish, a pattern of failure. So then – '

JACK: 'You hypnotize him or her, and tell them they can remember a previous life.'

JOHN: 'Right. So they experience a previous epoch. They're convinced they lived then. They populate it with characters symbolizing the people they've known in reality. They fill it with events representing the suppressed traumas of their actual life, so that these can at last be confronted and overcome.'

JACK: 'Yet so far as you're concerned, it's all invention on their part. You don't believe in reincarnation, do you? How can you honestly practise PLT?'

JOHN: 'While I'm engaged in therapy, perhaps I believe – in the sense that a novelist believes in what he's writing while he's busy writing it.'

JACK: 'You don't help them make up their story?'

JOHN: 'Oh no. Their own creativity wells up from within. The past lives they recount are often the greatest exercise of artistic creation during their whole lifetime. Sometimes the only such exercise. That's why this form of therapy is usually so positive and life-enhancing, even if the subject matter consists of misery and tragedy. It's like dreaming aloud, in a lucid way. My rôle is to offer a stage for this, using hypnosis. Then I help them interpret their past life.'

JACK: 'Without blowing the gaff. You leave them believing in reincarnation.'

JOHN: 'Well, I'd have to, wouldn't I? I'd like to emphasize that PLT often works dramatically well in cases where orthodox psychiatry has failed. Ultimately any type of analysis is a fiction, you see. It's one possible construction out of many. Freudianism might be ideal to repair the damaged psyche of patient A. It's no use for patient B, who has different problems. The Jungian approach might be fine for B; or useless. No school of therapy has a

8

monopoly on the truth. Consequently: *if it works, use it*. Suppose Freudian or Jungian or Adlerian analysis has led to a big brick wall, then roll on PLT.'

JACK: 'But you still programme your patients with a new belief system: reincarnation, multiple lives.'

JOHN: 'It rarely comes as a shock, let me tell you. Deep down, most people believe they're immortal in one way or another. When apparently compelling evidence bubbles from their lips, this doesn't so much astonish – as provide a sense of recognition. I'm merely channelling immortal yearnings down one particular route.'

JACK: 'Which you choose for others, but reject for yourself.'

JOHN: 'If a person's been drifting in limbo, perhaps it's no bad thing to gain a belief system. People don't really function effectively without some belief system or other to organize their lives. *My* system has one great advantage over other faiths. Born-again Christianity, Marxism, whatever. Mine doesn't include any set of dogmas. Its only creed is *karma*, the notion that your actions in life have consequences and shape your psyche – with which no one can argue. This can only promote a sense of responsibility, for yourself and for other people.'

JACK: 'Thank you, Dr Cunningham. Witness may step down.'

JOHN: 'So may you, Jack. So may you.'

Tony was thirty years old, with wavy sandy hair on which he obviously lavished care and style. That was his good feature. Despite a smart turn-out – well-cut light-grey suit, striped blue shirt with fawn suede tie, and yuppie grey trainers – he still looked awkwardly, batteredly adolescent, with a pinched, spotty, bruise-eyed face. That's how Jack would describe him in a story.

As I'd expected, he was taking a fair while to read through all those pages . . .

9

2

or *Jingling Geordie's Hole*, begun

On the cinema screen: a grey atoll in grey south seas. A bulb of light expanded suddenly; boiling cloud rushed skywards. Within moments the screen rocked at the impact of an implacable, blasting hurricane.

'This is the first moment of the thermonuclear age!' said the newsreel announcer, proud and cheerful as ever.

Ted Appleby felt such a thrill rush through his whole body at the power unleashed. The eleven-year-old paid scant attention to the rest of the newsreel: the Queen touring her Commonwealth, the French Foreign Legion losing a battle in some country called Indo-China, British troops successfully rounding up Mau Mau suspects in Kenya, a woman athlete running round a cinder track. The therm-o-nuclear explosion continued to boil through Ted, seeking outlet, expression.

Curtains slid across the front of the proscenium, luxuriously hung in tiers of pleats, spotlit in pink and orange and green. The main Art Deco lights came on, illuminating Egyptian-style papyrus columns and friezes. A recording of Mantovani's string orchestra playing *Charmaine* began. Ted tagged on to the crowd of children stampeding from their seats, squeezing through the foyer to erupt down mock-marble steps into the bright breezy salty June daylight.

He'd come to the cartoon matinée on his own. As half-expected, Gavin was waiting some way down the street pretending to look in a newsagent's window. Gavin wouldn't wish other boys, who might be from the same

10

school, to see them meet; so Ted loitered, to let the mob clear away.

It was thus with all the older boy's interceptions of Ted; Gavin wanted the two of them to talk alone, to walk alone. Gavin Percy was sixteen. A fortnight earlier a couple of other sixteen-year-olds had surprised Gavin chatting to Ted at a time when Gavin thought they were safe. The older boys had started kidding on. 'Got a big sister, then, titch?' Ted had, as it happened: Helen. He nodded. So far as he knew, Gavin had never even set eyes on her. 'Percy's after her – watch out!' Gavin had flushed with embarrassment. 'He must be, mustn't he?' Ted had agreed with the tormentors. Gavin had looked relieved at Ted's comprehension, at this evidence of his young friend's complicity.

A lot of smut was talked about girls at that school, a day school for boys only. Lately Ted had been growing ignorantly interested in girls; obviously his own sister didn't count as an example, though the mysteries of her life would be regarded as fair game by any other boys. Bill Gibbon related that his older brother Brian and chums would go to a chum's house when the parents were out at the cinema and would undress a sister and pour ink over her then bath her clean *thoroughly*. They would stick a carrot up her then make white stuff into the dirty bathwater where she lay. Later, after they'd dried her down *thoroughly*, Gibbon said that they tied a lump of carrot to a string, put this up her to stop her having a baby then stuck their cocks into her. When Ted told Gavin about this game, Gavin had looked offended – resentful at his friend having such things in his mind.

In Ted's classroom ball-fights were the rage among half a dozen of the boys, chiefly Gibbon who once exposed his cock in class under cover of his desk. Ted steered well clear of ball-fights which seemed excruciating. Two fighters would square off, each with one hand cupping trouser-clad balls, then would dart at each other to claw the other's defences aside and squeeze his knackers. Howls of pain went up from the loser.

'Hullo,' Ted said to Gavin.

The newsagent's window display consisted of a row of sun-faded paperback westerns and war stories, a line of pens and pencils, and a box covered with red crêpe paper. On that box stood a glass of water and a yellow plastic ostrich a few inches high. The ostrich slowly dipped its beak into the water, raised its head, dipped it, raised it.

'I wonder how that works?' mused Gavin. 'Perpetual motion is scientifically impossible. Something to do with water and sunshine, I suppose.'

Ted stared in trembling fascination. The novelty ostrich reminded him . . . of the crane on the pier!

From where they stood he couldn't quite see the pier. The clock tower at the bottom of the street was in the way, as was part of the miniature Gibraltar behind which housed the Castle, a small base, and the ruins of the Priory. Turn right at the clock tower and descend the steep road alongside the grass slopes of the Castle moat, and into view would come the great north pier of granite blocks, high whitewashed lighthouse at its seaward end.

The massive wheeled crane rested on several sets of rust-bobbled rails running along the mid-section of the pier, high and low. Anyone walking out to the lighthouse had to pass underneath its looming, girdered bridge then along beneath its hundred-foot jib. These days the crane never rolled to and fro nor swung its jib out over the sea. Why had it ever done so in the past? To unload boats tying up formerly at the lower stone quayside, safely clear of the Black Midden rocks?

Many steel hawsers as thick as a boy's arm tethered the crane to iron rings in the pier walls; at these points the granite was streaked orange with salt-water rust. The crane had to be chained like some mechanical Samson or winter storms could smash it into the bay. Wild waves sometimes broke clear over the top of the crane, even over the top of the lighthouse. But perhaps the machine couldn't move, ever again; perhaps it was rusted in place. Ted sincerely hoped that this was so, but scarcely dared believe it. Whenever his parents had taken him and Helen for a walk along to the lighthouse of a sunny Sunday afternoon, the passage under crane and jib was fraught with terror. He was sure that the crane's many wheels might creak into life, and start rolling, that the jib would duck down, dangling chains like octopus arms, to snatch him, crush him. He'd endured several nightmares about that iron giant which brooded over the pathway out to sea.

He imagined a therm-o-nuclear explosion hurling that metal monster into the bay where river met sea-tide, drowning it safely, though bits might still protrude.

Ted's Dad had told him that a tunnel ran all the way along inside the pier; that's why there were those opaque green glass slabs set periodically in the concrete path. But how, even in a dream, did you get inside the tunnel which would protect you from the crane?

The ostrich ducked its head into the glass of water, rose erect, ducked, arose, hypnotically.

'I just saw the H-bomb test,' Ted told Gavin and imitated the rush of a hurricane, as he imagined it.

'Oh,' said Gavin. 'Are you walking home or catching the bus?'

Buses departed from beside the clock tower. A crowd from the matinée horsed around the bus stop; a mêlée. Ted knew that Gavin wouldn't want to mingle with that.

13

'May as well walk and save the fare,' said Ted.

So they strolled away together from the hidden sea, past a closed fish and chip shop with amber Tizer bottles lining the window, past a barber's dustily advertising Durex sheaths, a gaunt Congregational church, a small shrubby park with floral clock. Then came a dingy pub, The Dolphin, smelling of stale beer, with a blue star mounted outside on a bracket; next to a grocer's and a greengrocer's. The plate glass reflected Ted and Gavin both dressed in dark blue blazers with crimson badges framing three black anchors, both wearing grey flannel trousers, in Ted's case short ones – but he'd been promised long ones when his next birthday came around. Both with close-cropped haircuts: Ted's hair chestnut, Gavin's gingery. Gavin was slightly plump; Ted was slim. Gavin's face was freckled; Ted had the complexion of an angel, so his mother said embarrassingly. She used to say cherub, which was worse.

They entered the wrought-iron and dirty glass cavern of the small railway station and climbed the wooden bridge over the rails, pausing at the summit to watch an electric train pull in below. Gavin produced a red-bound school book from his blazer pocket and showed it: *Edward the Second* by Marlowe.

'We've started reading this for the exams.'

'A play.' Ted regarded the volume with mild disgust.

'It's exciting. It's the best play I've ever read. Part of it happens right here – down by the Castle. Edward's best friend sailed from France and landed here to meet the king.'

France seemed a great distance from this northern port. Such a voyage – in an ancient sailing tub – made very little sense. If the king's friend had been coming from Norway, that would have been a different kettle of fish. But then, old plays often didn't make sense either.

14

'All sorts of things happen. Do you want to know how the king gets killed? He's in a dungeon up to his ankles in filthy water. They bring in a table, hold him down with a mattress – then they jab a red-hot cooking rod up his bottom.'

'That must hurt.' Ted felt sick. Another image had arrived to join the crane in nightmare land, one which he knew his mind would dwell on.

'Maybe we could read a bit of it together, another week? Act it out? It's terribly good.'

'Yes,' said Ted.

They descended the far flight of steps and headed through streets of houses, each with a tiny walled front flower garden, most with stained-glass panes above the doors. From a number of chimneys identical aerials rose in the form of a large capital 'H'. Those homes, unlike Ted's or Gavin's, boasted television sets. The 'H' reminded Ted of H-bomb.

'Pow!' he exclaimed, and made a noise like rolling thunder.

Beyond those streets was a large, tree-dark park with bowling green and pet cemetery as prelude, and a soot-blackened institution set within iron railings as finale. The old workhouse, from Victorian times, was still tenanted by aged paupers, mostly ailing. Some of the residents were sitting on park benches, passively. A few stood watching the bowling, over a low hedge. The players – more prosperous pensioners in white Panama hats and club blazers – ignored their derelict audience of shabby overcoats.

Ted wondered whether any work was performed in the grim building known as the workhouse. He imagined old women knitting sweaters for sale to Norwegian sailors, old men whittling wooden boats, or maybe sewing mail-bags. He'd heard that husbands and wives were kept separate inside, spent the nights in separate phlegm-racked dormitories. Only when they were let out could a married couple meet.

Presently Ted and Gavin came abreast of a hunched figure in greatcoat and cloth cap shuffling slowly along. This Methuselah with rheumy red eyes held a huge vile handkerchief at chest level to catch a constant string of grey gluey drool proceeding from lips or nostrils; Ted couldn't bear to look more closely. He had passed this fellow on other occasions and presumed that he and his like were the reason why this park, which dropped away steeply to the south down a leafy ravine with cascading stream in the direction of the fish quay, was known as Spittal Dene. On account of the sputum.

Soon they were in sight, over treetops, of the roofs along the river bank: those of ships' chandlers which supplied the trawlers, of wholesale fish merchants, the smelly guano works which manufactured fertilizer from tons of imported bird droppings, the Jungle Arms public house ill-famed for Saturday night fights, and Hood Haggie's rope factory, staffed mostly by notorious women.

Gavin also was staring at the roof of the rope factory. He licked his lips.

'Do you know what Brian Gibbon in my class heard happened at Hood Haggie's last month? There was a new supervisor on the job – a young chap. The women pulled his trousers down and fitted an empty milk bottle over his cock. Then they pulled their skirts up over their waists to excite him.' Gavin was sweating, nauseated and excited. 'His cock swelled up stiff inside the milk bottle, and wouldn't go down again. He had to go to hospital in a van

16

to get the bottle off. You know about cocks swelling up, do you?'

Ted nodded.

'Does yours, sometimes?' Gavin asked.

At this very moment it was trying to, and Ted walked on awkwardly. Just the other evening, in his room, he had drawn a naked woman on a sheet of paper torn from an exercise book. A woman with breasts and a smooth sweep of flesh between her legs, like a flap glued down. Soon he had ripped the drawing into tiny pieces and flushed them down the lavatory in case his mother discovered. Some scraps had floated; he had to flush the pan again and again.

'I haven't told my Mam, but I've got hairs growing on me down here,' he said to Gavin.

'Have you? That's *natural*.' Somehow Gavin looked as though he deplored this development. 'So have I,' the older boy added after a while. 'They're called the short and curlies.'

The sky had been clouding over. A hooter sounded from the river, just as an air-raid siren might sound.

A thought occurred to Ted. 'Do women have short and curlies too?'

'Yes!' snapped Gavin, a peevish note in his voice. 'Gibbon brought a picture magazine to school last term. I glanced at it.'

Ted brooded about his drawing. It had been copied, to the best of his memory, from a photo of the statue of a goddess in an encyclopaedia. And it had been *wrong*. No wonder he had felt so odd about it, and baffled as to what a husband and wife were supposed to do, as regards that seamless flap of skin down there.

'I'd like to see a magazine like that.'

'What for?' asked Gavin.

'You'll not laugh?'

17

'I promise I won't.'

Ted explained about the drawing. Gavin smiled.

Rain started to spit in their faces. A Vespa putted along the nearby road, the rider perched upon the scooter's ample casing as though upon two creamy metal buttocks.

Dreams could trap and trick you. Ted was hastening through the giant crane's shadow. He could hear noises up there: rattling, clanking.

He had to look up! Scrambling out along the jib above him was . . . Bill Gibbon, bare body bristling all over with hairs. A 'gibbon' was the name for some kind of ape, Ted knew. Therefore Gibbon was a hairy beast. The person overhead looked as massive as a gorilla. Could that be Gibbon's elder brother? Or both of them fused together?

Now that Ted had spotted him, Gibbon began gibbering and capering. One huge paw grabbed his groin in preparation for a ball-fight. Catching hold of a loose hawser, Tarzan-style, Gibbon swung down.

Ted fled towards the tall white lighthouse which seemed far away. Gibbon easily overhauled him.

A paw clutched at Ted's cock and balls, to squeeze. Pressure mounted, painfully – but also thrillingly. Squirming to turn, Ted found himself pressed against not Gibbon, but the naked goddess of his drawing. Her breasts squashed against his face; the hair at the base of her stomach prickled him. A bright light, bright as the sun, crescendoed somewhere. He felt wet, and woke. Down inside the bed his fingers touched his groin which was soaked with hot sticky liquid. He smelt a salty-sweet tang.

Gavin didn't coincide with him, the next school day; but the day after he was hanging about near the park gate. Ted hadn't wanted to tell his mother what happened in bed, but now he told Gavin.

Gavin nodded. 'That's *natural*. It's called a wet dream. Was I in the dream?'

'You?' asked Ted, puzzled.

'If Gibbon was, I thought I might have been.'

'The woman I drew was in it. I told you.'

Gavin shook his head dismissively.

Above the school playing field was a small wide grassy plateau with precipitous sides. The boys called it 'the Lost World' and occasionally agile disobedient pupils such as Bill Gibbon would climb up there to lie hidden on top. The headmaster had put the plateau out of bounds, as a boy once fell off and broke his leg. Cricketers who weren't yet in to bat were supposed to stay near the green-painted pavilion, with its scoreboard and changing room. Those who had already batted could watch play from anywhere around the fringes of the field, on the flat.

As Ted, in white shorts, shirt, and sandshoes, was sprawling on the grass eyeing bowlers and batsmen in total boredom and watching a ladybird climb a green blade, Gibbon and his chum Malcolm Davies loomed over him.

'You're sucking up to that Gavin Percy,' Gibbon said. Even Gibbon Junior was much burlier than Ted. 'You're his pet, hoping he'll help you with your homework.'

'No,' Ted said feebly. 'That isn't true.'

'I'll tell my big brother about you and him if you don't come up the Lost World with us after the game. We're going to tie you up with strong grass and leave you. You'll miss your tea, and get five hundred lines and the slipper for being up there.'

The two boys ambled off, leaving Ted hollow and scared.

Strong grass braided together would cut wounds in his wrists and ankles if he tried to free himself. Gibbon might debag him too, steal his shorts. If he didn't do as they said, *Brian* Gibbon would be told. Ted worried desperately.

After the game, however, he ran off home. In bed that night he fretted for ages because he hadn't gone up the Lost World and wished morning would never arrive, when he must go to school to face Gibbon and Davies.

He turned up as late as possible, nearly missing the school bell. Though he was full of jitters all day long, oddly neither of the bullies paid any attention to him. Could they have entirely forgotten something which preoccupied Ted so desperately? Although he still worried a bit the next day too, nothing at all happened. That evening, walking home, he realized that if the headmaster had discovered about Ted being tied up on the plateau, then he would have demanded to know *who else* went up there with him and tied him up. Davies and Gibbon would have been punished too; tanned with the slipper, kept in for an hour or two to write lines.

Following the cartoon and news matinée the next Saturday, Ted met Gavin in the usual place, beside the ostrich which Ted tried not to notice. An early bus had cleared everyone away from the clock tower so Ted and Gavin went to perch on the edge of the stone horse trough dated 1841 below the tower. The trough was bone dry, empty apart from a screwed-up fish-and-chip paper; buses didn't drink from horse troughs.

From that vantage point they could see a stone man standing in mid-air: statue of a commander in Nelson's navy, a victor of Trafalgar now surveying the river protectively from a high column. The column rose from an imitation castle, and Ted could make out one of the cannons from a man-of-war which poked riverwards over mock battlements.

Gavin took out a red book; his play.

'You don't have to go home yet, do you? We could climb up to the monument and act a bit. It's super. Would you like that?'

'All right. I can only stop for half an hour.'

As they climbed the wide, crumbling steps to the battlements, the sun shone bright. Up top, a fresh wind blew, to discourage other visitors. Over the river herring gulls and kittiwakes milled and screamed. The kittiwakes nested on all available upper storey window ledges along the river front, distempering walls with their droppings.

More sheltered spots might be basking in warmth, and the beaches to the north of the real Castle, though rather exposed, would no doubt be spotted with fly-specks of plodgers and sunbathers. Not the Haven nestling below by the pier, however. The Haven's sand was a mess of washed-up cork, sea coal, black weed, driftwood, nubs of polished glass, on which hulls of beached yachts rested. Several yachts were tacking out in the bay, with tiny crew. Otherwise, the scene seemed deserted of people.

They sat by a cannon, its wheel sunk in concrete and muzzle plugged likewise – as though someone might otherwise vandalistically fire a stone ball at a trawler.

Tilting the open play towards Ted, Gavin read aloud:

'Like sylvan nymphs my pages shall be clad;
My men, like satyrs grazing on the lawns,
Shall with their goat-feet dance an antic hay.'

Ted felt confused. Was there straw spread to dance on, to stop the satires from spoiling the lawn with stiletto heels?

'Sometimes a lovely boy in Dian's shape,
With hair that gilds the water as it glides,
Crownets of pearl about his naked arms,

21

And in his sportful hands an olive tree,
To hide those parts which men delight to see – '

Gavin broke off. 'Those parts. Do you understand that, Ted?'

'Sort of. He's talking about . . . down here. Is the boy hiding behind the tree?'

'No, tree just means a bit of a tree. A bunch of leaves, to hide his parts. It has to rhyme.'

Ted grinned. 'Maybe the boy has a lot to hide.'

'I shouldn't think so. The men want to see . . . and touch his parts. Shall we explore the tunnel down below?'

The false castle was hollow. An empty space the size of a train tunnel circuited the square core of the column. The entrance side was dingy, the other three sides pitch black. Ted had only once stepped through that entrance and taken a few paces into the thickening gloom. The floor was of dry soil, and just inside the entrance he remembered clumps of dogs' dirt, some of it white because the dog had distemper. He'd heard Bill Gibbon say that youths took girls into the tunnel under the monument for a feel.

'I brought a torch,' Gavin said. 'To show those parts, down below.' From his blazer pocket he produced a small flashlight.

Ted shook his head. 'Dogs do their business in there. You could catch distemper from touching it. Look, I'll have to go. I said I could only stay half an hour.'

'With the torch, we can keep clean. Let's just explore quickly.'

'I can't! Next week, maybe. I have to run for the bus.'

Ted dashed down the flaking stone steps away from the looming cannons.

That night Ted dreamt he was tied up, on the Lost World. It was twilight; Venus shone. He could see the

22

stone man looking in the wrong direction, atop his column, unable to turn round just as Ted was unable. The rope of grass bit into his wrists which were fastened behind his back, so that he couldn't touch those parts. Those parts itched and swelled painfully. Touch would change the pain to pleasure, relief.

He woke, to find that he'd been sleeping with his palms squashed under his buttocks. His hands were paralysed, two dead animals fastened to his wrists. Soon they prickled and stabbed with pins and needles.

3

Jack was in between books at present, so he was hungry for a new theme to get his teeth into between six and nine of an evening. Though he had lent a hand with *Jingling Geordie's Hole* I felt duty bound to deny him any further joy with the material. That bore the seal of the confessional.

Jack didn't agree. We'd had a bit of a set-to about this in our upstairs study the evening before.

JACK: 'After you've solved Tony's problem and dug out the root cause, maybe you could ask his consent?'

JOHN: 'That would mean revealing your identity.'

JACK: 'You're so damn middle-aged, John. So sedate, so neutral. Why don't you let your hair down? Take a risk! Kick your heels. You did let me go to that Fantasy Fayre.'

JOHN: 'In disguise, Jack. In disguise.'

Hmm. He was referring to the previous autumn. Jack Cannon rented a post office box at the Central Post Office beside St Nicholas's Cathedral for all dealings with his publisher, Mandarin Books. (No agent was involved.) Mandarin hadn't known a bean about Jack beyond the fact that he lived somewhere in Newcastle upon Tyne. He had never supplied any bio or photo and always politely declined invitations to lunch in London dangled by his editor, Sally Butterworth.

Anyway, forwarded through Mandarin came an invitation to be guest of honour at the annual Fantasy Fayre held in Birmingham. Jack's five books to date had earned him a name. Damn it but I decided to let Jack attend.

I drove down in our Volvo to Lichfield, where I'd

booked a hotel room for the night. Arriving by mid-afternoon I had time to visit Dr Johnson's house and the Cathedral. Then I retired to my room and put on the disguise which I'd already practised. I dyed my hair a more vigorous black. I slipped out my contact lenses and put on the old bifocals with dark brown frames which I'd kept. I pasted on a rather convincing black moustache. Folding John's sober suit away, Jack dressed in denims.

By then the night staff were on duty, so nobody was surprised to see Jack Cannon head out for a few pints and an Indian meal.

I had paid for the room on arrival. Skipping breakfast, Jack slipped away early next morning unseen, simply leaving the room key on the desk.

For the first time, Jack enjoyed a spot of public celebrity. He met other fantasy and horror authors, illustrators, editors, fans. Drank with them in the bars of the Midland Hotel, noting how many pick-ups still seemed to be going on in spite of AIDS: businessmen and girls from off the street. You can't teach every old dog and young bitch new tricks. Durex machines must have been humming.

He ate hickory-smoked seafood with his new-found 'colleagues' at the American Food Factory along New Street.

To my way of thinking there were two sorts of Tynesiders. Those who left the flat, cold, downbeat place as soon as possible and avoided going back unless forced. And those who went away briefly once then hurried home with their tails between their legs, telling friends, 'Wey, man, it's treacherous doon south.'

I recalled one bright brisk summer's morning down on the seafront with the slightest of blue swells hissing some foam on to the sands. A man muffled

25

He gave a well-received speech on the theme that horror transfigured the ordinary, the ugly, the banal, and rendered contemporary life luminous with significance; and answered questions, even personal ones, which he fielded with a smile.

'I'm forty-eight, I'll tell you that much. Born and bred in the North-east. Worked for a shipping firm since I was sixteen. Clerical stuff. Portage accounts, cargo insurance, seamen's wages. Accepted early retirement last year. Glad to see the back of it. Horror kept me sane.' (Laughter.) 'Wife, yes. Two teenage kids. Two cats, an aquarium, and a parrot.'

Without warning Jack, Sally Butterworth had travelled up from London on the Saturday to meet her mystery author. Did she suspect that he might have backed out of Fantasy Fayre if she had told him in advance? Now she could buy him dinner at last.

Sally was chubby, fresh, effervescent, and talked with

in overcoats had warned, 'Watch oot, it's treacherous on the beach.'

Ambitions were drenched with cold water. 'You're flyin' too high!' Odd ideas caused the lugubrious comment, 'Ye'll bring aboot the downfall o' nations!'

(The shipping clerk was my patient, Derek Davies, sacked for dipping into the petty cash and later prosecuted for fiddling the Social Security. His past lives included being a highwayman, who was hung and gibbeted, and a teenage cutpurse who got cut up in turn. A pattern of shabby-romantic unsuccessful crimes.)

I didn't quite place myself in the second category of Geordies, but I'd certainly gone to the local college instead of braving strange pastures.

(JACK: 'What do *you* know about horrors, John, old son?')

And here I was, still living in Newcastle,

half a brick in her mouth. Roedean, then straight into publishing. What could she know about ultimate horror? Aside from possessing a publisher's nose for the marketable sort?

So Sally and accomplices whisked Jack off to the House of Mr Chan in Bromsgrove Street for stuffed crab claw followed by crispy duck with plum sauce.

'My God, did you really work in a shipping office for thirty years?' Sally asked him, laughing. 'You know, you've never supplied Mandarin with a publicity pic.'

'He wouldn't even send us one for the programme book,' chipped in Walt Keeley, chairperson of the Fayre.

Cameras had been popping that weekend already. Sally pulled hers out from a patchwork leather shoulder bag.

'Would you mind, Jack? For Mandarin? And for me?'

Moustached, bespectacled, Jack grinned and allowed it.

'You'll send me a copy, won't you?' he said. Flash. Flash.

unmarried, with my elderly widowed mother sharing the house. True, I'd achieved a certain modest notoriety thanks to PLT. But wasn't my own life passing prematurely by? Apart from practising unconventional therapy, why had I not *dared*? To marry, really to believe in reincarnation, emigrate to California, become a popular guru? Whatever. Such dreams were treacherous. I'd be flying too high. I'd bring about the downfall of nations. Look at the mental and social mess which my patients got themselves into! They needed a stable, unhectic personality to face them in the consulting room.

Now of course, with AIDS, the whole world was becoming . . .

(To remind me what I looked like – in case I needed to look the same again.)

(Helen Daggett, under hypnosis, had related an

'Of course. What's your wife's name?' asked Sally.

'Helen,' he told her.

'So what does Helen think of your secret life as one of the country's prime horror scribes? I presume she *knows*?' teased Sally.

'She used to resent it a bit when I cloistered myself. But the money's useful.'

'She reads your books? Has opinions on them?'

'She prefers Catherine Cookson.'

'And your children, Jack?'

'Philippa and Paul.'

'Do they read their father's books?'

Jack smiled enigmatically. 'Life's hard for kids these days.'

'Sally,' murmured Walt, 'is it true that Toby Cook and Roxanne have AIDS?' (Who were they?)

'I'm afraid so. Yes. The virus must have been dormant for years.'

'What about their kids?'

'They're being given tests. It isn't as though Toby and Roxanne slept around in recent years. God, where will it all end?'

extremely pious life as a nun in medieval France.)

. . . was becoming ever more constrained and scared. To dare was – treacherous. Treachery stalked the streets, since if you had an accident and needed blood, well! Treachery lay in bed with you, withering you. Though to be sure, I dared let Jack rip writing horror stories!

(Two kids who lived next door in Jesmond Road. People who called their first-born 'Philippa' really wanted a boy, a Philip. Philippa was their female boy.)

Horror stories were a kind of therapy too. Looking around Tyneside, you might wonder how a person could ever dream, ever imagine anything extraordinary. As soon as you put on horror glasses immediately the view altered. The whole place glowed with potential significance.

JACK: 'Horror liberates your viscera, man.'

JOHN: 'Do I shit in my pants? Do I crap on the carpet in fear? I've hardly ever been in a *sickness* hospital, have I? Mental hospitals aren't exactly Holiday Inns but they don't nauseate. They only disturb. What I do in the consulting room . . . well, there can be terror and sweating and crying out in a trance – but it's spoken terror. It's words, words. Images cast by the mundane upon a wall of mist I conjure.'

JACK: 'Horror's a bit like the Phantom of the Brocken, isn't it? Travellers on the Rhine saw their own shapes cast huge upon the mist. Horror casts a hideous shadow to chill us with our own worst fears, with a sense of sick lunacy – till the sun burns away the mist.'

JOHN: 'So you said in Birmingham. The vomit, the blood and guts, is quarantined in horror novels.'

JACK: 'There's no reason why you should be mopping up actual puke. Don't flay yourself. That isn't what I meant by letting your hair down.'

JOHN: 'That's why Tony's story – the horror of it – is such an intrusion. It's as though something dreadful has crossed a boundary from yourself, Jack, to me.'

JACK: 'The stuff's symbolic. Said so yourself! Let me handle the material. At full length, as it deserves. I'll illuminate it and transfigure it for you. I'll lock it up where it belongs – in pages where there are safeguards, eh? In the shape of ironic distancing devices? The average reader mightn't suss that I'm being ironic, but sometimes I laugh out loud at the horrors. I chuckle and slap my thighs. And that's good. Keeps nightmares at bay, eh? The foul passions, the clutch of evil. I use nightmares to shine a searchlight, a black beam.'

JOHN: 'Passions can be harmful, can't they? Especially now that the imp of AIDS is loose from Pandora's pot. That's what Gavin found out. Yet without ecstasy and passion-fire there is no world, no future.'

JACK. 'Avoid touch, lad. Mutate the passion. Speak it in the voice of horror. That's what we're up to, you and I. And don't feel guilty. Let me rip.'

Jack hadn't typed a word all evening. I had been preventing him. I heard a bell tinkling. Mother was calling me to say goodnight. But yet I hesitated. Mother wasn't impatient. She would wait. I hadn't thought sufficiently about *Tony*'s life. Too preoccupied with my own. With both of my lives.

Why, during these special hours of evening – these Jack hours – should I think of Tony Smith?

Ah, that was because Gavin had spoken out in Jack's native language.

Tony hadn't totally screwed up his life, but nor had it exactly been a success story. Under-performing at school. Making the wrong friends there (in so far as he made friends), leading to some drug taking, shop lifting, and probation. His only adolescent success with girls was with one whose principal interest was in smoking dope and sniffing cocaine.

'Did he choose her,' I'd written speculatively in my case notes, 'so that he could pursue heterosexuality yet at the same time avoid it?'

Yet Tony had seemingly pulled himself together in spite of bouts of migraine, fierce sick headaches that recurred at the end of each winter. He had landed a job in Fenwick's, and now he was in charge of the audio section. LPs, pop singles, tapes, compact discs.

I suppose that *did* identify Tony Smith. Say rather: a job in a smart department store.

He went to discos, and drank, but kept off the drugs. A couple of years ago he had married a younger counter assistant who thought he was romantic, broody, brill, Byronic.

Carol – the assistant – should have wondered why Tony

30

hadn't chased girls more energetically. Within two years
he progressed from premature ejaculation to impotence.

The bell again. Mother's bell. Not yet the plague bell.

'Oh that cave,' groaned Jack . . .

4

It rained a lot during the next week, so that he didn't meet Gavin at all, only spying him once or twice in the distance down school corridors. However, the following Saturday was a scorcher. When Ted arrived for the matinée, Gavin was already waiting near the cinema.

'I've got one of those photo magazines to show you,' said Gavin. 'You know? It's in my pocket. I can't take it out where anyone might see. Why not skip the cartoons? That'll give us longer to look at it.'

'How did you get it?'

'From a newsagent's down on the fish quay. I went specially. Sailors must buy these.' From the strain in Gavin's voice Ted could guess how hard it must have been for his friend to sneak into that shop, down in rough territory, where at least he wasn't likely to be known. No doubt Gibbon Senior never had such qualms. Had Gavin worn his school blazer?

'Did the newsagent make it hard for you?'

'Not much.'

'Are there lots of pictures?'

'Quite a few. Some show everything.'

'Where shall we go? The monument?'

Gavin shook his head. 'How about the rocks below the Priory? It's more natural there. More beautiful. We could climb up into Jingling Geordie's Hole. We'd be private; it would be light and airy and clean.'

Jingling Geordie's Hole was a small cave a little way up the cliff face, which high tides lapped into. Legend had it that the cave drove deep into the headland on which

Castle and Priory stood; it had supposedly been used by smugglers, and was haunted by a ghost who jingled chains. According to an old book called *North Country Lore and Legend* in the Percy household, a young knight had once fought his way past demons into the pitchy depths to drink from 'the chalice of truth'. An engraving showed him wielding a sword which shone as bright as the sun, against beasts resembling pterodactyls and prehistoric crocodiles. In reality, the cave was only shallow.

'All right,' agreed Ted.

Ten minutes later they were crunching over shingle littered with torn-up bladderwrack, broad black whips with explosive air-pods. They skirted pools inhabited by button anemones, limpets, whelks, and small crabs, then clambered over tumbled white boulders to the towering cliff. Gentle waves slopped and hissed. The tide was barely on the turn, so they couldn't be cut off for another two or three hours. Further along the shore a couple of blokes were sea-angling from a spit of black rock, but a deep inlet of water carved its way in between. No one else was exploring *their* area; most kids would be at the matinée.

Past storms had tossed weed into the cave but no recent wind-whipped waves had reached as high, thus crisp black heaps matted the stones thickly. Hot morning sun had been warming the weed mattress. Gavin shucked off his blazer, encouraged Ted to remove his, and laid both down as rugs. From his inside pocket Gavin slipped a small folded magazine and creased it the opposite way to straighten the pages. On the colour cover: the upper half of a smiling naked suntanned woman with raven hair and big bouncy breasts.

'*Health and Efficiency.* It's for nudists.'

'Oh boy,' said Ted.

Inside were black and white photos. A dark-maned

33

young woman splashed naked in the sea, her bottom turned to the camera; Ted thought he saw a hint of hair between her buttocks. He felt those parts tingle and well. A blonde woman lay supine on a towel, her nearer leg raised to conceal her groin. Gavin turned the page. The same blonde was leaping in the air, but between her legs was only a blurred grey smear. However, on the right-hand page a flaxen-haired girl with little pointy breasts showed faint delicate curls on the mound where her legs met.

Gavin propped the magazine open on a hump of weed. 'You'll hurt yourself, keeping your parts squashed up like that. So will I. It's dangerous.' He opened his belt and unbuttoned his trousers; opened Ted's gently too, his hand brushing Ted's aertex-clad parts. 'Better let it right out. In fact, we ought to take our trousers and pants right off. We don't want to stain them.'

Remembering the hot wet gush in bed, Ted agreed. Soon their flannel trousers and aertex pants lay discarded. Gavin looked at Ted's now urgent parts; Ted looked at Gavin's hairs and swollen cock, then at the photo. Ted wanted to hold himself but Gavin pushed his hand aside. From his pocket he took a blue and white glass jar, unscrewed the lid, scooped a mass of Nivea skin cream on to his fingers.

'Watch the photo, Ted. Pretend I'm her.' Gavin massaged him teasingly with cream-smeared fingers. Presently he whispered, 'Lie over. Let's pretend you're a woman too.' Briefly he took his hand away to smear cream on himself, emptying the jar. Now Gavin gripped Ted's cock wonderfully; and a creamy cock butted up Ted's backside. 'This might feel strange. It's worth it.'

Ted stared at the photo in front of his face, moving his own parts up and down now in Gavin's fist. His bottom felt as if he was straining on the toilet with a huge turd stuck half way out, but this discomfort was secondary to the pleasure in his front part. He shut his eyes. From deep inside him something was rising, a snake of hot jelly that lived in his belly. Hotter, more urgently it rose. The therm-o-nuclear explosion was coming – the blinding light; that was why he had his eyes shut. For timeless moments boiling milk burst through the squeezing fist; he saw whiteness everywhere. Simultaneously the burning rod which killed the king entered Ted's bowels. Gavin gasped, 'Sweet Prince, I come!' Fiery stars exploded throughout the blank smooth whiteness, and Ted cried out.

The world boomed as though the cave was a bass drum which the sea beat upon. Ted felt that some door had been torn open in him – a door which was also in the backside of Jingling Geordie's cave. A dim tunnel stretched away. Far off, a transparent ghost gibbered and writhed. Ted's limbs were the ghost's, his gibberings and writhings, its. At the heart of the ghost floated an albino tadpole. Somehow that tadpole swam within Ted too.

Then the wild wave which had burst its bounds hissed back to its source. Gavin let go of him, turned him over, kissed him on the lips.

Ted drew away, and saw vivid blood streaks on Gavin's foamy cock like strawberry syrup on an ice cream cornet. As he drew on his underpants hastily Ted felt cream and blood ooze out to stain the cotton.

Feeling sore and awkward, Ted walked home alone, worrying about his underpants. There'd hardly been any need for Gavin to say so strenuously that he shouldn't tell anyone; he had no intention of telling. But his soiled pants! Maybe he'd stained the inside of his trousers too.

He detoured through the huge cemetery near his home.

Around the back of the chapel and crematorium was a shabby public lavatory; he could examine himself.

He generally admired the marble chips within the boundaries of graves: little lakes of emerald crystals, ruby crystals, ice, and amethyst. He usually enjoyed seeing the glass bells covering bowls of china flowers faded to pastel. Today he hardly noticed. Rooks cawed from their black stick-nests in the green heights of elms. Decaying wreaths lay heaped along one new grave; nobody had cleared the rotting flowers away yet. He hardly heard, or saw.

The men's lavatory was a short dark concrete tunnel with pee-stained wall and yellowed gutter sloping to a drain-hole. The stone floor was slicked with damp. Cocks had been pencilled on the wall as if to remind users – in vain – which way to aim. At the end: a door battered with bootmarks, carved with initials, a stout brass mechanism bolted to it. Ted fed it a penny.

Behind the door he found a china bowl with no seat, a string dangling from the overhead cistern, a piece of metal where toilet roll would fit, had there been any. He forced the bolt shut with difficulty, fearing that he might lock himself in. He undid his trousers, which to his relief were reasonably unblemished. But a big dark brown patch disfigured his underpants.

He recalled how much soaking and bleaching his hanky had needed, when he had a nose-bleed. He couldn't possibly clean this mess in secrecy. It mustn't be known that he had bled between his legs. His sister presumably bled – Gibbon told dirty jokes about tomato sauce – but that was different, and private. He wasn't meant to.

So he eased his trousers off, keeping them clear of the wet floor, removed his underpants and put his trousers back on. The underpants he stuffed behind the chipped bowl. Maybe his mother mightn't notice for weeks that he now owned only three pairs of underpants instead of four. If she did find out he would say that he messed his pants at school one day, took them off in the school bog and got rid of them. Because there was dirt in them. But he'd been ashamed to tell her.

A week later the summer term ended. In the hall the assembled school sang:

> 'Lord dismiss us with thy blessings,
> Thanks for mercies past received . . .'

Ted had avoided Gavin during that final week, and on the last day once again he caught a crowded bus home in company with a gang of boys rather than walking. For the first two mornings after the events in Jingling Geordie's Hole, he had found smears of blood on the toilet paper, but then no more.

During the first ten days of the summer holiday Ted mainly stayed at home, re-reading old copies of *Hotspur* and *Wizard*, sorting out his cigarette card collection, drawing pictures of therm-o-nuclear explosions. Though he was no nuisance his mother chased him out occasionally for a breath of fresh air. He stayed close to home, wandering round the wooded back lanes of the cemetery.

On the eleventh day the Appleby family set off by train to spend a week in Edinburgh. Ted's Dad, an electrician with the Council, was now on holiday; also sister Helen who had left school the year before and now worked as a dental receptionist.

The family stayed in a boarding house off Hanover Street, ate porridge and kippers for breakfast, explored the city. The Botanic Gardens of Corstorphine seemed to Ted a paradisiacal version of the cemetery back home. The tiny room Ted stayed in was directly behind the red neon sign, *Princes Guest House*, which stayed lit all night long, tubes humming and buzzing, bathing the room even through the curtains in a blood-stained light. Though it wasn't obvious from the street below the sign was thick with spiders' webs and hundreds of insect corpses.

On the fifth morning of the holiday Ted was sick before breakfast. He vomited clear bitter liquid into the tiny wash-handbasin and couldn't face kippers or porridge. Likewise the next morning.

'You must be off colour,' his Mam observed. Ted wondered if this could be some reference to the neon sign outside his window.

On the train home he felt nauseated, then better once they had returned. He carried on reading, drawing, walking in the cemetery, daydreaming about the botanic gardens of which he'd bought picture postcards. He wished he could live there forever, camping in the orchid or fern house, after a therm-o-nuclear war which had killed everyone else. Since that would include his Mam and Dad, he cried a little. Soon it was September, and the new school term began.

'Have a good holiday?' Gavin asked, meeting him in the corridor near the physics lab.

'We went to Edinburgh. I was sick a few times.' This stuck in Ted's mind since he had hardly ever been sick before, and never on just getting out of bed.

Gavin looked hurt, as though Ted said this to reproach him.

'We went to the Lake District,' said Gavin. 'I thought about sending you a card but I decided not. Your parents might have asked. I bought you a present.'

A tin of butterscotch with a picture of a hill called Helvellyn.

'I climbed that mountain. Early on, I found a sheep lying on its back in the bracken. I rolled it over but it

38

couldn't stand up. I thought about you at the cairn on the top and added a stone for you. Are you going to the matinée this Saturday?'

'I don't know.'

Noisy boys were clattering in their direction. Gavin slipped away into the lab.

On Saturday Ted set off for the cinema, since his Mam expected this; but he went to the cemetery instead. Parking himself on a bench, he read most of the stories in a new copy of *Hotspur* and ate all the butterscotch. Careful that no one saw, he chucked the empty tin under a laurel bush before returning home. For several hours afterwards he had indigestion.

Playing Rugby that winter, Ted soon got puffed out and could only trot around after the ball. The crush of the scrum bruised and scared him. Bill Gibbon often shouldered into him, tried to trip him.

Ted was very hungry these days, sometimes gobbling four slices of bread and marg with his Mam's meals. He sneaked biscuits from the pantry. He always bought chocolate bars with the money he saved by missing the cartoon matinée; these gave him the energy to endure the cold of the cemetery.

Towards Christmas his Mam said, 'You're putting on weight,' and it was true. His trousers – long ones, since his October birthday – pressed cruelly into his waist. He hadn't seen much of Gavin at school; Gavin seemed offended by Ted's long trousers instead of admiring them. Ted found that the trousers tried to cling together at the turn-ups when he walked; he waddled, legs apart. The turn-ups filled with fluff which wadded into felt, but he couldn't bend to clean them out with his finger. If only his elastic belt, with the silver snake-clasp, would stretch still further.

39

In January as the new term started his Mam said, 'You're becoming a fatty. You shouldn't eat so much. But maybe *that* isn't it, maybe it's glandular. It can be, with boys of your age. Maybe we should take you to see the doctor.'

'No,' said Ted, 'I feel fine.'

He didn't. Rugby games were a nightmare, made slightly less so only by the general indifference of the sports master. On sports day Ted longed for rain, then the class would stay in the school doing prep. As often as not, it did rain; or sleet. Worse, now there were marks on his belly like thin red worms as though his skin was slowly tearing. His Dad had a feeble, brief word with him about the facts of life, embarrassing them both.

The radio news announced how British troops were leaving the Suez Canal Zone, and how France was sending thousands of troops to Algeria. Ted felt proud for the French. Their Prime Minister, who was also called France, was making everyone drink milk because it was healthy. Ted used this as an excuse to persuade his Mam to order an extra pint bottle a day all for him. But the British hadn't done so badly after all; tommies had crushed the Mau Mau who butchered settlers with long knives. In Algeria the natives threw bombs into cinemas. In America President Eisenhower was guarding Formosa against the Red Chinese. By the autumn of that year there would be television with adverts, just as at the cinema. Ted wished there was a TV set in their house, and a big 'H' on the roof, so that he could see all the newsreels he was missing; but his Mam said they wouldn't get one while he was still at school with homework to do. Helen didn't seem to care whether they had a set or not; she was a dull, boring sister who read *Woman* and *Ideal Home*.

Ted always locked the door when he had his weekly bath; he never let anyone glimpse the red worms on his tummy. He didn't dare go to the surgery because he already knew what Dr Robson would discover. Nocturnal visions of a tunnel and of a white tadpole – coupled with furtive reference to a big maroon volume titled *The Home Family Doctor* which was kept on a high shelf – had made it plain; and if Dr Robson found out he would find out what Ted and Gavin had done.

Ted was having a baby.

5

The carpet in my consulting room was a light blue Wilton, which I had chosen to suggest Heaven. Some patients reported that the soul floated in a blue void between one life and the next. Angels, or else a committee of wise old codgers, would debrief the dead soul, sort out its karma, and advise about the next incarnation.

If the carpet was sky, the net curtains were clouds veiling Jesmond Road. An ambulance passed outside, lights strobing, piercing my clouds.

We were now living through the Scourge, the plague years. Reincarnation not only opened up a wealth of supposed past lives. (Which might not be wealthy at all! They could be utter cans of worms, and often were. None the less, they deepened a person.) Reincarnation also promised future lives, lives of possible ecstasy and fulfilment once the present ghastly epoch had run its course.

Ghastly indeed. Time of dread. The death of joy. It hadn't escaped my attention that the anti-sexuality – both homo and hetero – apparent in the tale might be expressing itself in such horrific terms because of the AIDS pandemic which now haunted the human race and scythed it down.

I'd noted the previous Great Fear, of nuclear war, sounding its bugle at the beginning of Gavin's story. Yet that source of dread was relegated almost to the back burner. People could co-exist with the nuclear threat, awful though it was. They could ignore it for weeks on end, while they got on with their lives. Whereas AIDS struck home more intimately. Already it had altered our whole society and our social relations in a way that nuclear weapons never did.

From around the globe, as we heard of more medical services faltering and breaking down amidst travel restrictions, xenophobia, triage, and mass burials, so the economic dominoes of society were rocking on their bases, slumping further. The lives of today's children were going to be utterly different from anything we had imagined, in the straitened, repressive, death-filled future. Unless there was a miracle, an elixir of life.

Was it odd that Jack Cannon should still have an audience eager for horrors? Perhaps not. In Jack's books Evil – preposterous but plausibly presented Evil – entered the zone of normality and tormented it. In the end Evil was usually expelled, exorcized. The pins were pulled out of the fetish doll. The devil was driven back into the pit. Nightmare was overtaken by daylight. The ordinary reasserted itself. In the end.

Maybe it wasn't surprising that Tony experienced his 'past life' as though it was a horror novel. Other patients of mine also betrayed AIDS-dread.

Yet they did not express themselves in horror terms. Really, Tony should not have been able to tell me a horror story while he was on my couch under hypnosis.

Which is why I had called in Jack. The material seemed so ideally suited. I hadn't allowed Jack to invent or add or rearrange anything, yet in letting him polish the raw material perhaps he had given it more authority than it had actually possessed for Tony until now? More substance, more physical presence, landscape, and solid setting. The original account had been closer to a nightmare, with some of the logic of a nightmare. Now it wore persuasive everyday clothes.

Tony, shuddering, was coming to the end of Jack's novelette. During our session the previous week Tony had trembled and sweated and appeared terrified at times as he talked. Now I could see how scared he was by the upcoming ending. (If only every reader of Jack Cannon reacted likewise!) For, what ending would the story have? In fact it didn't have one. Not as yet.

You don't usually challenge or try to verify the details of a previous life. I knew I would be treading on thin ice, but in this case I felt I had to make an exception since Tony had ended our earlier 'séance' in abject terror.

He turned the final page. He let the typescript fall on to the carpet and stared at the window.

'You're quite a writer,' he said. 'You could do it for a living.'

My heart skipped a beat. However, his tone was numb rather than accusatory.

With the fingers of his right hand he worried the cuticles of his left hand, tearing scraps loose. Tony didn't bite his fingernails. Those were kept neatly trimmed. What he did was nibble the skin around the nails into tiny traumatized arrowheads, than flay off little strips of raw flesh.

'I drove down to Tynemouth on Saturday,' I told him. 'There used to be a cinema where you say. The Carlton. It was demolished years ago to make way for a block of sheltered housing. Obviously someone could have told you about the Carlton.'

'Yeah? I've hardly ever been down to the coast. Bloody stupid freezing sea. Can't stand it.'

'Still, you might have heard mention of the cinema. I also visited the library in North Shields, and I looked up microfilm copies of the old *Evening News* for early 1955. A boy called Ted Appleby did go missing. And a few weeks after that, an older boy called Gavin Percy . . .'

Tony had gone white.

'Gavin's body was fished out of the river – or sea – somewhere between the piers.'

44

'So I drowned myself! I escaped.' Tony sounded so relieved.

'Gavin Percy drowned himself.'

And even this Tony could have known. He could have heard some aunt reminiscing when he was a toddler; seen an old newspaper . . . a hundred possibilities. The human mind was a sponge that soaked up billions of bits of data and stored them in the attic of forgetfulness. I had no wish to undermine his trust in PLT – Lord knew, he needed help – but what appeared at first glance to be proof of reincarnation almost invariably wasn't. The evidence usually had a more normal explanation.

'This reincarnation business must be true,' he said. 'I was reborn three years later, in '58. My other Mam and Dad might still be *alive*.' He calculated. 'They'd be in their mid-seventies, I suppose. Don't we get old quickly? 1950 sounds fairly recent. Yet they'll be old. Almost dead.'

'Does that matter,' I asked gently, 'if we live again?'

'If one of them's alive – '

'You might cause a lot of distress, Tony. And confusion. As you say, they'd be old.'

'Doesn't make them gaga. I could describe my bedroom in their house. The Swiss chalet clock.'

I shook my head. 'We aren't searching for proof.'

'Then why did you go down to Tynemouth and Shields to check up, eh Dr Cunningham?'

Because of the horror. Because of the impossibility. Fortunately he didn't repeat his question, for the horror flooded back upon him too.

'Hey,' he exclaimed, '*I* escaped by throwing myself in the river. But Ted will still be locked in the rock! He'll still be with that creature.'

Oh God. Don't think along those lines.

But Tony shuddered desperately.

45

'I couldn't go near there. I couldn't, I couldn't.'

'No one wants you to. It wouldn't help.'

'Now that I've remembered, mightn't the creature reach out to me like it did before I killed myself?'

There can't be any such creature in the cliffs underneath Tynemouth Priory. It's out of this world. Dared I say that to Tony? What would one of Jack's devil-possessed characters advise?

'Listen,' I said finally, 'you experienced your past life the way Gavin experienced it. But Gavin was under an enormous strain. When you're under a huge strain – '

'You can crack your pot. Lose your screws. Become looney. Am I a looney in the making?'

'No, no. Gavin's view of reality – not *yours* – obviously became distorted.'

'Did I kill Ted? Is that what you mean? Did Gavin imagine the creature because he actually strangled Ted, to stop Ted telling on him? Then did guilt make me chuck myself in the sea? The sea which I now hate!'

Careful!

'That may be closer to what happened. Perhaps.'

'So there's no monster. The monster was me.'

I smiled. 'You'd make a fair psychologist, Tony. The monster equals a knot in yourself, in your subconscious. To untie that knot, we need to go back to an even earlier life where it was first tied. We have to find out what tied that knot in the first place.'

The central trauma of life as Gavin – the buggery of another boy and the awful consequences – most likely represented Tony's own sexual problems; and we mustn't forget the vitriol of AIDS-dread nowadays. According to the theory of PLT the same pattern could crop up in several successive lives. By regressing Tony further into the past we should come to the crux event which first

46

established the pattern – dramatizing whatever it was in Tony's early life which had knotted him.

Maybe this would be sexual molestation by an uncle or an older boy, a memory long suppressed. A Freudian would expect something of this nature. However, Tony had already been 'shrunk' ineffectively by a Freudian as a condition of his probation twelve years earlier. Having interviewed Tony in some depth before I hypnotized him, I knew all about that episode.

Maybe the therapist in question had been sloppy. Maybe Tony hadn't co-operated, the way he could co-operate with me. The beauty of PLT was that terrible events happened to a stand-in, a representative, 'another person'. But I mustn't become technical about *catharsis* and *cathexis*. Mainly I needed to pull Tony loose from the electric charge of horror which he had built into his life as Gavin – becoming like one of Jack Cannon's characters, not that Jack ever imagined anything quite like this!

'We'll do that next week, shall we?' I glanced apologetically at my watch.

Mrs Amanda Harvey from Benton was due in five minutes, to relive her experiences as a child prostitute who died of pox in eighteenth-century Bristol, back in those days when sailing ships brought sugar and rum and syphilis from the slave estates of the West Indies. Was this another reflection of the grim reaper, AIDS? Amanda was scared of catching AIDS from her husband in bed, afraid of their little daughter being infected. No real reason why either event should occur. But still she feared. And froze.

Just as Tony, for his part, was impotent.

The black blur of a hearse slipped past, followed by a sleek Rolls full of mourners. The cemetery was just along the road. Hearses passed the house all the time. They always had.

Amanda's past life wasn't exactly attractive. Still, there was a definite appeal in the notion of being able to lead more lives than one. Hence – speaking agnostically – my own cohabitation with Jack who believed all kinds of occult things, at least while he was typing them out.

'The *creature* in the rock . . .'

'Be quiet, Jack. Stop moaning.'

Tony bid me a shaky good-day.

6

or *Jingling Geordie's Hole*, concluded, for the time being

One day he met Gavin after school. The older boy no longer seemed to like Ted so much, not only on account of those long trousers but because Ted looked swollen and blotchy as well as being a bit taller. They walked the streets together as of old; unlike as of old.

'Gav, I have to tell you something.'

'Yes?'

'I'm having a baby. I think it'll come in March.'

Gavin grabbed Ted by the shoulder. 'You can't! You aren't a woman. What do you mean?'

Ted began to blubber.

'What's wrong with you?' Gavin had gone white.

'Scared.'

'Why?'

'I told you. It's because of what we did in Jingling Geordie's Hole.'

Now Gavin seemed furious – though scared, too. 'You're making this up. That's scientifically impossible. You don't have a womb inside you. You're saying this to make trouble!'

'I must have something that's imitating a womb. I've got so fat. I told you how I was sick in the mornings during the summer hols – that's morning sickness. I looked in a medical book. There are all these red marks on my tummy, because it's stretching. Can I show you them?'

'I don't want to see.'

'Won't you help me, Gav? My Mam wants me to go to the doctor.'

49

A cunning look crossed Gavin's face. 'You haven't told your Mam?'

'No.'

'Women drink stuff to get rid of a baby. I'll find out. But you mustn't tell anybody else.'

Ted winced. 'Ouch, I felt it move.'

'*What?*'

'In my tummy. Feel it, Gav!'

'Here in the street?'

'Feel while it's moving, or you aren't helping me!'

Gavin glanced up and down the deserted street, scanned the nearby net-curtained windows. Hastily he stepped close to Ted, let his hand be guided clammily.

'Do you feel it?'

'Something's shoving, kicking,' the older boy mumbled, bewildered and terrified now.

Two days later, by the deserted chilly bowling green, Gavin said, 'I've asked Brian Gibbon.'

'He'll tell his brother.' Ted felt betrayed.

'No, he won't. I gave him my new fountain pen. I'll do homework for him, and I promised him some of the money I got for Christmas if he helps. Gibbon knows about girls and babies. It has to be him, Ted. Anyway, I didn't mention *you*!'

'So what did you say?'

Gavin sniggered bitterly. 'That I got a girl into trouble. She's threatening to tell her Dad. Gibbon respects me now, because of that. He wanted to know all the details. He would!'

'And?'

'I pretended she's a friend of my cousin's. I said I took her to one of those concrete pill-boxes from the war, along the dunes among the spiky grass, and we did it there. Last term. I thought she might only let me have a feel but she took her knickers off and let me do it all.

That's what I said.' Gavin looked disgusted by his story. 'Gibbon'll find a way.'

Ted thought about carrots tied to string, and milk bottles. His tummy curdled. Gavin too looked haunted with anxiety. Let him be haunted!

He whispered to Gavin, 'If I have a baby and people find out you're the father, the police'll take you off to a reformatory.'

Gavin bit his lip.

'Gibbon says it's done with a bottle of gin and a bent wire coathanger,' Gavin told Ted. They were on the railway bridge. 'The woman drinks the gin to upset her stomach then someone pushes the coathanger up inside her and scrapes the pregnancy loose. The thing comes out.'

This news filled Ted with alarm. 'You'd shove a coathanger up my bottom?'

'Gibbon says that only works properly in the early months, and the woman sometimes bleeds a lot. He said if the baby's bigger it's best to stick to the gin, to try and cause a miscarriage – '

'Hey! I thought you told him that girl and you did it last term.'

'Yes, but I asked him "what if?" and he told me. The baby would get born prematurely, and die. It could be buried or chucked in the sea. Gibbon'll get the gin for me from an off-licence if I pay him.'

'I'd be drunk. My Mam and Dad would know.'

'It takes three or four hours for a miscarriage. You'd probably have got over being drunk. We can do it this Saturday if you can find a good excuse for being out all day.'

'I'll say I've been invited to a birthday treat. Matinée in the morning, fish and chip lunch in a café, and the skating rink in the afternoon. Where shall we do it?'

'We'd need to be alone. What about the cave? My Grandad mentioned the tide won't be very high this weekend – I'll find out what time it's rising. The sea would cover the rocks but it wouldn't reach the cave.'

'Are you sure?' Ted imagined coastguards, soldiers, police climbing down the cliffs on ropes to rescue them. Even the lifeboat being launched and a breeches-buoy hauling them from drowning.

'Unless there's a storm.'

But there was no storm. When they climbed into Jingling Geordie's Hole that Saturday at ten o'clock the sea was already sluicing across the boulders. White foals – only junior horses – capered along rock-broken, breeze-flicked waves. In deeper water, swells and gulfs of dark green glass undulated frigidly. The sky was a dismal uniform grey.

The cave was damp though not too chilly. Ted had on his thickest jumper as well as blazer and mac; Gavin likewise, with the addition of a woollen scarf. From his deep mac pocket Gavin pulled a bundle wrapped in the *Shipping Gazette*, unwound a bottle of Gordon's Gin almost as darkly green as the sea; then he produced a small First Aid tin with some bandages and gauze in it. Finally, a chocolate bar and mince pie for himself.

Ted disgorged a crumpled envelope with birthday card inside and something in gift wrapping.

'It's a Dinky tank. Fires matchsticks. Cost my Mam four and sixpence.' Ted tossed the wrapped present aside.

Health and Efficiency and the empty Nivea jar were still where they had left them, though the magazine was now a damp wad, the pages sticking together.

Ted thought of other places where they might be doing this. In a pill-box along the dunes? With its machine-gun slits facing the beach where concrete blocks still lay slumped, waiting to repel the Nazi tanks brought on landing craft from Norway . . . a pill-box with no door, where courting couples went for a feel. There was nowhere else.

Gavin uncapped the bottle. 'Don't swig it like lemonade or you'll cough it up again. Gibbon said so. Get as much down as you can, slowly, and keep on getting it down.'

Ted started swallowing gin.

Though Ted was laying flat he felt desperately ill and dizzy. The cave roof rocked from side to side. The walls rotated. The largest of the slapping waves just below tossed their icy spittle inside, which gave some momentary relief. He sweated, he shivered. His tummy burned and churned. He longed for it to spew out everything, including that living creature that lurked there. But it would have to come out of his bottom, like the biggest turd ever.

Suddenly he did vomit. A stinking flood pumped out over Ted's mac and over weed, as convulsively as though his guts were unreeling through his mouth. Gavin had squirmed aside, swearing, 'Bloody *fuck*!' Even after nothing more would come, Ted was still racked by gasping spasms, deep down in him now, doubling him up on his side.

Gavin began to press Ted's midriff excruciatingly. 'You can do it, you filthy little tyke!' he screamed. Ted hardly heard. Waves of pain were squeezing downward rhythmically.

Gavin hadn't *entirely* believed till now. Even though he had felt those spasms in Ted's tummy. The younger boy was loopy because of what he and Gavin had done together. Gavin knew that people could make themselves ill by imagination. If only he could purge Ted, 'catharsize' him – just as Mr Brennan the English teacher said that a tragedy like Marlowe's was supposed to do to the audience. *Drive* the nonsense out of Ted which had cost Gavin a fountain pen, money, extra hours of homework, worst of all: obligation to Gibbon. Make Ted utterly sick of it! This had been in Gavin's mind as a safety valve of sanity alongside the mad steam-boiler of Ted's impossible pregnancy. A safety valve, till now.

Now Gavin unbuttoned Ted's spew-smeared mac and his blazer and hauled his flannels and underpants off over the shoes. If Ted was to give birth – to *believe* he was giving birth – he must be naked from the waist down. The sight of Ted's parts gave Gavin no joy now. Swollen, red-streaked tummy. Shrunken knob, wrinkled nuts, hairs. Ted seemed to have passed out, but his midriff convulsed; with each flux the boy's legs slid further apart – and his bottom gaped. Now there could be no doubt in Gavin's mind: the boy *was* giving birth. Having a baby, in a cave cut off by the sea. Gavin backed away up against the cave wall, chilled with dread and disgust.

He forced himself to look.

Ted's anus had split open amidst reeking shit, blood and yellow juices. Something rather smaller than the boy's head had forced its way out and lay between the spread of his legs, writhing, wriggling.

Was that a miscarriage? A premature baby?

Premature meant feeble, weak, unable to survive. Let the thing stop moving, let it die! But it wouldn't; or not immediately. He should snatch it up and toss it in the sea; he'd have to touch it, though. Or bash it with a stone.

Ted looked dead. *I've seen my Teddy bare and now he's dead; the stuffing has come out of him. I didn't kill him!*

Roll Ted's body into the sea? The corpse might float, pointing at the cave where Gavin sat imprisoned.

The thing between Ted's legs thrashed about as if to right itself; as if growing stronger. Gavin crept closer, then jerked back. The baby looked more like an octopus

54

with bulbous body, suckery arms. Or legs. How many? Where the coat of blood and shit had rubbed off, it was white as cow-tripe, white as cooked cod. Made of strong white rubber. A glossy patch might be an eye; a puckered ridge: a mouth. It was a monster, a terrible deformity. Gavin scrambled to the back of the cave where a hill of stones was piled, rubbed smooth by years and years of sea-grind at highest tide. He cast about for a suitable instrument with which to destroy it. The stones were jammed into a lumpy jigsaw. When he tugged loose an ostrich-egg of speckled, salt-whitened granite another stone shifted of its own accord; then its neighbour, and the next. As if that particular granite egg had been a keystone the whole top of the pile started to slide, scraping and grinding. As Gavin jumped clear, dropping his bludgeon, it almost seemed that the stones were being shoved from behind. High up, an opening appeared – big enough to crawl through.

The creature slithered up over Ted's body. Floppily, fast, it squirmed up the tumbled hill – Gavin shrieked and dodged – and disappeared through the gap.

When his heart stopped thumping Gavin re-armed himself. Cautiously he climbed the slope, having to duck as he came to the gap between stones and roof. The opening appeared to give on to a rough tunnel – faintly visible, extending away upward into almost-darkness. If only he had brought his torch today.

Maybe he was just seeing a rear section of the cave, one which the stones had blocked off? Surely there couldn't be a tunnel – not an actual Jingling Geordie one! Why, it would have been discovered years ago, explored, and barricaded with a padlocked iron gate, not with a heap of stones. Its existence would be common knowledge, not some legend printed in a nineteenth-century tome. Yet he perceived a tunnel. Yet a faint foetid breath wafted against his face.

The creature's breath? If such creatures breathed. He couldn't see it anywhere, though he could see little enough. As his vision adjusted, however, a blob of grey appeared to flee uphill.

Gavin descended to where the half-naked boy lay sprawled with filth and blood between his legs. Discarding the stone, he shook Ted, slapped his cheeks, tried to find a pulse, tried to find a heartbeat. Ted's flesh felt unnaturally cool; bleeding had apparently stopped.

No one knew they were here. Gavin dragged the boy towards the rear of the cave, humped him up the slope. Using all his strength, he eased the body through the opening until Ted's weight finally pulled him down out of sight.

Quickly Gavin collected Ted's trousers and pants, the wrapped present, the card, and stuffed those through the gap, too. After he had crammed the opening tight with fallen stones, he sat to await the sinking of the tide, trying not to think of what was behind him.

An hour later, having looked to see that no one was visible on the pier, he climbed from the cave and worked his way over high slippery boulders, still sloshed by the waves, back to safety; to the stone steps with their rust-bobbled rail that led up from shingle to where the granite pier rooted into the land.

In the early hours Gavin sat up in bed in a sweat of fear. With blankets dragged up to his throat, he pressed his spine against the wallpaper. The bedside lamp, which he'd switched on with a panic hand, illuminated the same familiar bedroom: blue imitation velvet curtains, untidy work-table, chair with flat orange cushion, full bookcase, calendar of Canadian scenes sent by an aunt that

Christmas, tick-tocking Swiss chalet clock with chain weighted by a metal fircone, a long framed school photograph: four ranks of tiny faces all topped by caps, one of them Ted.

Gavin had just dreamt the worst dream of his life, and knew that Ted was linked to him by an invisible cord which could stretch for miles, miles which had no meaning.

Gavin had been within Ted in that dream much more deeply than he'd been within him the previous summer. This time, he'd been wholly inside his skin.

He woke, half-naked on cold rough stone. His tummy, and beneath, was a cavern of dull pain. His head ached.

Light. More in the distance than close by, as though light needed to gain depth before it could show him his surroundings; a tunnel in rock, stretching one way and the other way to the limit of the light, the limit of his eyes.

Ted knelt on bare knees. He noticed clothes nearby. Staggering to his feet he reclaimed his underpants and trousers and managed to draw them on, over a kind of emptiness as though something was missing from him. His mac stank of stale spew; he dragged the raincoat off and dropped it.

Some way along the tunnel he noticed movement. Something small, complicated, and white was climbing along the floor towards him. Pulling, sucking itself along.

He mustn't let it reach him! He began to limp away – but now ahead of him he saw another white thing, twin to the first, an afterbirth, only the second creature was retreating from him as if filled with loathing. As he moved, the thing behind advanced, the thing in front fled. He was a kind of mirror between the two. The one ahead wanted nothing to do with him. The one behind – they were both like swollen white balls dangling long soft cocks – was doing its best to reach him, touch him, cling to him. He feared it would join itself to him suckingly, and though he sensed a hole in himself he didn't want *that* inside him ever again.

Therefore he must trudge along the tunnel, to escape from one white thing while tormenting the other white thing by pursuing it. He hadn't the strength to overtake the creature ahead, unless it stopped to welcome him; and he hoped it wouldn't. If he himself stopped, the creature behind would catch up. The tunnel seemed to extend from forever to forever, perhaps because space and time had changed.

Night after night Gavin dreamt the same dream, as if Ted was calling to be let out from behind the wall of stones.

Police visited the school to question Ted's class-mates. In assembly the headmaster said a prayer for the missing boy and his family, and warned of the dangers of not confiding in one's own parents. Word went around the school that Ted Appleby had killed himself – probably by jumping in the river – since he was depressed at putting on weight and being useless at games. No finger pointed at Gavin. Bill Gibbon may have felt scared and guilty at having persecuted Ted a bit. So if *he* knew any other explanation, he wasn't saying – even to his big brother.

Brian Gibbon asked Gavin furtively whether the gin had worked.

'Like a bomb,' said Gavin. 'But maybe she wasn't really knocked up in the first place! I think she was having me on.'

'They do. Slags! Did you use a coathanger?'

'She refused. She just drank.'

'She just wanted the gin.'

'She got pissed as a newt and sick as a dog. Serves her right, I say.'

Gibbon nodded, approving Gavin's new worldly wisdom.

The next Saturday Gavin went back to the dreadful cave, to try to purge his dreams. Scrambling to the top of the stone pile at the rear he began pulling the salty granite eggs loose one by one, tumbling them down behind him. Within five minutes he had cleared the upper reaches. He shone his torch.

On blank rock.

No opening, no tunnel, no body, no octopus-baby, nothing! Just the solid back wall of the cave.

For a moment, in spite of his clear recall that there was one cave and one cave only in the cliff, he wondered wildly whether there might be another, very similar, a few yards away. Then his gaze lighted on the empty Nivea jar. Frantically he began unloading all the loosened stones, tossing them out of the cave mouth to crash and bounce down the boulders. Then he attacked the bulk of the pile.

He worked hard. Half an hour later the cave was bare. He had even torn up the weed matting from the floor. He stood gasping for breath in an empty hollow, a barren stone womb. The only way out or in was the way he had come already.

Gavin sat on the stone floor and wept.

That night in the dream for the first time Gavin's perspective altered. Now he himself was the terrified, nauseated creature which groped and sucked its way along that dim tunnel – to escape from the zombi figure of Ted which lumbered helplessly after him.

Images began to form in Gavin's mind. He saw that something ancient existed behind that hollow pocket in the headland known as Jingling Geordie's Hole. It could open up its own spaces when it wished. The previous summer the creature had opened a door from its stone depths, to enter Ted; to put part of itself into him, to grow there for a while. Two weeks ago it had opened the door again, to reclaim itself. And to claim Ted, its spent host.

Why? Its thoughts weren't human thoughts. Maybe it wished to escape, but didn't know how. Maybe it wanted to taste the outside world, like an octopus poking an arm from its lair then pulling it back in again, a phantom, ectoplasmic arm emerging out of stone.

Now it was claiming Gavin too, sucking him through the cord which joined him to the dead boy; who wasn't exactly dead. Just as the creature, though cased in stone, wasn't dead.

Gavin glimpsed a fossil: of a primeval, mutated octopus-thing which possessed strange and terrible persistence, a suction upon existence; which had somehow stayed alive in stone. Imprisoned under prehistoric mud, its flesh had changed to rock during a million years but its whole pattern persisted, the pattern not just of body but of *will*.

Yes, he saw this image clearly now! – as a distant, mute beckoning, from the far end of the tunnel – though really the tunnel had no end. Its earlier stretch and its later stretch were the same, eternal stretch.

It must get lonely inside that rock. But the everlasting creature didn't seem to be imaginative. Or insane, or sane. It merely exerted power over the space around it, and over time; power which caused it to survive. People in the past had sensed its presence: the 'knight' – a naïve medieval youth on a quest for some holy grail? – and the old-time smuggler, Geordie, with his trinkets clinking about him, whom it swallowed into the rock as he was stowing kegs of rum or whatever. Possessing them both.

As it had possessed Ted, and was now beginning, from a distance, to possess Gavin . . . until one night soon he would find himself out of bed, dragging coat and shoes on, tiptoeing from the house, hurrying helplessly through the darkness down to the sea, to climb into the cave for one final, everlasting time. The door to the tunnel-which-wasn't-a-tunnel would open and close behind him, and he too would be encased in stone, a fossil continuing to think clinging thoughts, and dream, and sense existence. In the grip of the octopus-wraith, near the ghost-fossils of Ted and the knight and the smuggler who must be insane long since, buried alive in their solid, perpetual, cold hell.

'Only a therm-o-nuclear explosion right above the pier could melt us out of our rock! Turn us to gas and dust, and end us. Could kill the white stone octopus. Bomb the Priory, Gav! Get in the crane and rip the cliff open!'

Ted's thoughts were reaching Gavin! Gavin was thinking the boy's thoughts now. Their minds were mingling. Or was the octopus-creature transmitting Ted-like thoughts – which it hardly comprehended? Whichever, Ted and he would have ages together to think such thoughts, ages haunted by a foul noise of monotonous, circulating reverie, degenerating yet never fading. Unless a thermonuclear war broke out.

As if the fear was parent to the deed, the next night Gavin woke to find himself standing in near-darkness. He was out of bed. Something soft clutched at his arms.

Gasping with panic he blundered towards the hidden light switch. Iron fircone and Swiss chalet clock flew askew. With his brow he butted the switch. Light blossomed. The thing that was gripping him was his own raincoat, half-donned. His sockless feet were stuck into unlaced shoes.

Tearing off the mac and kicking the shoes away, he

plunged back under the blankets where he shivered with dread.

That night, or the next night. That week, or the next . . .

Deep within mad Jingling Geordie's Hole, there in the young knight's hell-bound corridor, next to the cracking fossil of Ted: forever the stone ghost waited. Ghost out of ancient Carboniferous seas, prehuman, perpetual. Potent – and imbecilic.

Forever its petrified prisoners whispered their crazed memories of the greed or fierce desire or yearning which had led them into that cave, and which had spurred the living fossil to open its stone door.

7

It was a week later, as arranged.

'*Rewind!* Go back to the previous life before you were Gavin.'

I had found it a handy trick to instruct my patients while under hypnosis as though their minds were tape recorders or videos. I would explain this to them in advance, and run through the commands I used so as to programme these in.

'Who are you now?' I asked Tony.

'Me name's Harry Bell. Aa live with me Mam in Front Street, Tynemouth, alang from Missus Halliday's. That's where aal the important folks come to visit Miss Martineau in hor sick room. She's too ill to step ootside the hoose, but ye can see hor telescope at the window watchin' everything as gans on. Miss Martineau's deaf too, ye knaa, so she can read lips. With that telescope she can tell what the sailors is sayin' half a mile oot.'

Harry's accent was much broader than Tony's, or Gavin's. That meant little. Any Tynesider could put on the voice.

'Well, Aa had a bigger ear trumpet than hors – in the shape of me own two lugholes, God help me. An' Aa spied more than she ever did with hor telescope! Only, there's some sights nay boogar should ever see; an' Aa saw o' those sights last year. It's laid its finger on me – not as it had any fingers to speak of. It's hooked its clarty grappers in me buttonhole, an' Aa canna shake loose. It's slid itsel into me heed, where the dreams are.'

'How did this happen, Harry?'

'It was the fault of owld Shanky Elwes! It was him as wagered that Red Indian fella, Van Amburgh, when he came to Shields last year, that he couldn't winkle what lives in Jinglin' Geordie's Hole oot of its nook an' tame it. Trust Shanky to knaa aboot what's in that cave in the cliff! Elsewise, just a few smugglers an' wreck-scroungers an' their hinnies knaa'd. Sartinly not them soldier lads struttin' aroond the Castle up top wi' their minds on loose tarts as fancies a uniform.

'Van Amburgh got away scot-free. That's cause he had the knack of a mesmerizer when it came to wild beasts. Aa suppose ye'd have to call the thing in the cave a beast, though it wasn't like any other beast on Earth. And nothin' breathin' ever put one over on Shanky. But Aa'm afraid the creature's fettled me. The dreams, man! Aa could use some o' that mesmerizin' mesel, same as Miss Martineau's gannin' in for – '

'Pause! What year is it, Harry?'

'Wey, 1844.'

So the traumatic event which happened 'last year' occurred in 1843. I was disturbed to find that damned cave cropping up again. Two persons could often pop up in tandem from one life to the next. Bitter enemies, thwarted lovers, or victim and murderer. Why not a person and a place? Plainly the hole in the cliff represented a locus for Tony's primary neurosis.

I was also bothered by the mention of 'mesmerizing'. This seemed like an intrusion from the present, a reflection of the therapy situation. What I needed to do first of all was sort the wheat from the chaff.

'Fast forward, Harry. Go almost to the end of your life.' Assuming that he had lived a good few years beyond 1844, this could establish some perspective. 'What year is it now, Harry? How old are you?'

'It's 1888. An' Aa'm sixty-two.'

'Where are you, Harry?'

'Aa'm in the bloody workhoose. Aa knaa that much. Aa'm drivellin'. Slobberin'. They call us a lunatic an Aa knaa's it's true. A pauper an' a looney. On account o' the dreams. Last year Aa couldn't keep away from the cave any longer. Aa've been fightin' the pull of it aal me life. Aa got hold of one o' them bombs as they've been tryin' to blow up the polliss stations with. Aa knaa'd who was involved. Anarchists! When yor trampin' the streets an' the fish quay an' docks ye hear things if ye keep your lugs open.

'Ye knaa how they tried to explode John Matheson's hoose at Hebburn with gunpowder back in May last year? Him as manages the shipyard, Messrs Hawthorne Leslie. That was just afore the big Jubilee Exhibition up in Newcastle on the Town Moor. An' they had three attempts at polliss buildin's includin' the courthoose in Hebburn. They'd cross over on the Ha'penny Dodger ferry to hide oot in North Shields. Aa knaa'd who they were. As said Aa'd tell unless they gave me a bomb – to blow up Tynemouth Castle with, that's what Aa telt them. But Aa blew up the cave in the hill. Aa did. Wey man, Aa sealed it tight. Folks thowt it was a fall o' rock. It worn't.

'It ain't over, though. The creature still thrashes aboot in me heed. The horror, man, the horror! That's when Aa finally snapped. Noo Aa'm stuck in the workhoose, drivellin'.'

'Pause!'

The workhouse. Was that the 'Spital? The same place had figured in Gavin Percy's life, haunting and disgusting him. Here it was again, with Gavin's predecessor confined there.

I buzzed Brenda on the intercom to ask her to postpone Mrs Amanda Harvey, with profound apologies. Brenda

Jarvis was my receptionist and secretary – though certainly not secretary to Jack Cannon, about whom she knew nothing. From the neighbouring room Brenda also acted as a kind of chaperone to my hypnosis sessions, not listening in on them but available. Brenda would nip upstairs every hour to see to any needs of my mother.

'Rewind, Harry. Go back to 1843.' To the year when he had seen the sight which sank fish-hooks into his brain, the date when he had supposedly encountered that creature in the cave.

The afternoon's session with Tony stretched out to well over two hours. That evening – and several evenings thereafter – my right hand, Jack, was pressed into service again.

In 1819 a certain William Henry Elwes inherited the title of baronet, though without any fortune or lands to go with his nobility. The new Sir William was thirty-five years old and a singularly handsome fellow. In size and general appearance he closely resembled King George IV – apart from the fact that William Elwes possessed exceptionally long legs, which had led to him being nicknamed 'Shanky' just as Edward I had been dubbed 'Longshanks'.

Unfortunately Shanky was a spendthrift and a scapegrace, bane of his mother and a terrible trial to his friends and family. His two younger brothers were both promising army men, though their careers were sadly cut short. Lieutenant Henry John Elwes of the 7th West India Regiment died of illness at Nassau in the Bahamas. Lieutenant John Raleigh Elwes (71st Highland Light Infantry) succumbed to battle wounds twelve days after Waterloo. Shanky was no such model of good conduct.

A few years after the defeat of Napoleon the gay and attractive young reprobate – newly ennobled but totally penniless – was invited to a ball in the seaside resort of Largs on the Firth of Clyde. The ball was hosted by officers of the 71st Highland Light Infantry; there Shanky had the good luck to captivate a Miss Bannatyne. She and her sister had been brought up in style at Mauldslie Castle, between Carluke and Wishaw, where their education was overseen by the Earl of Hyndford's aunt. The Misses Bannatyne's father had been a deputy-lieutenant of Lanarkshire and a close friend of the Duke of Hamilton; thus the daughters had mixed with the very best of local society, not to mention being frequent guests of the reformer Robert Owen.

Maybe Miss Bannatyne imagined that she could reform Sir Shanky. If so, she was blinded by love to all the pleas of friends and relatives. Wedding Shanky in haste, she repented – not exactly at leisure. Strings were pulled to provide commissions for her husband but he ruined every opportunity by running up debts, resulting in him being regularly thrown into prison. A divorce was finally arranged, however the strain had proved too much for the former Miss Bannatyne. She was to die in a lunatic asylum.

Sir Shanky wandered to North Shields, where he became a notorious local joke. This joke would have been nastier if Elwes had not retained his habitual charm and good manners. He married a Mrs Thompson who already had three children to cope with, and to support his extravagances he set himself up as an informer.

Shanky was forever to be seen striding about the town on those stilt legs of his, poking his nose into everyone's affairs. He was the terror of shopkeepers who used short weights or who stocked smuggled items. He was the bane of every street huckster and hawker or higgler, as well as of the smuggling fraternity whose goods came ashore by night in the river mouth. He knew all their complicated signals and signs. Shanky was most particular that the Crown should not be defrauded of any revenue – so that he could himself be duly rewarded at the going rate.

In the years before the building of the railway he would station himself on Coach Lane, the route from Newcastle, to observe the stage coaches passing by. These were only licensed to carry so many passengers. One person in excess on board, and Shanky would be off post-haste to the Town Hall in Sidney Street where the supervisor of excise, Mr Robert Ridley, grew as familiar with Shanky as with a twin brother. Whenever a case was proved against a coachman, the informer must receive half the fine.

Shanky continued to borrow on the strength of his title and his good manners, whenever he could find a suitable dupe. Creditors might as well hope to squeeze blood from a stone, as to be repaid. Some angry optimists did try to gain recompense at law. Thus, from time to time, it was back to prison for Shanky – not that these experiences disheartened him. While he was in Morpeth Gaol for debt in '26, he wrote to a firm of tailors in London ordering an expensive suit to be made to measure and despatched to 'Sir William Henry Elwes, Bart., Morpeth House'.

It was from one of the Tynemouth in-shore fishermen, who supplemented his income by rowing out to meet ships by night to bring back brandy, that Shanky learned of the unnatural creature that roosted deep inside Jingling Geordie's Hole. The smuggler had actually seen the beast, and felt its feelers touch his mind.

('Aa knaa's this on account o' how Aa heard Shanky tellin' the Red Indian, when he wagered him – ')

Shanky had surprised the fisherman at some nocturnal antic. As bribe to buy silence, the man offered this information. Shanky demanded proof. Reluctantly the man accompanied Shanky to the cave, down there below the Castle and the lighthouse on Pen Bal Crag, swearing that the beast would sense him coming.

Whatever Shanky experienced at the cave convinced him. But it did not curdle his brains. In his blithely unscrupulous way Shanky was imperturbable. Gaol? Phooey. Wife gone insane? Shrug of the shoulders. I'm Sir William Henry Elwes, Bart.

Shanky kept the knowledge to himself for a while, till he could work out how to make some profit from it – an opportunity which only came in June 1843, by which time Harriet Martineau had been languishing on her sofa in Front Street not so many hundred yards away for somewhat over three years . . .

8

'You work so hard,' said Mother. 'Typing all evening. I hear you.'

Not me, but Jack.

'In a way the evenings are lonelier than the days. During the day I see Brenda quite often. She's a good girl. It's a shame she never married, and now she's getting on a bit.'

'She isn't a girl, in that case,' I said with a smile.

'With this disgusting AIDS thing, that's better. It's safer. You need really to know the person, know their habits. How long has Brenda been with us now?'

'Going on for seven years, I suppose.'

'Yes, she's settled in. Now she's thirty-six. You aren't too much older than her. It does get a bit lonely in the evenings.'

'Are you in any pain?'

Mother lay abed against plumped-up pillows. An old cloth-bound book, which I recognized all too well, sprawled on the eiderdown. The TV set was as blank as it had been earlier. The remote control peeped from behind a few other books on the bedside table. I had brewed both of us an Ovaltine, and had set Mother's mug amidst the pills and Kleenex and carafe of barley water.

Mother's arthritis still permitted her to use the en suite bathroom, which was adapted for her disability, and to go to sit on the sofa or in the armchair by the window if she preferred. That window looked out towards the huge, wooded cemetery. The ever-busy main road in the foreground counteracted the possible melancholy of the view.

Mother's hair was entirely white. Her face was thin, though not unduly grooved by pain caused by her joints. Age had shrunk her, emphasizing her bones and sharpening her nose, so that she looked like a bright-eyed, snow-feathered bird, a spry neat bird of winter with her faculties still intact. She wore a white angora bed-jacket.

I thought briefly of a gull in a glass case in the Hancock Museum up the road. Mother's bedroom had become something of a museum too, filled with her treasures. A glass cabinet of miscellaneous ornaments: Dresden ladies with parasols, rows of ribbon ware, fat green old paperweights . . . bookcases, photograph albums . . .

She said, 'It was kind of Brenda to stay here while you visited that psychology conference in Birmingham last year. Kind, don't you think?'

'Yes,' I agreed. 'Though I paid her.'

'It was no trouble to her.'

I had told Mother that I was going to Birmingham for professional purposes.

Mother wanted me to marry Brenda Jarvis. Then, there would be a helpmate always in the house. A daughter-in-law. Maybe even a grandchild? Jack didn't wish any of that. It would hamper his whole existence, the free play of his imagination.

'I'm forty-eight, she's thirty-six. That's too much of a gap.'

'Oh no! A woman is usually younger than her husband.'

'Which is peculiar, since women live longer than men.'

'Don't they?' agreed Mother. 'They outlive their husbands by years – of loneliness and solitude.'

Father had died twelve years earlier, just shortly after he had retired from Boots the Chemists where he had spent most of his working life as a dispenser.

Subtly Mother changed tack. 'I'm not trying to interfere with your work, John. I know how important it is. Nor am I trying to interfere with your chosen life. But, well, shouldn't you have *more* life? I confine you to this house – except for that weekend last autumn.'

'Enough varied lives come into this house to satisfy anyone, I'd have thought! Lives lived in the Middle Ages, in ancient Rome and Egypt; just you name it.'

'But why don't you go out more of an evening? You used to like a drop of beer.' She managed to look both pained and encouraging.

'I can just as easily drink at home. Some of the pubs in Newcastle these days after dark . . . it's Dickensian. Broken glass, blood-stains.'

'I'm sure you could find a decent one. Why not invite Brenda out for a drink? I'm not a total cripple. I wouldn't panic. Doesn't draught beer taste best?'

I shrugged. 'I drink Brown Ale these days. Why go to a pub for a bottle?'

'For the company.'

Ah, but I had company. Jack's.

'Speaking of ale . . . would you read a little to me?' She indicated the book on the bed. How deviously and stubbornly her mind still worked. Her thoughts were spiders' webs, fragile yet very tough if you were a fly.

'A poem by your namesake. You know he always amuses me. Read that poem in praise of Newcastle beer, will you? Maybe that's where you got your own taste for the stuff – from your earlier incarnation! I wonder who I might become in my next life? And will we two know each other again?'

Mother accepted the idea of reincarnation because I made my career out of it. She consistently failed quite to grasp the theory. I had only ever once broached my own mixed feelings on the subject. I shouldn't even have tried. My words had wounded her, as though I was pretending cruelly not to believe in what I obviously must believe.

72

Mistake, mistake. Mother could confide my agnosticism to Brenda. Brenda might mention my attitude outside the house, though not out of disloyalty. Complications could ensue.

That old nineteenth-century edition of the poems of another John Cunningham of Newcastle underlined my problem with Mother's subtly oppressive brand of wishful thinking. Why should I *not* have been that eighteenth-century poet, now reborn into a more successful life? And if my previous life was so easily identifiable, then why should Mother and I not both meet each other again in a future existence?

'I've never known a case,' I told her, 'where a person has the same name in different lives. People just aren't reborn into the same families.' (That would be psychically incestuous, wouldn't it?)

'Same family? What same family?' Mother sounded sentimentally wounded, as if I was rejecting her. 'The other John never married or had children.'

Just like me, eh? Therefore, why should I not be repeating the same pattern? His weak, shy pattern.

Who on earth would want to have been the poet John Cunningham? True, he had enough merit to have been memorialized in stained glass in St John's down in the city a whole ninety years after his death. But really the man's life had been a cruel comedy.

I picked up the book, found the poem she wanted, and read aloud:

'When Fame brought the news of Great Britain's success,
    And told at Olympus each Gallic defeat,
Glad Mars sent by Mercury orders express
    To summon the Deities all to a treat.
        So the Comus was placed
        To guide the gay feast,
And freely declared there was a choice of good cheer,

73

> Yet vowed, to his thinking,
> For exquisite drinking,
> Their Nectar was nothing to Newcastle Beer.'

It's an eighteenth-century TV commercial,' I joked.

'You should heed it, John. Read on.'

Which I did. However, when I got towards the end, the last two jingling verses struck me as utterly sinister that night.

> 'Ye youngsters so diffident, languid, and pale,
> Whom love, like the colic, so rudely infests,
> Take a cordial of this, 'twill *probatum* prevail,
> And drive the cur Cupid away from your breasts.
> Dull whining despise,
> Grow rosy and wise,
> No longer the jest of good fellows appear,
> Bid adieu to your folly,
> Get drunk and be jolly,
> And smoke o'er a tankard of Newcastle Beer.'

Yes, the young people were languid and pale with fears of sex, with AIDS-dread. In the pubs they were drinking to chase Cupid away. Increaseth the desire (maybe!) but taketh away the performance. Good, good, get sodding drunk!

> 'Ye fanciful folk, for whom *physic* prescribes,
> Whom bolus and potion have harassed to death,
> Ye wretches whom *law* and ill-looking tribes
> Have hunted about till you're quite out of breath,
> Here's shelter and ease,
> No craving for fees,
> No danger – no doctor – no bailiff is near;
> Your spirits this raises,
> It cures your diseases;
> There's freedom and health in our Newcastle Beer.'

74

Physic had no prescription nowadays, none. Newcastle beer couldn't cure the disease, though it certainly did take a lot of minds off it – the minds of the lost, the lovelost generation.

Mother chuckled appreciatively.

'Now read "Kate of Aberdeen" – and then "The Withered Rose".'

My namesake John Cunningham was born in Dublin in 1729. His father coopered wine barrels for a living. Being unlucky enough to win a lottery – an earlier incarnation of the Irish Sweepstake – Cunningham Senior promptly set himself up as a full-blown wine merchant, and quite soon went bankrupt. Young John was hauled back home from his new grammar school half-educated and with no prospects. He hung around the Dublin theatre, and out of his soul at the tender age of seventeen there blossomed a play called *Love in a Mist*. This went down great guns in Dublin, and on tour in Newcastle too.

John was fired with a craze to be an actor. This, despite his absolute lack of acting talent – and of physical grace. His face, with its cow's eyes, horse's nose, and mouth of a parrot, could have curdled milk. His voice resembled a corncrake's.

Nevertheless he joined a company of players who specialized in touring the North of England. The only roles he ever played with any success were comic cranky Frenchmen. However! While acting on the Edinburgh fringe in the early 1760s the ugly duckling began to publish swan-like verse.

A London bookseller offered to sponsor him. John rushed to London, to find that the bookseller had suddenly gone bankrupt. Back in Edinburgh again, John enjoyed better fortune with the actor-manager of the Theatre Royal, Mr Digges. Digges commissioned prologues and epilogues to be recited by himself and by the lovely Miss Bellaney.

Perhaps certain rhapsodies which John penned in praise of Miss Bellaney's charms began to irk Mr Digges? At any rate, John removed himself to Newcastle, scene of early triumph, a town for which he had always felt a soft spot. He scraped a living by acting, supplemented by minor commissions from the amiable then-owner of the *Newcastle Chronicle*, Thomas Slack. Wealthy local admirers of John's melodious poetry chipped in.

1766, *annus mirabilis*! John's collected poems were published by subscription. So instead of taking the advice of every sensible friend and dedicating the volume to his most generous local patroness, Mrs Montagu of Denton, John inscribed the book instead to the country's greatest actor, David Garrick, hoping that a suitably flattered Garrick would make the awkward corncrake into a star of the London stage.

John had a copy of his poems sumptuously bound and walked all the way to London to lay it at Garrick's feet. Garrick gave John the bum's rush. He treated him almost like a beggar, and in lordly style sent the poet packing with a couple of guineas.

John trudged back to Newcastle, and spent the money drowning his sorrows. Mrs Slack boxed John's ears for not tossing the guineas back in Garrick's face.

Downhill from there on! Depression, premature ageing, and too much Newcastle beer. John still managed to do a spot of acting and write some verse, and the Slacks always loyally supported him. They even housed him; and Mrs Slack would empty his pockets before letting him out of the door in case he gave away the pittance he had, either to someone in worse distress or else to a barman.

One Sunday a portly churchman surprised John fishing in a tributary of the Wear, and harangued him for fishing on the Lord's Day. With gentle inoffensiveness John begged pardon, since his only chance of a dinner lay at the bottom of that pool.

Being so extremely ugly, John had always resisted having a portrait made. A few days before the poet's death, however, Bewick the engraver spotted him shambling along a Newcastle street clutching a scrap of handkerchief with a herring in it. By guilefully overtaking and loitering and overtaking, Bewick succeeded in sketching dying bard with fish.

I read:

> '"Why call us to revoltless doom?"
>   With grief the opening buds reply;
> "Not suffer'd to extend our bloom –
>   Scarce born, alas! before we die."'

That was the last poem John Cunningham wrote. AIDS, I thought. The lovelost generation.

'But we live again,' said Mother, 'don't we?'

'Mmm,' I said.

'So that's all right.'

9

Harriet did not enjoy a happy childhood in Norwich, where her father manufactured cloth during the first decades of the nineteenth century.

Mainly the misery was of Harriet's own making. Although the early onset of ever-worsening deafness hardly helped her morale, Harriet convinced herself quite falsely that she was despised compared with the other children of the family. She was sixth in a complement of eight. She became sullenly petulant.

For years on end she failed to protest at this non-existent assessment of herself – or even to mention or query it. If she had done so, the mirage might have vanished. In actual fact she was given a far better education than most girls of her time.

For years she wished ill health upon herself – not in order to gain attention, which obviously she didn't merit, but merely masochistically.

At times she seemed almost pathologically alienated, for not only was she disconnected from human voices by her ear trouble, but often she couldn't even see what other people were pointing out to her in plain view. She enjoyed exceptional eyesight, quite unimpaired by any amount of close needlework and book learning, yet she developed her own strange (and mortifying) species of blind spot.

At the age of seven, on a family visit to far-off Tynemouth, she could not for minutes on end perceive the vast surging sea at the foot of the very slope where her family were gathered, gazing admiringly.

At the age of nine, she completely failed to be able to spot the great comet of 1811 which everyone else was goggling at night after night through the big windows at the top of her father's warehouse.

Was this done in order to cheat herself of pleasure? Or to rob her family of enjoyment? Maybe not! Maybe it was a defence against anything unusual and remarkable.

As an even younger child the oddest things could terrify Harriet. The Martineau children would frequently be sent to walk on Castle Hill in Norwich. From there they could watch the local residents beating their feather beds down in the vista below. There was always a tiny, inexplicable gap in time between the sight of a blow with a stick and the dull thud of sound (she wasn't deaf yet). This gap horrified Harriet, as though the world was coming unstrung. Yet it never occurred to her to ask about it. She never thought of mentioning her fear and hatred of that walk. Thus she could silently reproach her parents with lacking the kindness and the sympathy to guess the circumstances that persecuted her – provoking her to so much illness and ill temper.

But no matter. Up by her own bootlaces! As a girl she had struggled to codify the principles of the Bible, and to tabulate these into a set of moral theorems worthy of Euclid. She developed an obsessively methodical streak. When the family business collapsed and her father died, ill health obviously forbade Harriet from becoming a governess like her sisters. So she pitched into local journalism to save the family home.

She allied method to imagination. Now that her imagination was given a playground, and a workshop, she became much more amiable, sweeter, and more considerate – though never anyone's fool.

Hey presto, Harriet was winning not one, not two, but all three prizes in a Unitarian competition for essays on

79

how best to convert Catholics and Jews and Moslems by reasoned argument to Unitarianism.

Hey presto again, she was best-selling author of a monthly series of semi-fictional booklets with settings from Demerara to Siberia expounding all the principles of political economy.

She was famous, she was lionized by grinning idiots (something she disliked). Her friends and acquaintances were a roll-call of reformers and authors and thinkers: Malthus, Robert Owen, Carlyle, Babbage, Darwin . . . Government ministers pressed blue books of statistics on her, begging her to propagandize.

At the age of twenty-four Harriet might have married, but her fiancé – John Hugh Worthington – suddenly went insane and died mad within a few months. Thereafter, Harriet was happy not to have married. She rejoiced in her emotionally unencumbered life and her clear mind; not that she ever saw eye to eye with Mary Wollstone-craft, self-proclaimed champion of women. Miss Woll-stonecraft raised such a furore about how she, as a female, was a social victim – when really she was the victim of her own noisy, hectic, self-centredness in Harriet's opinion.

Harriet's industry multiplied, accompanied by a putter-ing 'liver' complaint. In 1834 she sailed to tour America for two years. She grew so involved in the anti-slavery cause that she might have emigrated permanently to America, had it not been for her illness of 1838. This affliction crept up on Harriet amidst much political and social bustle, including her American travel book, her first novel, and further travelling in Scotland and Europe. She was sure that the illness was due to a tumour of the kind that generally originates from mental suffering; that was her diagnosis and she stuck to it for years.

Harriet collapsed in Venice and was quickly repatriated to the house of her brother-in-law, Dr Greenhow, in

Newcastle. Thomas Greenhow was surgeon to Newcastle Infirmary. He cared for Harriet in his home for six months, but then she was transferred away from the grime and bustle of the city to the seaside. She took up residence in Mrs Halliday's boarding house, where she was to lie on a sofa for more than five yers.

And to sit, too, with her telescope as a peephole on the world. And accompanied by her books, especially of travel. (Little did Harriet realize that thanks to mesmerism she would later be hiking vigorously through the Lake District in the depths of winter, and touring Egypt!) And consoled by her framed print of Scheffer's *Christus Consolator*, a gift from actress Adelaide Kemble who visited Tynemouth and sang 'Auld Robin Gray' by Harriet's couch. (But Harriet was already well along the road from her early primitive Unitarianism towards eventual, comfortable free thought and Comtian positivism.)

And of course she was attended by poor orphan Jane, Mrs Halliday's long-suffering and much-bullied niece.

One spring morning after a night of severe pain, through her sitting-room window raised high on its sashes the invalid saw . . .

Lo, sunshine flooded through the ancient, empty window-holes in the ruins of the Priory. The sun danced diamonds on the harbour mouth, and lit the yellow sands across the Tyne.

Hands on hips, neighbour Mrs Bell strolled complacently down to the bottom of her garden to feed her pigs and milk her cows. Next Mrs Bell would let the cattle out of their shed to graze upon the furrowed downland which rose, emerald as Ireland, to the Spanish Battery ridge overlooking the Black Midden rocks.

Harriet still had occasional nightmares about her

mother walking off that precipice into the invisible sea
. . . but wine and laudanum eased such fantasies.

To the eastward the ridge dipped steeply into Prior's
Haven with its chimneyed bathhouse. The only minor
interruption to the view was a solitary sycamore, stunted
by winter storms and exposure. Not another tree to be
seen until those on the uplands beyond the southern
shore! Yet she could exchange the beauty of trees for that
of the sea. Her chosen lodging place offered a fine
segment instead of a whole horizon vast with glaring, eye-
stunning ocean. *That* would have been excessive, and
numbing to the spirit.

Panning her telescope upward from the southern shore,
she gazed at the heath where gangs of boys often flew
kites, where young men and women would saunter a-
courting, where gossipy washerwomen would mount the
lanes towards the houses of the gentry with great white
bundles perched on their heads. At this early moment
only one solitary sportsman was abroad, with gun and
dog.

A puffing billy came careering along the railway line
beyond, past hedges and trees. The engine panted steam
as it laboured upward and away between hills. Mr
Stephenson's vindication! How the sophisticates of
London laughed at the uneducated Stephenson when he
first addressed them in his uncouth accent. Oh, they had
hooted and split their sides. Now hundreds of miles of
new railway were being opened, and George Stephenson
took his well-deserved ease at Tapton, growing melons
and tropical flowers and winning prizes for his giant
marrows; while Harriet, becalmed, watched his brainchild
bustle out of sight.

She angled the telescope higher still. On the heights of
the hills were paddocks, yards, and dairies of several
farms. A windmill. A lime kiln in a rock-strewn field. A
church tower. And a colliery where driverless wagons

rolled along their elevated, sloping tracks under the guidance of gravity.

Topmost of all was the tip of Pensher Hill. Soon that little peak would be graced by a suitably noble monument to poor, honest Lord Durham – so tragically broken by political treachery and insult. The Masonic lodges of England were raising a private subscription.

And now Mrs Bell was heading back, bearing two pails of frothing milk. She paused to cast a proprietorial eye over the rows where her son Harry had sown their radishes.

Abruptly a pair of twittering redbreasts alighted amongst the hyacinths in the flower box outside Harriet's window. The birds squabbled fiercely, scarcely heeding her. Mrs Bell glanced up and saw Harriet watching. Forcing a smile in spite of her pain – which had indeed faded considerably – Harriet withdrew. She walked through the sitting room with all its pots of blooming tulips and narcissi, back to the darkened bedroom at the front.

There, she parted the curtains upon Front Street – to catch sight of the penny-postman . . . and of that officious busybody, Sir William Elwes.

Elwes! It was he, *he* – presuming on his title of noble breeding, when he was no better than a common informer! – who had scented a profitable game at Harriet's expense. It was he who had set the tattling, double-dealing Mrs Blagdon to thrust herself upon Harriet in the delicate matter of the testimonial fund which friends were raising on Harriet's behalf.

The intrusion was so energetic that Harriet's two dear aunts had to come expressly, to lodge close by. One or other aunt must constantly be available for summons by Jane, should Mrs Blagdon call. The aunt would hurry on the instant to Mrs Halliday's to forbid mention of the fund, and to bear witness that Harriet remained quite innocent of the progress of the scheme, far from being its initiator and grey eminence.

Did Elwes hope to catch the postman in breach of some petty regulation? He was scanning a sheet of paper as though it was a letter he had discovered lying in the gutter.

Was he covertly studying Mrs Halliday's? Elwes did indeed glance across the street to where Harriet kept watch; but then he directed a long gaze down Front Street towards the Castle, while thoughtfully he rubbed his chin.

Elwes suddenly thrust the paper into his pocket and strode the opposite way. That would lead him soon enough past Mrs Blagdon's door.

Harriet spotted Harry Bell hurry across the wide street. The lad ducked into the doorway of the confectioner's, from which he peeped out after Elwes. Harry began to *follow* the man. So it looked, at any rate.

Harriet pulled the knob on the wall to jangle a bell and summon Jane.

Poor Jane. She had sat up late the previous night to occupy Harriet in her wretched discomfort. If the girl was dozy this morning, one must hope that her aunt wasn't treating her sourly and savagely, as so often. Young Jane was a treasure: truthful, ingenuous, without a grain of dishonesty or tarnish in her soul. Mrs Halliday abused and scolded Jane unmercifully, all of which the girl bore with sweet cheerfulness. Sometimes Harriet's heart bled.

True, Jane was forever a mess: face dirty, hair a mop. And Harriet's rooms lacked for proper dusting and tidying. Yet the girl's eyesight hardly allowed her to perceive a cobweb or a smut on her own brow. Those rheumy, sickly eyes – the irises seeming to be covered in tissue paper – were Jane's other cross in addition to her ignorant and selfish aunt.

Jane arrived, blear-eyed, in a rumpled dress.

'Wey, good mornin', Mistress! How are ye feelin'? Shall Aa pull the curtains? Here's the post an' the paper for ye.'

Jane held out a tray. Upon it, last night's *Newcastle Chronicle*, a trio of letters, and handbill.

'Yes, do open the curtains, dear Jane, or we'll neither of us see what we're doing.'

That handbill . . . surely it was the same piece of paper that Elwes had been scanning with such apparent interest? Harriet read:

THE WORLD-FAMOUS LION TAMER!
Van Amburgh of Kentucky
WHO CAN TAME ANY KNOWN CREATURE
Will soon visit Sunderland, Newcastle,
South Shields, North Shields, Blyth,
Morpeth, Alnwick, and Berwick, et cetera
Accompanied by Titus's Magnificent Managerie!
Comprising Fierce Lions & Lionesses,
A Royal Bengal Tiger, a savage Black
Tiger, two Panthers, et cetera.

There was more in small print.

The postman had been delivering these bills and he ought not to have been. A boy should have done the job, instead of a public employee accepting the shiny shilling. Now Elwes would likely be off to the post office to report on the man, supposing there was a share in a fine.

So perhaps Elwes wouldn't be paying a call on Mrs Blagdon to further the annoying conspiracy . . .

Had Harry Bell set out in pursuit of Elwes so that he could run back and forewarn . . . Jane? Harriet was puzzled.

Laying the handbill on the mantelshelf, she took her letters and the *Chronicle* through to the other room. Jane remained, to tidy a bed disordered by Harriet's tossings

85

and turnings, laudanum notwithstanding; and to tend the hearth, doubtless smutting her fingers and face.

Sinking on to the sofa, Harriet scanned the return addresses. One letter was from the ever amusing Sydney Smith, now alas old and failing. Another was from deaf Bulwer Lytton. A third, from Thomas Carlyle. But first Harriet opened the *Chronicle*, that excellent publication of the liberal Hodgsons in Union Street.

'Ah!' she cried.

Jane hurried through. 'Ma'am?'

'Fine news! It is as I hoped. There is to be a petition to Parliament against Mr Bright's failure at Durham. We must trust this will lead to Lord Dungannon's election being declared void!'

'Mr Bright is the gen'leman again' the Corn Laws?'

'Yes. He and Mr Cobden. You recall how Mr Cobden visited us here in February, together with Colonel Thompson?'

'Mr Cobden, the Member of Parliament, wey aye, Aa knaa.'

During the course of Harriet's illness visitors and correspondents had confided many deep matters to her discretion. Cobden hoped that she might apply her pen to his cause; which was also Harriet's cause. Cobden and comrades spent so much of their time lecturing and lobbying that they had little chance to chart the actual future of free trade, following a repeal which must surely come.

Only lately, Bright and Cobden had held a great meeting in the Music Hall at Newcastle, one of an infinity of such meetings around the country. At least *their* reception in Newcastle had been much more hospitable than that accorded to Robert Owen in January. When Mr Owen expounded his utopian socialism in the Nelson Street Lecture Room, that meeting was broken up by a mob of Irish residents wielding sticks and bedposts and chair legs.

Taking a cue from this fracas, the rabidly Tory *Newcastle Journal* was doing its best to stir up violence against the freetrade campaigners. According to the deplorable *Journal*, Bright was a 'disaffected vagabond' whom all 'stalwart yeomen' should feel no compunction in thrashing. Hence the importance of John Bright being elected Member for Durham.

'I will explain this to you,' Harriet told Jane. 'Then perhaps you could explain something to me?'

The Durham seat had been vacated by Captain Fitzroy when he accepted a Government appointment. But it was a difficult target for any Liberal. Bright had hesitated until the very last moment about accepting the Liberal nomination. Meanwhile the Tory campaign hoisted all its sails. Brass bands marched the streets for several evenings preceded by flags in Tory red. Newspapers, especially the *Journal*, were promising a walk-over for Lord Dungannon and predicting that no Liberal would even dare show his face. By nomination day itself, Monday, 4 April, the day of the Spring Assizes, Durham was red with Tory flags and ribbons.

However, Bright did accept. On the day, he arrived – to find a miserably small wooden hustings tacked together outside the Town Hall, and a crowd speckled with red ribbons mostly worn by miners, who were freemen employed by the Marquis of Londonderry at his Rainton collieries. These miners raised a constant uproar at Bright, until Lord Dungannon condescendingly appealed for a hearing for 'the stranger'.

When the Mayor called for a show of hands, however, this went in favour of Bright. His Lordship's agent, William Lloyd Wharton, immediately demanded a formal poll. The poll was to result in a majority of one hundred for the Tory candidate.

Subsequent enquiries by Liberal agents revealed how

voters had been invited to visit the Wheat Sheaf Inn at Claypath, where they could queue at a window to mark the poll book and receive a golden sovereign each.

The Liberal agent supreme, Mr Coppock, travelled up from London to collate the evidence of bribery.

'So now a petition is being launched,' concluded Harriet.

'Wey, what dishonesty there is in politics! What acrimony!'

'Alas, I am no stranger to people's dishonesty.' (Would that Lord Durham had been less innocent! she thought.) 'Nor to acrimony, either.'

Sir Robert Peel, so stubborn about the Corn Law question, had insultingly accused Cobden in public of being responsible for *assassination*. Cobden, inflamed against Peel, was replying in kind . . .

'Long ago, Jane, I resolved never to let acrimony poison me; but always to proceed moderately and reasonably, though firmly.'

If only Cobden and Peel – those two great men! – could be reconciled. Meanwhile, ill as she was, Harriet had agreed to Cobden's request to attempt some writing along the lines of her political economy series, as her own contribution towards repeal.

'Should Mr Bright enter Parliament,' Harriet added, 'he hopes to form a committee on the game and forest laws. Those are so much more detrimental to our farming class, and to our whole national food production, than any foolish fanciful grievances about the supposed demerits of free trade. Mr Bright would supply evidence for my pen.'

'If he's elected. Aa follows ye. An' if yor illness allows.'

'Which seems unlikely . . . Now, dear Jane, speaking of acrimony, I must ask you: have you by chance confided my problems regarding Sir William Elwes and Mrs Blagdon to young Harry Bell?'

10

The following Sunday was a day to remember. The morning was bright though breezy. Once church was over, gay crowds thronged the opposite shore. Slack bonnets were bowled away, to be chased with a laugh and retrieved. In Front Street, too, the good citizens of Tynemouth, and those not so good, strolled about. Some headed down to the Haven, others up to the Spanish Battery where mercenaries from Spain had once been billeted as garrison. Down at the Castle yard the Union Jack fluttered on its flagstaff, as it did every Sabbath. Raffish soldiers chatted to flighty girls.

Harry Bell, natty in Sunday best, was in conversation in the street below with an untidy, diffident Jane.

Jane had indeed let Harry know the nuisance which the town snoop was trying to foment. Elwes was hoping to glean some scandalous intelligence regarding Harriet's funds. This, he could sell to the *Journal*. Mud might stick to Harriet's political friends and might even soil the scutcheon of the Anti-Corn Law League – in which Dr Greenhow had lately become prominent.

Oh mud could be sprayed all over! A few years before, Harriet had refused the offer of a pension from the public purse. How could she write objectively on political matters if she accepted? If favouritism seemed to have been shown her? Promptly the Tory newspapers had heaped abuse and mockery on the 'ungracious' and 'proud' Miss Martineau. Never mind that she was now an invalid disabled by pain, Tory editors would love to flay her – and her friends – again. And Elwes knew it.

So, out of loyal affection for Harriet, Jane had confided in Harry. How flattering it must have been to poor Jane that Harry paid any heed to such a sickly-looking raggle-taggle. Yet the boy genuinely did, perceiving her sweet nature. For this reason, Harriet felt reluctant to rebuke or interfere.

Harriet was aware that the lad had had a good 'eddi-cashin', in local terms, at the Royal Jubilee School in Shields opposite Christ Church. Two years since, its headmaster Thomas Haswell had called on Harriet to discuss pedagogy, and to beg Miss Martineau to write something or other to sway opinion, particularly about the odious tax on paper.

'My boys have to search the shore,' he had told her, 'to find any substitute for slate pencils. They have to forage the docks for chalk, which we bake in the school oven – as well as for wood-chips and logs to fuel the oven.'

Yes indeed, the difficulties and obstructions Mr Haswell faced – as a new and radical broom! As soon as he took over the Jubilee in '39, Mr Haswell had paid a lad sixpence per night to hold a candle while a master painted two huge hemispherical charts on the walls from floor to ceiling. He was determined that future seafarers should have some notion of geography and astronomy.

A candle! He wasn't allowed any gas lighting in the school. Though the streets and numbers of houses were now equipped with artificial light, this was still frowned on by the school managers. They were of the generation which fought vigorously to keep their town and Tyne-mouth in darkness. It was only two decades since the inhabitants presented a fine silver snuffbox to Mr John Motley for his sterling work in resisting the newfangled notion of lighting the town.

'As you may know,' Mr Haswell had related, 'I erected a mast and ropes in the school yard for physical exercise;

and I prevailed on a drill sergeant from the Castle to supervise. What poor health the majority of my pupils suffer! If they are not hampered by rickets or deformities, or impetigo, scabies or vermin, then their faces are tied up on account of nerve aches, carbuncles, boils, and abscesses. Every winter their warty hands and feet are cracked and bleeding with chilblains. It is abominable.'

'I agree,' Harriet had assured him.

'The Health and Towns Act is just not carried out – because we are not incorporated as a borough. The death rate is thirty in every thousand per annum. If only you could write something . . .'

Harriet had sighed. 'I am ill, myself, Mr Haswell.'

Harry Bell was a much less snot-nosed, vermin-ridden specimen of scholar. He had walked the mile or so to the Royal Jubilee for several years, with his parents' full blessing, and properly clad; and had been one of Mr Haswell's best monitors, passing on his lessons to the younger pupils.

Thus Jane had now made him her knight errant in shining armour, who might somehow 'see that Shanky off'. Never mind that Harry was only seventeen, as she was, hardly a match for a rogue like Elwes.

'Shall I,' debated Harriet, 'pen a note to my brother-in-law to ask him to visit, to discuss the dangers posed by Elwes? Only a twenty-minute train journey to Shields, for fourpence. Then a quick trot onward by horse omnibus . . . Shall I, shan't I?'

She was loath to involve herself in *any* knowledge of arrangements regarding the fund. An even greater disincentive to embroiling Thomas Greenhow was that, if he came down to Tynemouth, her mind would inevitably be on the topic of Bulwer's letter. She had no desire to annoy Dr Greenhow again by broaching the matter of mesmerism.

Taking paper from her writing case, which had been the gift of Miss Nightingale, Harriet settled on the sofa and began to compose a reply to Thomas Carlyle, instead.

As ever, Carlyle was agonizing in that cauldron of Babel which was his house in rowdy, foetid Chelsea. Smiling, Harriet polished the signet ring which he had bought for her. So typical of the man! – to have instantly squandered the money which Harriet had put into his hand, as though a little money made him feel awkward.

Harriet had brought back from America cheap pirated copies of his *Sartor Resartus* and sold these at the English price. When next she imported a parcel, she converted the assets into liquid form: namely best French brandy. Carlyle loved to make a hot brandy toddy. So this time he actually enjoyed the proceeds.

Harriet wrote: 'I beg you to find an airy quiet country house set upon a *gravelly* soil. It is the dankness of that Chelsea clay which afflicts your health and Mrs Carlyle's . . .'

His recent letter recounted how he had gone a-house-hunting at long last, on a fine black horse lent him by a friend. Thus he could range the whole countryside around London. To show willing, he also equipped himself (Germanic thoroughness!) with no less than five maps. Three of the British Isles and two of the World. In spite of this, she doubted whether Carlyle would overcome his old stubborn Chelsea habits.

Bulwer, object of her next reply, was just as stubborn. This, in a department where Harriet had a wealth of personal expertise – namely, the department of deafness. Generous-hearted though he was, Bulwer was also preposterously vain. He refused to admit that he could no longer hear, and claimed that contemporary conversation simply wasn't worth listening to.

She would not have dared offer Bulwer advice. Yet, as it happened, he was advising her; urging her earnestly for the sake of her crippled health that she must travel to Paris to consult a somnambule.

This was as much out of the question as a simple journey across the Tyne. However, there were mesmerists in England who readily visited all the main cities. The reports she had read . . . there must be something in mesmerism! Alas, Thomas Greenhow was utterly set against such 'quackery'. Likewise his wife, likewise the aunts.

'What action could I possibly take about this matter, when I would surely cause a family breach?'

Harriet was writing this to Bulwer when Jane banged on the door and entered.

'Eee, Miss Martineau!' Jane was clutching a copy of that handbill. 'Wey, lions and tigers is comin' to Shields! Isn't it excitin'?'

Harriet smiled. Harry must have told Jane, since with eyesight like hers she could hardly have deciphered the advertisement.

'An' the tamer, as sticks his head in their mouths, is a real Red Indian!'

No need to reach for her ear trumpet when Jane addressed her! Whenever a Tynesider was enthused, the accent grew shrilly pitched. All to the good was the local habit of adding as many extra vowels as possible to words; since vowels were all that Harriet ever heard with any ease.

Before she settled in Tynemouth it had only been with Sydney Smith and Malthus that she had been able totally to set aside her ear trumpet – or its predecessor, the speaking tube. Luckily so, in the case of Malthus! – for one could not decently press a speaking tube to a hare lip. However, Malthus's other defect – a cleft palate – quite robbed him of consonants, leaving his speech as a slow and sonorous procession of gratifying vowels.

93

'Did ye see any wild Indians when ye was in America? Did they ever attack yor party?'

'No, Jane. The danger of attack when we were in the woods of Michigan came wholly from civilized mobs – who were inflamed against the abolitionists. *They*, not the savages, would ambush coaches and bludgeon the occupants.'

'Were ye attacked by mobs?'

Harriet had to laugh. 'To date, I have only been assaulted by newspapers!'

'Harry might take me to the beast show, if his Mam goes too.'

'Ah Jane . . . I'm not sure that I approve of wild animals being caged and enslaved – any more than of the same circumstance happening to negroes.'

Jane looked so crestfallen that Harriet immediately regretted her reproof.

'Let me tell you about *lions*, Jane. I speak from experience. A lion is a *celebrity*. The saddest such specimen of lion is to be seen at a reception or at a country-house weekend. It is the author or artist who allows himself to preen before a crowd of simpering, shallow adorers. Or else the lion in question may be a polar explorer or a Hindoo rajah or a Polish refugee. It matters not. It is all one and the same to the lion-hunters. It is *they* who should be tamed with a whip – and all literary lions should be promptly released from their cages, of drawing rooms!'

Jane goggled at Harriet. 'Why's that? A bit of attention's nice.'

'If the artist's vanity lets him believe that he is a superior creature, distinct from the mass of society, then he wounds himself. He wastes his time and saps his true vitality. Society suffers too, since superficiality is encouraged as admirable behaviour. And of course society will

94

cast the lion down as readily as it takes him up; so he is always disappointed in the end.'

Jane looked unhappy. This was all somewhat outside of her experience – unlike the prospect of that beast show in Shields in a few weeks' time, with herself perhaps on Harry's arm? If only her aunt would allow.

Harriet's bowels grew sluggish with inactivity. As she lay on her sofa, suffering, the weather underwent a fearful change. Squalls buffeted her window. The earlier breeze quickened to a shriek from across the German Ocean. The sky darkened fast.

In hope of relieving her knotty cramps, she rose and gazed out. Now myrtle-green, the sea swelled and tumbled, driving ashore. Balls of foam were whipped by the wind over the pebbles of the Haven and sped like balloons up the slope towards the houses. With each moment the waves grew wilder and darker. By three o'clock that afternoon the vista was almost as gloomy as night, and breakers were crashing deep into the Haven, exploding against the headland to drench the grass.

This unseasonably late storm was as awful as any winter tempest – and as unexpected to any vessels unfortunate enough to be caught between the Scylla of the deep and the Charybdis of the rocky coastline. While sheets of rain advanced and spray billowed far inland, a collier reached the safety of the river. Two steam-tugs were now standing by, to render any assistance.

Harriet hastily removed the window cushions and laid cloths to soak up the wet already oozing in through every cranny.

Here, through the fierce murk, came a vessel in distress. A wooden paddle-steamship. Surely she was the Norwegian mailboat! After years at her telescope with a reference volume beside her, Harriet was as familiar with the language of flags as any ship's captain. She had learned the signals by heart; and with all her heart.

'I require a pilot.' 'My vessel is healthy; I require a free pratique.' 'You are standing into danger.' 'I am disabled.' But all flags had been ripped from that ship's masts. Her barque-rigged sails were streaming out, torn. Harriet pressed her telescope against the rain-spattered glass. One of the two paddle wheels was damaged, splintered by the rolling and the crashing against tons of angry water. Waves even broke over the funnel; were the boiler fires doused?

She must be the mailboat. Harriet saw the characteristically long forward run of the clipper hull rising high – the headsail-bowsprit tilting a lance at the black sky – before the vessel crashed into a vast trough.

She was being driven wallowing in the worst of directions, towards the Black Middens. And now the tugs were steaming valiantly out to meet her.

Harriet could see men climbing into the rigging to cling tight – one person at least was swept away – and other brave or desperate sailors were hauling their way to the drenched bows to receive the lines fired over by rocket from the tugs. Somehow these were secured. In vain! Puff as those tugs might, they could not haul the vessel up into the throat of the Tyne away from the rocky teeth.

The masts angled. She had struck. She was heeling, savagely pounded. Breakers were tremendous.

Yet the two starboard lifeboats had been swung out on the davits. Now these were lowered with a freight of refugees. Slanting deck and rigging remained crowded with desperate souls.

Shedding their lines, the steam-tugs puffed as close as they dared. Oars dipping into mountainous waves, the lifeboats rowed to rendezvous and transfer passengers.

The terror of it; the frustration. Harriet's own soul cried out, urging the mariners.

But now here came the Tynemouth lifeboat. And from across the river, the South Shields lifeboat came too. Along the clifftops spectators were gathering, careless of the wind and rain. Figures ran across the down to swell the crowd.

Praise be for lifeboats! – much improved in design since North Shields' native son, Willy Wouldhave, first invented the mariners' salvation . . .

In the year of the French Revolution the *Adventure*, out of Newcastle, was lost on Herd Sand over the river. Out of the thousands of spectators present, not one person dared offer help at any price. One by one, the frozen and exhausted crew had dropped from the rigging to their deaths, till none remained to save.

In the wake of that tragedy a committee of South Shields gentlemen raised a public subscription and offered a prize for the plan of a safety boat, small and of shallow draught. The initiative came from Nicholas Fairlies, JP, who was later murdered near Jarrow Slake.

Only two real contenders were in the running for the prize. One was shipwright Henry Greathead. The other was Willy Wouldhave. Journeyman painter and jack-of-all-trades, Willy was poor and uncouth, flighty and brilliant, heedless of the morrow, as bouncy as india-rubber, and habitually foul-mouthed towards his so-called superiors.

Willy's humble model was buoyant and self-righting. Mr Greathead's professional model floated bottom-up. So the committee awarded a consolation prize of two guineas to Willy, and commissioned Mr Greathead to get on with the job – which he did after adopting Willy's notion of a curved keel.

Honours, medallions, gifts, and grants were heaped

upon Mr Greathead by a grateful Lloyd's and Trinity House and Parliament, and even by Czar Alexander I of Russia; though these did not prevent Henry Greathead from going bankrupt, thus achieving almost the same condition as Willy had existed in all along. Willy died penniless in 1821.

The fate of the true inventor of lifeboats was much in Harriet's mind. Willy's only daughter, who eked a living in penury as a seamstress in South Shields, had only lately been granted fifteenpence a week by the parish in recognition – which made Harriet consider her own circumstances, and the matter of the testimonial fund . . .

Within an hour, the great majority of passengers and crew seemed to have been taken safely off, and the ship had broken up entirely. Perhaps a thousand spectators watched. Amongst them, enlarged by the telescope, Harriet had spotted the unmistakable shape of Shanky Elwes. He had stared avidly as waves claimed the cargo.

Dinner, of roast beef and Yorkshire pudding, was understandably delayed beyond the usual hour of four. After she had dined, Harriet was able to observe files of men and women and boys passing along the sands and over the ridge, laden with bundles of sailcloth, shoulder-loads of planks, armfuls of spars.

Gladly she barred her shutters, closed the curtains, and lit the gaslight.

The wailing wind slackened. In the wee hours of the morning, still tormented and twisted by discomfort, she arose to see the sky calm and clear, the sea a pond flecked with driftwood, and a gibbous moon climbing over the ruins of the Priory in the black-blue heaven. This spectacle soothed her spirit so that finally she slept.

11

Wild beast shows were by no means unknown on Tyneside. Back in 1568, an Italian exhibited the corpse of a monstrous serpent fully sixteen feet long, with the girth of a horse. This creature had supposedly gobbled up a thousand Ethiopians and ravaged their country, until the Turkish authorities put paid to it.

In 1732 a giant cassowary was on view in Newcastle, along with a huge vulture, several big cats, a Mountain Monster, and a possum with a false belly where her young could take refuge.

1734: a camel. 1747: a rhinoceros visited Newcastle. 1750: a porpoise, accompanied by a mermaid and a mummy.

In 1780: a zebra – plus the return of the Grand Cassowar. The six-foot-high bird would visit the house of any nobleman or gentleman upon payment of one guinea (up to a total of twenty-four guests, a shilling a head thereafter). While the bird stood in the drawing room being admired, its proprietor Mr Pidcock would declaim a poetical effusion, ending up:

> 'Yet each brute seen on this terraqueous ball,
> The beauteous Cassowar exceeds them all!'

Mr Pidcock invested his guineas and shillings wisely. He was back in 1799, accompanied by an extremely sagacious elephant, though this did not enter drawing rooms.

The prime entrepreneur was definitely George Wombwell. Shoemaker by trade, he was enraptured at London

Docks by the sight of the first pair of boa constrictors ever imported. He bought them for seventy-five pounds, and within weeks had gained his investment back. Soon whole menageries of his beasts were touring the British Isles. Not without ultimate tragedy; Chuby the elephant killed George's nephew in '42, while a tigress fatally mauled his niece.

A beast-tamer ran such risks. In the revised, expanded edition of *The World as Will and Idea*, Schopenhauer related how an inquest was held at the Phoenix Inn, Morpeth, in August 1830. One Baptist Bernhard of Venice had been vengefully crushed by an elephant, into whose cheek the Italian had inadvertently stuck a fork four years earlier.

(By 1830 Shanky Elwes had long since quit Morpeth Gaol, however his genteel son Henry was working as an under-boots at the Queen's Head in Morpeth. The sensitive and penniless boy originally scraped a living by carrying coals. Then he had signed on board a collier, only to be appalled by the obscene crudities of his shipmates. Being an under-boots was paradise, after that.)

The coroner fined the guilty elephant five shillings – the money to be devoted to pious purposes. This was a so-called deodand penalty, invoked whenever dumb chattels caused the death of a sapient being. Yet, as Schopenhauer pointed out, the elephant had acted with intelligent premeditation.

And let's not forget Hilton and Wright's menagerie, which gave pride of place to a large Siberian wolf kept in the same den as a sheep beneath a sign, *The Scriptures Fulfilled*.

However, no tamer of beasts was more notable than Isaac Van Amburgh, and no show more splendid nor better publicized. Van Amburgh could bend any known creature to his will with preternatural panache.

Van Amburgh's grandfather had begun life as Tangborgon d'Oom which meant 'Great King of the Woods' in the language of the Tuscorara Indians, of whom he was one. Tangborgon happened to save a Dutch settler from a lethal attack by two wild pumas, and was invited by the grateful fellow to his home in Kentucky. The Indian converted from paganism, adopted the name Vorboys Van Amburgh, settled down, and got married. Yet baptism did not dispel his power over the beasts, which his grandson Isaac inherited much enhanced.

As a child, Isaac wasn't interested in childish games, only in flies and wasps and maybugs. As a boy, he became lord of the rats and mice in the local storerooms. The rodents would all dance to his tune. By the age of twelve, the wildest horses of Kentucky were being brought to Isaac to be broken. He was in such demand that he could have been set up for life.

Yet he was restless. Roaming the Kentucky woods in his spare time, he tamed foxes and ferrets, coyotes and wild pigs, and wolves. He established a Forest Police of animals. If any carnivore made off with a goose or lamb, Isaac and his brute constables would trace and punish the criminal, and as often as not recover the victim in one piece, and even alive. So the local people swore on oath.

Presently Isaac joined Titus's Menagerie, the largest in America and in the whole world. Immediately he distinguished himself by taming an intractable lioness, sticking his head inside her mouth as proof.

In '38 Titus shipped Van Amburgh over to England in company with his most impressive lions and tigers, who would obey their tamer's slightest nod. The twenty-seven-year-old beastmaster was lionized, painted by Landseer on a commission for the Duke of Wellington, and was showered with money by young noblemen for instructing them in the art of taming. Only the caution of the London magistrates stopped Isaac from ascending in a balloon over Vauxhall together with his favourite tiger, then jumping out by parachute. Deprived of Isaac's gaze, the tiger might have eaten the balloon pilot, causing the contraption to descend who knew where, releasing jungle violence upon the city.

On a fair June morning, Jane was out at the farthing pant to fetch water for her aunt's establishment. So was a whole queue of hinnies, bickering about priority at the wretched pump and gossiping about Van Amburgh's show, which was at last about to arrive in Shields.

'They say as he gans in the cage wi' the Bengal tiger, an' then torns his back – '

'Will ye let me gan forst, Missus Jackson? Aa've left the bairn in the cradle, an' there's nobody else in the hoose.'

'Aa divvent believe ye!'

The superintendent of the pant, widow woman Hulme, presided in a sentry box within easy reach of the pump, cannily turning it off after each customer and on again only on receipt of a farthing. Her key was as big as a bargee's windlass.

Mrs Jackson duly tendered her coin and the slow process of filling her six-gallon skeel began.

It was just such a skeel which Willy Wouldhave had helped a woman hoist on to her head at the Field House Well – after he had first observed how a bit of broken wooden dish which happened to be afloat in it always turned itself points-upward no matter how he interfered. This inspired his idea for the self-righting lifeboat. Out of a skeel, a new concept of keel.

At last Mrs Jackson's container was full. Gripping the

wooden tub by its single handle, and her other hand beneath, she weightlifted the burden up on to the cushion perched on her head, and waddled away. All hinnies in quest of water wore those padded weezes on their crowns in place of their usual bonnets. The queue shuffled forward.

'Can Aa pay ye tomorrow, Missus Hulme?'

'Aa durna, hinny! They've varry partiklor at the offis.'

The huge key was not turned. The petitioner trudged away towards the closest free public pant, a third of a mile away.

'Hullo, Jane,' said Harry Bell.

'Ye shouldn't be here!' she hissed. 'Watter is women's work.'

'Oh, aye, an' yor skeel weighs a ton. Aa'll carry it for ye, an' divvent argue.'

Jane didn't argue, since she dreaded the strain of hoisting the skeel. Miss Martineau said that Jane's muscles looked like strings of dough; and Jane rarely more than half-filled her skeel, provoking her aunt to fury.

'Me and me Mam's gannin' to see the beasts arrive this arternoon. When Mam delivers Missus Halliday's milk an' eggs, she'll ask if ye can gan alang with us.'

So in spite of Mrs Halliday's peevish complaints, Mrs Bell and Harry and Jane took the horse omnibus that afternoon to Chirton Green, where crowds were gathering . . .

Here came Van Amburgh now along the road, driving a team of ten fine vigorous horses harnessed two abreast. Those mettlesome cream-and-piebald stallions obeyed the least flick of his reins like docile ponies! Behind followed a procession of caravans which were decorated green and gold and pulled by other fine steeds, their harness ornamented with silver.

'Wey, it's Cleopatra's royal progress!' exclaimed Mrs Bell.

It was indeed. Save that in place of a barge, there were caravans hauled by equine slaves. Rather than the Nile, the Tyne glinted in the distance. Instead of a 'serpent of Old Nile', those wagons conveyed royal beasts that roared and growled ferociously.

Isaac Van Amburgh wore a suit of silk fleshings, a dashing scarf, and a shirt of pale blue satin. He didn't look particularly muscular – in fact not robust all. Yet his eyes: his eyes commanded. There was iron in his gaze, and there was Indian magic.

The procession turned into a field. With military precision camp was quickly pitched. The great marquee was raised.

All of the borough's hucksters and hawkers were circulating to sell toy harlequins, flags to wave, wind wheels and paper serpents, sugar fish, chocolate lions, fudge bears, and marzipan tigers and cigars. And oh yes, Shanky Elwes with a top hat on his head was stalking amidst the parked caravans and the penned horses and the rising Big Top. He hummed to himself. To Harry's eye, Elwes looked intent on some scheme.

It couldn't have been more than an hour till the first crowd was admitted.

'Eeee!' cried Mrs Bell, as Van Amburgh bounded into the cage.

'Eeee!' agreed the crowd; then hushed.

The tamer walked towards the wild beasts. He held out his whip at belly height, and kept his gaze fixed on the grumbling animals. Though not hefty, Van Amburgh stood just short of six feet tall. His silk- and satin-clad body seemed to crackle with *will*.

104

He called out loudly, 'Trajan!' – and the fully-grown Bengal tiger advanced and obediently leapt over the whip.

'Jezebel!'

The tigress took her turn.

Next the lioness, Sheba, followed by two leopards, Nero and Hannibal. All leapt the whip. But the full-maned old lion Samson lay glaring murderously at Van Amburgh, refusing to shift. Van Amburgh cut at Samson with the whip. Roaring like a discharge of cannon, Samson was on his feet . . .

'Me blood's freezin'!' Mrs Bell gripped her son's arm tight.

'What's happenin'?' begged Jane. Her eyes had blurred.

The lion sailed over the whip and returned to his place.

An assistant pushed a hoop through the bars. While Van Amburgh brandished this, one by one his beasts leapt through it, even Samson. The man's gaze constantly darted, arrowing at each animal in turn.

'He must be magnetizin' them!' declared Jane. 'Wi' mesmerism!'

Indeed, the whip did appear to Harry like the needle of a compass as it swivelled from one fierce brute to the next. With soft taps of that whip, Van Amburgh tumbled each animal till all lay on their sides or on their backs. They were like some basketful of gigantic, diverse kittens. He lay down amongst the recumbent beasts, striking one pose then another. He pressed cheek to jowl with Jezebel. Samson's mane served as a pillow. Leaping up, he stepped upon the prostrate lion and the tigress, one foot balanced on the head of each.

'Wey, what a power has Man!' sighed Mrs Bell. 'What a dominion!'

Now Van Amburgh knelt and teased Trajan's jaws wide open with the whip butt. He placed his head inside the tiger's mouth. The beast's great teeth were poised around the tamer's skull, which they could crush in a trice. Trajan rolled his fiery coals of eyes, yet otherwise moved not a muscle.

At last Van Amburgh backed away. Throwing open the iron wicket of the cage, he leapt out fast as lightning; fastened the barrier, turned and bowed. In that same instant the wild animals threw themselves at wicket and cage wall, shaking the iron rods so violently that these seemed to bend beneath the blows. The enraged roaring competed with the thunder of applause.

As a stream of amazed and satisfied spectators left the marquee, a second crowd just as huge thronged outside waiting for the next performance.

'Wey, what's it like?'

'Bloody smashin', man!'

Harry drew Jane aside. 'Aa have to hang aboot. It's aboot ye-knaa-who. Aa'm shore he's up to somethin'. He's aal anxious and excited.'

Jane's eyes shone in a watery way. 'Yor so clever, Harry. An' brave.' Her best bonnet was askew. 'Ye dee what ye have to. But be careful!'

'Aa have me jacky-legs, if need be.' Harry patted his coat pocket, feeling the shape of the clasp knife. 'Mam,' he said, 'Aa've some important business. Will ye see Jane hyem?'

'Business, is it? Ye wouldn't be thinkin' o' runnin' away wi' the circus, would ye?'

'Na, Mam. Ye knaa Aa'm gannin' to run away to sea!'

Mrs Bell chuckled. Her husband, Captain Bell, was skipper of the snow-brig *Amphitrite*, plying between the Tyne and London, and Harry was due to follow in his father's footsteps after his next birthday.

'Only if that's aal reet wi' Jane here,' she said, 'you bein' hor escort.'

'It's aal reet, Mrs Bell,' Jane assured her.

So Mrs Bell gave her blessing, and Harry melted away into the crowd.

'If ye like,' Mrs Bell said heartily to the girl, 'Aa'll buy ye a bag o' winkles to eat as wor gannin' alang.'

'Aa wish ye was me aunt,' replied Jane, with a sniffle.

'An' ye can tell me aal aboot this mesmerization, an' why Miss Martineau's folks is so keen to stop hor.'

It was early evening when Shanky Elwes at last ascended the steps of Van Amburgh's personal caravan. Penned in their individual cages again, the big cats growled and roared impatiently while a couple of men made the rounds with pails of meat or offal.

Harry ambled to the far side of the caravan and lounged by an open, net-hung window, nonchalantly nibbling at a marzipan tiger.

'. . . a wager,' he heard, 'which I am sure that a redoubtable gentleman such as yourself will not decline! No indeed; lest it become known to the public that there is one instance where you dared not meet a challenge – one case where your magic fails you. Magic is decidedly needed, make no mistake, sir! Magic!'

For a person who could shout so stentoriously, Van Amburgh's voice in reply was surprisingly soft. A gentle American burr. Harry pressed closer.

'Have you perhaps discovered a unicorn, Sir William? Look closer, and you may find that it is one of your Chillingham wild white bulls which has lost a horn! I am curious to see those on our route from Alnwick to Berwick. And to take a walk amongst them. The aboriginal ox, eh? Too pugnacious to serve men's will.' The American chuckled.

'This is nothing of the sort,' said Elwes. 'This is no natural creature. It is a supernatural beast; and I have seen it for myself in its cave home by the sea. Underneath the ruins of the Priory, below the lighthouse. I shall wager my twenty sovereigns to a hundred of yours that you cannot exert your will over it.'

'Odds of one to five? That rather puts you at the advantage, Sir William.'

'Not in the least! Yours is the fame, and the rich reputation. To wager at evens would diminish your glory, should word of this venture ever leak out.'

'This would be a secret wager? Why should I be interested in secrecy?'

'On account of the satanic nature of this beast,' replied Elwes, 'and the scruples of the Godfearing people of this town.'

'Your cave denizen is notorious?'

'Not at all, sir. Only a few people know that the legend has tangible substance. The fewer the better.'

Harry scratched his head. Wey, he thought to himself, there were legends aboot the Castle rock an' Priory ruins. Owld hinnies said as the place was haunted, an' fairies used to live there. But he'd never seen any. When he was a bairn he recalled his Mam tellin' him a tale by candle-light at bedtime aboot a brave young knight who fought his way into one o' the caves in the rock as was guarded by monsters . . . That was just a story from the olden days. What Shanky was sayin' was eyewash an' baloney. Soldiers guarded the rock an' the harbour mouth. Mind, they was aal up top – an' not even concerned wi' smug-glers who could always sneak in, of a dark neet, doon below. But that the British Army was axually campin' on top of a supernatural beast, unawares . . . !

'Besides,' continued Elwes, 'I believe there may be a treasure-trove deep in that cave. In the event of publicity the Crown would show a legitimate interest, this being so close to the shore. We should agree to divide any treasure

108

between us. That is why we must shun notoriety and go there alone, the two of us.'

'First, Sir William, you *threaten* me with publicity – and now you counsel the very opposite. It occurs to me that a venturesome blackguard might lure a man of note to a lonely spot, to have him waylaid and held to ransom.'

'You hurt my feelings, sir. I'm a man of distinction in this town.'

Van Amburgh laughed. 'You're a rogue. I see right through you.'

'In that case, bring a trusted companion. Let him be armed to the teeth! One pistol shot and the whole garrison would be roused, I assure you.'

'Like all good rogues, you win in either event. You either gain a hundred sovereigns in wager and as sweetener to keep your mouth shut, not least regarding attempted fraud against the British Crown; or, you reap half-share in a treasure for the puny outlay of twenty pounds! Hmm, but you claim to have witnessed this supernatural beast? So what does it resemble?'

'That's hard to say,' replied Elwes.

'And now I do begin to believe you.'

'No, listen. It appeared to change shape. At times it was like an octopus . . . at times like a giant white coily worm, with legs. It can . . . touch the *mind*, sir.'

'Oh . . . indeed?'

'*Yes*. To resist it and bring it to heel and enter its den would call for all the will-power of such a man as you. I swear this is so! Is there a Bible handy? Well, no matter. Let me tell you how I found out about it . . .'

Harry listened, enthralled.

12

Elwes and Van Amburgh had finally made their wager the previous evening. The beast-charmer's curiosity was piqued by the account of the fearful, slithery, mind-touching creature.

'If no crittur shows, all bets are off,' the American had insisted.

'It'll show,' Shanky had promised. 'I've met it, so it'll smell my thoughts. Not in its nose – if you follow me – but in its mind. That's why it came out the first time, because it smelled the fisherman. Now it knows me too. You have a mind for beasts' thoughts, don't you?'

Van Amburgh had allowed that he did.

The menagerie was due to stay at Chirton Green for two days of performances before heading for Blyth. So the next evening Van Amburgh and a companion would ride down to Tynemouth to meet Shanky at the Salutation Inn in Front Street. Hearing that, Harry had rubbed his hands. Shanky was going to give him an opening – for a lever to prise that rogue away from the affairs of Jane's beloved Miss Martineau.

Now, next morning, as Harry sat over his bowl of crowdy pudding, he said to his Mam, 'Dee ye recall tellin' me aboot some lad in armour as went into Jinglin' Geordie's Hole an' fought monsters for a treasure?'

'Aye, Aa does.' And Mrs Bell reminisced: 'When *Aa* was a bairn, me own Mam had a long poem by heart aboot the Hole, as she recited to me. The poem was published too, ye knaa? Shortly after yor Dad an' I got married, Robert Owen wrote it aal doon. Mr Owen was forever traipsin' roond collectin' owld nonsense.'

'That's the Robert Owen as caused the riot in Newcastle wi' his lecturin'?'

'Na, ye daft booger. This Robert Owen lived in Shields twenty years ago. He used to gan aal over the Borders, until his health gave way. That's when he handed his collection over to Willy Hone, as was publishin' a table book in monthly parts. That's hoo the poem saw print.'

Harry spooned up the last of his scalded oatmeal and milk, warm from the cow. Mrs Bell removed the bowl.

'Aa'll fetch yor kipper, son.' She headed for the kitchen. Soon pungent fish smells were drifting through.

Harry sat contemplating the scale model of the *Amphitrite* on the chiffonier and thinking about his father, imagining a model Dad bellowing orders on deck.

Captain Bell had carved and rigged that ship during voyages carrying coal to the capital. The *Amphitrite* had been built at Shields in the same year as the Americans declared their independence. She was a twin-mast brig of the type called a 'snow', with her spanker set on a small mast close to the mainmast. His Dad had explained all of this in great detail to Harry, who knew the snow-brig's history by heart.

Originally she was a single decker displacing 221 tons. In 1802 she was outfitted with a new bottom, new deck, and uppers. Five years later, after a close encounter with rocks in a storm, she needed another new bottom as well as extensive damage repairs. In 1820 she was part doubled and lengthened; and recently she had undergone another refit that included a new deck. Nowadays the *Amphitrite* displaced 305 tons, and was Class AE 1 in the London transport service. Mr Laing of Dockwray Square owned her. Crew of eighteen. She was named after the Greek sea god's wife.

Harry would be joining another of Mr Laing's ships as an apprentice. He would study for his papers and become a skipper himself one fine day – even a skipper to foreign parts, not that London itself wasn't fairly foreign according to his Dad. That was the way Captain Cook had started his career, on the Tyne-to-London coal haul.

If Dad was at home right now, should Harry confide in him? Ask the Captain to accompany him when he trailed Shanky that night? Supposing there was a rough house, his Dad would put up with no nonsense. But Dad might tell him to keep out of it, keep his nose clean. The Captain didn't regard his son's affection for orphan Jane, who was no Greek goddess, with the same equanimity as did Mrs Bell.

Dad wasn't due home for another two days. Till then Harry was man of the house.

'What are ye gawpin' at the shefferneer for?' Mrs Bell placed a plate with a juicy golden kipper in front of him.

'Nowt, Mam. Ye was sayin' aboot the Hole an' the monsters. What sort o' monsters? Aa've forgotten.'

Mrs Bell smiled, and sat down opposite him.

'Wey, this is the story. Young Walter was the son of a famous knight who fought on the Borders. Walter wanted to dee somethin' famous too. So his Mam telt him aboot this huge store o' wealth in the goaf under Tynemouth Priory, guarded by infernal spirits set there by a powerful sorcerer.'

'Was it a genuine goaf?'

'Na. It was *like* the void that's left in a mine after the coal's taken oot. Well, various other knights had tried to break the spell, but none ever came back into the light o' day. They was aal doomed to remain in the rock forever.

'So one midnight durin' a fearful thunderstorm young Walter gans doon to the shore. He's wearin' a coat o' mail, an' a helmet shaped like a basin that's called a basnet, with a barred visor. He has his shield an' a sword an' a burnin' brand.'

'Didn't the storm extinguish his brand?'

'Ye used to ask that when ye was a bairn! Not in the story it didn't, son . . .'

With a single leap Walter gained the entrance to the dismal tunnel. As he proceeded inwards, goblins yelled louder and louder.

('That could be the sound o' the thunder reverberatin', said Harry.)

Of a sudden these goblins were all around him, dancing wildly, blue flames darting out of their eyes.

('That's reflections of his torch on the damp walls?')

However, the young man slashed these goblins out of the way. Next, fierce scaly dragons threatened him. These dragons had great sharp teeth and forked tongues; and fire belched from their throats. But when Walter rushed to hack at them, they vanished.

('Oh aye.')

Hell hounds raced towards him, baying furiously. Their breath stank of sulphur fit to suffocate him. These also vanished as soon as he attacked.

('If there's enough foul air in there to dizzy him, he might imagine anythin'!')

Inward went Walter, and inward. Far off in the murk he spied the glimmer of a lamp. He hurried towards the light – and stopped short just in time. He was on the brink of a wide chasm! Impossible to tell how deep it was. While he halted, demons clustered round him invisibly, gibbering and jeering.

To rid himself of excess weight, Walter tore off his basinet and his coat of mail. Then he backed up and sprinted and launched himself over the chasm. No sooner had he landed safely than other phantoms assailed him.

Indescribable snaky monstrosities were twisting among his feet, coiling round his limbs. By now he realized that all these monsters were shadowy things such as dreams are made of. They were images in his mind. They could only destroy a man who allowed them power over him through faint-heartedness.

Walter prayed silently to his patron saint, John the Baptist. It was the eve of St John's nativity. He forged on into the shrieking, slithery gloom.. Not even the crash of a rockfall deterred him. That too was an illusion.

At last Walter reached the lamp. This hung above a closed door, in between a golden cockerel and a bugle hanging from a golden chain. He seized the bugle – and it became a writhing serpent. The mouthpiece was full of poison fangs. This too must be an illusion, so Walter blew one blast then another. And at the third blast the golden cockerel awoke and flapped its wings and crowed. Immediately all phantoms vanished, and the door before him crashed open. Beyond stretched a huge hall lit by golden lamps. Chests of treasure stood all around: mounds of emeralds and diamonds and opals, heaps of gold.

Young Walter gathered up as many of the jewels as he could carry.

('That couldn't have been too many – not when he'd left his basket hat, an' had a chasm to leap back over!')

Well, he certainly took enough to buy himself a splendid domain of forests and meadows and cornfields and several castles. Thus he was able to wed a beautiful, clever wife who brought him handsome, loving children. At the end of a highly satisfactory life, Walter founded a monastery on the rock above the cavern, right where the ruins of Tynemouth Priory now stood.

* * *

Harry had finished his fishy on a dishy, and was mopping up the juice with a crust.

'Mind ye,' concluded Mrs Bell, 'it's aal tommy-rot since ye didn't have any knights in armour back when the Priory was built. That wasn't lang after the Romans left. An' even though the Vikings burnt it doon, it was aalways a sacred place – Priory Chorch o' St Oswin, eh? – not somethin' built over a den o' magician's monsters; which were aal imaginary, as the story tells us.'

'So who was Jinglin' Geordie? Dee ye knaa that, Mam?'

'Oh, he'd be some daft destitute as lived in the cave. Like that heathen Lascar, as gave his name to Spotty's Hole at Roker. He'd be a sailor as skipped ship an' couldn't even speak English. Or maybe he was an escaped convict wi' his chains still on him, so when he skulked roond at neet foragin' he'd clank and jingle. So much for yor phantom monsters.'

Phantom? Was Elwes hoping to *fool* the American? Maybe there would be an accomplice hidden in the cave dressed up as a white monster . . . or some hideously crippled child hired for the occasion . . . Maybe there'd be clouds of opium smoke.

And yet Elwes had sounded so utterly convincing the evening before.

A canny swindler would, wouldn't he?

'Aal tell ye why else it's tommy-rot,' said Mrs Bell. 'Mister Owen telt me Mam there's exackly the same sort o' tale aboot Dunstanborough Castle up the coast. Mister Owen even wrote his own poem about it, though it never got printed.'

'Why not?' asked Harry, who was somewhat interested in the world of letters thanks to Jane's account of Miss Martineau's career.

'Accordin' to Mister Owen, that scandalous fella Lewis – him as wrote *The Monk* – had aalready published *his* own poem on the subject. Lewis's poem went into aal sorts o' foreign languages, such as Danish an' Jorman. Maybe Mister Owen was daft to write the same poem!

'Anyhow, there was supposed to be a goaf under Dunstanborough with an enchanted maiden sleepin' there in a crystal coffin. Merlin the magician had mesmerized hor. This goaf was guarded by serpents an' ban-dogs an' fiends an' phantoms just like here at Tynemouth.

'One neet, durin' a wild storm, a knight called Sir Guy took shelter. At midneet a door in the rock flew open. Sir Guy braved aal manner o' fiends till he reached a hall ablaze wi' lamps. There he saw the gorgeous maiden. Her crystal coffin lay in between two giant skelingtons. One of these held a sword in its bony fingers – an' the other held a bugle.

'So what should Sir Guy dee? Should he grab the sword an' smash the case? Or should he blow the bugle, like wor Walter did?

'He chose to blow the bugle. Instantly aal the lights went oot, an' voices from aal sides was mockin' him cause he'd called for assistance instead o' bein' bold, an' his own man.'

'How was he to knaa, Mam? He might have hurt hor, smashin' the crystal aal over hor.'

'He made the wrong choice, an' that's that. Poisonous gases knocked him senseless, an' he woke up in the mornin' ootside on the grass. He tried for the rest o' his life to find that door; an' afterwards too as a ghost.

'So it's the same story, with a bit of a twist. What's aal this aboot then, Harry? Ye aren't plannin' to impress Jane wi' some scary nonsense, are ye? She doesn't need that! Aa'm thinkin' yor aalready hor shinin' young Walter.'

But Harry thought about how the unfortunate Sir Guy had blown the bugle to bring help instead of taking matters into his own hands.

He shook his head. 'That was a smashin' kipper, Mam.'

13

Harry hung about in Front Street as dusk thickened. From under the wrought-iron portico of the Bath Hotel assembly rooms, he kept an eye on the front door of the Sal and on the archway into the adjacent stables.

First, Shanky Elwes strode towards the inn from the eastward. He wore boots and a long black greatcoat. On his head, a puffy-crowned black cap of the sort favoured by workmen and raffish sportsmen. Its stiff peak gleamed in the gaslight. Into the pub he went, perhaps to see whether he could con a free drink.

The town still talked of Shanky's cheek at Mr Haswell's alehouse. The baronet had asked Mr Haswell, 'Would you be kind enough to give me a glass of brandy?' and on receiving and draining same had promptly stepped towards the street. 'You have forgotten to pay,' cried out Mr Haswell. 'I beg your pardon,' came the reply, 'but I asked you to *give* me a glass of brandy. Good-day, sir!'

Before long, Van Amburgh and another fellow rode past Harry on ordinary hacks. Both men were wrapped in cloaks, and the former's riding crop looked excessive till Harry realized that it was the beast-taming whip. The men stabled their mounts and entered the Sal, but they did not remain any longer than the last trace of daylight lingered in the sky. Within ten minutes, the trio were heading down Front Street, shadowed at a distance by Harry. Soon they were beyond the reach of the street lamps.

He had expected them to choose the gentler route down into Prior's Haven, thus on to the rocks that skirted

117

the cliffs. Instead, they turned northward, passing the Gibraltar Arms which was rowdy with soldiery. They began to descend the steep grassy slope into Percy Bay.

Harry threw himself prone, up top. No moon stood in the star-studded, cloud-smudged sky, but still that bank and the wide sands below were exposed to view, should anyone glance back. The darkness wasn't quite sufficient cloak.

The tide was out, uncovering broad riven plateaux of black rock and tumbles of boulders which led out from those sands. The sea looked calm. On the tip of Pen Bal Crag the tiered lighthouse flashed as the revolving mechanism reflected the oil lamp.

Quitting his vantage point, he raced back along the road, passing the Gib and the Castle. He headed down the track into the Haven. Breath ragged, he reached the southern thrust of cliffs under the Priory. Scrambling on to the steep shingle beach he crunched across the scree till he reached slabs. He stepped in one rock pool, soaking his shoe. Skidding on slithery bladderwrack, he almost wrenched his ankle.

Then he froze. A bobbing of lanterns, ahead.

Using the great boulders to hide his approach, he sneaked closer.

'So there's our cave, Mr Van Amburgh!' A lantern beam shone up the cliff face, directed at a modest cleft. 'The beast's lair. I can sense it faintly.'

'Can you indeed?' Van Amburgh sniffed the weed-tangy, ozone-laden air.

'It's squirming and writing – in my brain. It doesn't want me, any more than it wanted that smuggler. I want it, though! There's gold behind it. Golden treasure. More than gold.'

The tamer extended his whip. 'Let's mount, and see.'

Once the men had vanished inside, Harry also climbed, and peered. The lantern-lit trio were advancing along the rough tunnel in Indian file, Van Amburgh in the lead. He was whistling, a teeth-on-edge sound which was at once teasing and sinister like whining wind. Harry slid inside, to crouch.

'Ah! Halt. I can detect something . . . vibrations.' Van Amburgh held the whip out in the manner of a fencer on guard. Softly he sang or chanted heathen syllables.

Inside Harry's skull there was also singing. The noise dazed him. When he thrust out a hand to support himself, the muscles of his arm were jelly. The rock he touched felt soft and squashy as if curtained in weed (which it certainly wasn't). Mesmerized by the song in his mind, Harry had shut his eyes. Now he snapped them open in panic.

No longer was he looking along a black rocky tunnel, but rather down a fleshy, phosphorescent tube – at the end of which the three men postured tiny as flies. For a while then Harry saw double. Something floppy was advancing towards him, humming that sickening song, rolling over and over on too many rubbery arms or legs. Something white as tripe. A fat coiled-up worm, with other worms clinging to it. The thing wasn't coming along the passage. No, it wasn't! It was sliding and tumbling slowly through the solid rock alongside. A worm that could pass through stone!

The creature was distant no longer. It was upon Harry – and he shrieked out. The thing was clutching his hand in a suckery, slobbery grip. It was pulling him. It was drawing his forearm inside the solid stone, transforming his flesh and bone to something ghostly.

The thing also sucked at his terrified thoughts, lapping them as a cat laps milk. It sucked his existence inside the stone along with it, inward, downward.

Cold, the cold! The locking cold!

Yet fires were a-burning. Fires in the heart of the world! In the lava entrails; in the interior oceans of molten rock. Fires which made gold flow like blood through veins! Phoenix fires, of power. Fires of foreverlasting. Oh no, not the fires of Hell – but fires which transmuted the stuff of coal into bright immortal diamond. Vital fires of the primal planet, before it scummed over with soil and fields, with trees and houses.

Creatures, incarnate forces, thrived in the boiling heart of Earth in extremest heat. Oh no, not devils, though people might think them devils. Born in the Venusian heat of early Earth, as the world cooled and as metals and mountains and meadows hardened, as clammy marshlands formed a skin, they had descended into the furnace depths.

These creatures could be called up from the stiff, molten depths – to writhe in cold exile seeking a means to return to the original fire; back from the cold, the locking cold. Fierce passions, wild desire, mad greed, fiery spurting blood, the burning of the brain which is insanity: needles of nightmare could pierce the cool skin of the world and let the exiled elementals return to the depths.

The chilly tentacles released Harry. His fire wasn't hot enough yet. It let go; yet part of the creature still touched him, and would continue to touch him, to stroke and stoke his fire, if only that could be made to burn mad bright.

If a fish is hooked up from its own cold depths, does it not fight to return? Particularly if the fish could sense the fisherman's feelings, and play these on a line . . .

A fish can flop for hours struggling for its breath while razor-air saws its gills; lying limp then thrashing again. A creature of elemental mercurial fire can exist out of its element for fossil centuries . . .

* * *

120

Harry writhed in bed, sweating the sheets. Memory and dream throttled one another.

'. . . You gain the wager, Sir William. I would not wish to win. What is in here unseen, should never be seen. The Indian tribes are aware of such . . . such ravaging forces from beneath nature. This is not a cage I would enter.'

'The gold . . .' Elwes' voice shook. Maybe his long shanks were knocking together, but he repeated, 'What about the gold inside?'

Van Amburgh snorted. 'Gold? Yes, I sense a kind of gold, and more. You have your gold, Sir William: one hundred sovereigns in payment for this encounter tonight. And should you try to earn extra by consulting the gentlemen of the press I shall return – and tame you with my whip! For the sake of every living soul, this business ends in silence. Understood?'

'I know you! You're Captain Bell's boy from Front Street. Why, you snooper, you've been spying on us! Get up!'

'The boy looks dazed out of his wits,' murmured Van Amburgh's companion.

'That he does,' agreed the beast-charmer. 'I think he may have experienced something which we only felt brush by us. You all right, lad?'

Harry gibbered, vomited.

'That'll teach you to mind other people's business,' said Shanky high-mindedly. 'What was your idea? Why, I ask myself? Ah! I begin to perceive. Master Bell . . . Mrs Halliday's slut of a niece . . . and a matter in which I concern myself in the public interest – regarding that friend of agitators, Miss Martineau, for whom we're supposed to feel such generous sympathy! The thread leads back, does it not? Does it not, indeed!'

Van Amburgh said sharply, 'I know nothing of these

121

circumstances. However, Sir William, despite your graceful airs you appear to be a deplorable person. Do you not see that this boy is badly shaken? His spirit has been mauled. Hand me your lantern, Brendan. Support the lad. Let us leave this vile place quickly, before worse . . .'

In his dream Harry was trapped in the rock. Jane's voice called out to him desperately, pleadingly. Drunken soldiers laughed at her.

'Look at that mad tart wailin' after hor sweetheart.'

'Can none of you heroes help me?'

'She needs a soldier, doon on the sands.'

'Question is, does a soldier need hor?'

'Harr-eeee! Harr-eeee!'

'What's the hot hurry, lass?'

Slowly, as if through suffocating mud, Harry was pulled by her voice through the mass of the Castle rock upwards towards air and life . . . and fire bubbled in his mouth.

The man called Brendan poured brandy down Harry's throat so that he jerked upright in the packed snug of the Gib, coughing and spluttering.

'I'm . . . I'm aal reet.'

Distorted red faces of soldiers leered and swam amid clouds of dizzying tobacco smoke. He shouldn't be here. What would his Mam and Dad think?

'Let me be!'

'There's gratitude for you.' Elwes fixed Harry with a malevolent eye that promised for the future. Something had twisted up inside Shanky, thought Harry. The man's carefree reprobate heart had been stained. Yet the baronet swiftly recovered his bright good manners and amiability.

'Speaking of gratitude, my good partner in adventure, hmm?'

'We'll settle our affairs at that other inn,' growled Van Amburgh.

'In privacy, I trust?' Elwes' glance at Harry was all benevolence now.

'Aa can walk hyem on me own.' Harry struggled up. 'Thanks, Mista Van Amburgh.'

'So you know me, lad?'

'Aa saw yor show. Aa'll not say nothin'. Aa must gan hyem.'

A red-hot worm forged through the bowels of the world, and through his own bowels. A white-hot worm swam in fire, its element. Harry found that he was holding his penis: a hot swollen worm had joined itself to him. He tried to pull this off. The image of Jane appeared in his mind, hectic with embarrassed desire.

'Escort her to my cave,' whispered the worm. 'Lie her down. Pull up her dirty skirt and her petticoats. Who'll notice any extra stains?'

The worm shivered. It was cold as ice, but it felt hot enough to Harry. The worm needed to plunge itself into the inner heat of Jane, her blood heat. He writhed, loathing himself, sick in the head. He couldn't. Mustn't. Wouldn't.

He passed out.

He had led Jane into the cave and his worm was mesmerizing her. Her mouth was agape, her eyes watered rheumily. Then he was turning her over on to her front, because of course he mustn't give her a baby. So instead he parted her tripe-white buttocks wide and thrust up from behind into the tight heat where no baby could be made; thrust until he burst.

He woke soaked and sticky, thinking in despair, 'She is not that person at all! I am not that person!'

However, his worm kept on touching him; the worm that corrupts.

14

On Saturday morning Jack wanted me to go to the Central
Post Office down by St Nick's Cathedral to check out his
mail. High time that Mandarin made an offer for the
latest addition to the Cannon canon, *Gorgon Gaze*. This
had been sent off a good six weeks earlier, a fortnight
before Tony ever came into my life.

On the street I noticed a good few more veils being
worn by women, some of whom looked like beekeepers.
This wasn't just another symptom of the new puritan
modesty being enforced by the scourge, which might
eventually transform our towns into Islamic ones. There
was a growing dread of being bitten by any midges or
mosquitoes which might be breeding in puddles on derelict land. Liked a nip of blood, didn't they? So they might,
might conceivably, transmit AIDS to a few people in a
million.

So might fleas. Since the new strain of AIDS had got
into part of the animal population, the number of domestic pets was declining. Moggies were being put down by
scared owners. People were shooting at cats with air guns,
crippling them. It was the Middle Ages again; the witch
fever, with cats as victims. Dogs were fumigated, kept
indoors, only walked with muzzles. Houses of former pet
owners were fumigated to kill fleas, since hungry fleas
could bite people, couldn't they, and sup their blood?
Memories of the Black Death. Irrational nonsense – but
it gripped people.

At the post office I collected half a dozen letters and a

fat Jiffy bag from Mandarin, which presumably contained copies of some French or German edition.

Usually I wouldn't let Jack open his mail until the evening. In this case I made an exception, since I'd spotted Mandarin's postal franking, first class, on one of the letters. So I walked along past the Lit and Phil Library to the Station Hotel in Neville Street to see whether the lounge bar was open yet. It was, and had no other customers. I took a small bottle of Brown Ale off to a padded corner.

Yes indeed, the letter was from Sally Butterworth. Mandarin were willing to offer £5,000. But first . . .

Sally wanted some changes; and she hated Jack's title.

'*Gorgon Gaze* sounds like a blend of *Gormenghast* and *Gorgonzola*,' she wrote. 'And it's confusing – not everyone knows what a gorgon is. Couldn't you simply call it *The Gaze*, to be in key with your other books? That would look much neater on the cover.'

Readers would know what a gorgon was all right, when they'd read the book! A woman whose look could petrify, who could turn a man (or another woman) to stone – psychically, and physically too in part or in whole. In the AIDS context the symbolism of the gorgon was obvious enough to me; however, I felt that Jack had handled the treatment subtly. There were some wonderfully disturbing scenes, but none in which a penis simply turned to stone.

Sally was also unhappy about the main character's 'casual promiscuity', as she put it.

She – the gorgon character – could hardly be otherwise, could she?

Well, these days sex had almost entirely vanished from advertisements on billboards, on TV, in magazines. (And Page Three was gone forever.) You couldn't sell vodka or perfume or fast cars any longer by suggesting that these products would increase your chance of scoring sexually –

not when that way lay (perhaps!) an incurable disease. The accent now was on health and efficiency, on family, on personal and spiritual fulfilment. Driving a fast car was a private, Zen-like high; sipping vodka was a way of imbibing the soul of Tolstoy and Chekhov. Plus, there were some very odd and creative attempts to evolve a new iconography of polymorphous-perverse fetishism. Romantic relationships with inanimate objects, you know? I could foresee sex-robots being developed quite soon for flexible, pneumatic gratification, if technology was up to it. These soft robots *would not necessarily* resemble the human form too closely, provided that certain curves and openings and protrusions were coded in satisfyingly.

The Gaze was Jack's problem. Likewise the other letters. I finished my ale and set off up Grainger Street. I detoured through the covered market, crowded with shoppers, because Jack enjoyed the sight and smell of blood and sawdust, and all the display of black and white puddings, knuckles of beef, tripes, faggots, hearts, livers, brains, half sheep's heads. These gave him ideas and images; nourished him.

On impulse, I decided to cut through Fenwick's. A few minutes later I found myself in the book area, where I stopped to check the titles in the horror section. Naturally Jack kept his works locked up in an oak cabinet in our study back home, so it was amusing to see those same books nakedly on open shelves. Why not rearrange some, with more covers facing outwards? I stooped to do so.

'Hullo, Dr Cunningham!'

It was Tony Smith.

Of course. The music department was just along from the books. He could have seen me coming.

'Do you read horror books, Doctor?'

'Um . . . not really. No.'

126

'Why are you looking at them, then?'

'A cover caught my eye.' I had my hand on *The Goblin* by Jack Cannon. An evil red flaming imp grinned and bared its teeth. Tony took the book from me.

'Could be psychologically interesting,' I joked. 'Maybe it's a book about compulsive eating.' (Oh no, it wasn't.)

'Oh yeah?' My joke fell flat. 'Jack Cannon, eh?' he read. 'Wonder who he is, when he's at home? Makes a bundle out of it, I bet! You going to buy this?'

'No.'

'Why not?'

'What a high-pressure salesman you are.'

'Maybe you don't *need* a copy.'

What the hell did that mean? How could he possibly suspect . . . ?

'You being such a good writer yourself already,' he added.

I realized that in my zipper bag were several letters and one whopping package all addressed to Jack Cannon. Was the bag zipped up properly?

('*Don't* look at it, you idiot!')

I visualized the bag spilling its contents over the carpet of the store, the Jiffy bag bursting open, exposing half a dozen identical copies of a German horror with Jack's name on it . . . Oh, so we get published in foreign countries so that nobody will know the truth in England?

'The way you wrote up about Gavin and the cave, Doctor – what did you think I meant?'

I glanced in the direction of the music department, where the jolly soundtrack of *Oklahoma* was playing. Two female assistants were on duty, by my count. The blonde one was serving a fat man. The brunette was arranging a cassette display. Which of the two was Carol Smith? Or was neither of them Tony's wife, to whom he could no longer satisfactorily make love?

127

('Fuck, John. Fuck.')

I returned my attention to *The Goblin*, as if I had never seen such a book before; as if Tony was recommending it to me.

('Tell him that you're here to sneak a look at him and Carol interacting. It's plausible. That's why you were hiding behind the shelves.')

'Why hullo, Doctor!'

It was Brenda Jarvis, with a canvas shopping bag.

('Bloody Piccadilly Circus today.')

Brenda wore her straight black hair to shoulder length, framing a somewhat ruddy face which I suppose indicated high blood pressure, not that she was under any particular stress that I knew of, either at home where she lived with her parents, or in Jesmond Road.

('Maybe she's frustrated, John. Pent-up.')

Mother didn't exactly *pester* Brenda. It was Brenda who ran upstairs at regular intervals. She had quite a trim figure. Brown boots disappeared under a long, dark-green tartan skirt. A tweed jacket cinched a tight pea-green pullover which moulded firm, moderately prominent breasts. She favoured a bright-red lipstick, but with her skin colour that wasn't too blatant. Not that much skin was showing; only her face. I noticed that she was wearing thin tan gloves.

'Buying a book, are you, Doctor?' She peered at the cover. 'I wouldn't fancy meeting him on a dark night!'

(No, I'm not buying a book!)

'This is my receptionist, Miss Jarvis,' I told Tony.

'I know. I've been in her office, remember? Fancy you both bumping into each other in Fenwick's.' Tony sounded suspicious.

('That's because Brenda's here to give a woman's assessment of Carol.')

I beamed at Brenda. 'Indeed, an unexpected pleasure.

128

Maybe you'd like a quick drink?' Anything to disentangle the situation.

Brenda beamed back. 'That's very kind. I'd love one.' she continued beaming, her face like a blush.

'We'll be running along,' I said to Tony. 'See you at the usual time next week, mmm?'

'Any reason why not?' Tony still held *The Goblin*. 'Do you think *I* ought to read this?'

'God, no.'

('Thanks a heap, squire.')

'Why shouldn't I?'

'Well, because . . .' Because I daren't let you! In case you recognize some mannerism of mine. Turns of phrase, attitudes, quirks of thought.

'Because,' I murmured to him, 'a horror novel – whatever's in it, and I'm sure I wouldn't know – could conceivably colour what you tell me next about you-know-what.'

'Do you think so?'

'Suppose one of your past lives was located in the Wild West, I certainly wouldn't advise reading something by J. T. Edson just at the moment! You mustn't read any horror novels. Right? Ah, we must see about that drink.'

In my confusion, I took Brenda by the arm.

So there we were in another lounge bar, myself with my second Brown Ale of the morning, Brenda happy with a Martini and lemonade; and with my company too.

'Do you mind if I call you John, while we're being sociable?'

'Not at all.'

We talked about my mother. More to the point, Brenda talked about my mother.

'She'll be delighted to hear about us meeting and having a drink. She's a bit worried about you, you know? Not

129

enjoying life enough, not getting out, she says. For a drink, or a meal, or a dance.'

'I don't dance.'

'Do you like Chinese food?' she asked.

'No. Indian.'

'Oh, I like Indian too. I hear there's a fabulous new restaurant in Newgate Street. The Star of Bengal. Could I invite you out for a meal, John? As a birthday treat! It's your birthday in a fortnight.'

Thank you, Mother.

'At my age, birthdays are best ignored.'

'Nonsense, John. You aren't old. You're a man in his prime.'

Oh gorgon you, I thought to myself.

'If you'd prefer,' she offered, 'we could go Dutch.'

'The event seems to be arranged.'

'Oh, I'm so glad, John.'

John, John, John.

When I got back to the house and Jack opened the Jiffy bag, it contained not a foreign edition but a new printing of his second novel, *The Nail*. New cover art showed a red hammer-headed fiend whose nails were exactly that, metal nails, dripping red to match the cover of *The Goblin*.

I'd totally forgotten this reissue was due. Maybe Jack hadn't, but I had.

Jack admired the copies for a while then locked them away safely.

15

On Thursday, 29 August 1844, Harriet pointed her telescope in the direction of Pensher Hill, trying her best to visualize yesterday's magnificent ceremony.

Yesterday the lens had allowed her the faintest, partial glimpse. But now the *Chronicle* confirmed how much sincere popular esteem dear Lord Durham had indeed enjoyed.

'No fewer than *thirty thousand persons* congregated to see the foundation stone laid!' she exclaimed to Jane. 'Imagine that.'

'It's a lot o' people.'

'Indeed.'

The *Chronicle* had printed the complete text which was engraved on the brass plate attached to that stone.

This stone was laid by
THOMAS, EARL OF ZETLAND,
Grand Master of the Free and Accepted Masons of
England, assisted by
The Brethren of the Provinces of Durham and
Northumberland, on the 28th of August, 1844,
Being the Foundation Stone of a Memorial to be erected
To the Memory of
JOHN GEORGE, EARL OF DURHAM
who
After representing the County of Durham in Parliament
For fifteen years,
Was raised to the Peerage,
And subsequently held the offices of
Lord Privy Seal, Ambassador Extraordinary and
Minister at the Court of St Petersburg, and
Governor-General of Canada.

He died on the 28th of July, 1840, in the 49th year
of his age
————————
This Monument will be erected
By the private subscriptions of his fellow-countrymen,
Admirers of his distinguished talents and
Exemplary private Virtues
————————
John and Benjamin Green, Architects

And erected it would be! A twice-size Temple of
Theseus one hundred feet in length, dominating the
skyline from the Tyne to the Wear.

'He's bein' done decent honour at last.'

'Oh yes,' sighed Harriet. 'At *private* expense.' She
could not avoid a note of bitterness.

'Aa remembers hoo upset ye was when his orphaned
dorters came to visit ye here, Mistress. It can be aaful to
be an orphan; though one has to bear it with a brave
heart.'

'You're a good girl, Jane. I wept unpardonably on the
day of their visit. But really, Lord Durham's story is the
most tragic I know. Such a bright start in the Commons;
such a triumph with the Reform Bill! He was so earnest
and heartfelt – yet so cheerful and so innocent of falsity.
Perilously innocent. Remain innocent, Jane, as you are
now! But be vigilant against malice.'

'Ye advised His Lordship yorself, afore he went off to
Canada, didn't ye, Mistress?'

'Went there at his *own* expense! – to save the colony
from chaos. And what did that false friend Lord
Brougham do, but joke with his toadies that Lord Dur-
ham's ship would surely sink under the weight of the
Governor-General's plate! Whereas the mission cost Lord
Durham ten thousand pounds out of his own pocket. Oh,
Brougham was happy to imperil the stability of Canada

132

just to stab Lord Durham in the back – and alas the Queen allowed this, and permitted the humiliation of Lord Durham on his return.'

'Aa can hardly believe it.'

'Lord Durham's Report was of unparalleled value. But would you believe he had to obtain copies for his own use by *buying* them at four shillings and threepence apiece? It is true. This was merely one of the insults. Malicious Brougham sent Lord Durham heartbroken to his grave – *and* Lady Durham after him. Beware of false friends, Jane.'

'Aye, Aa will.'

'For example, your previous hopes with regard to young Harry Bell – '

Valiantly Jane strove to change the subject.

'With a great big temple on Pensher Hill, the owld Lambton Worm itsel wud have a real sorprise if it came back, Aa'm thinkin'. Did your Lord Durham ever talk about his family's worm?'

'Once.' Harriet smiled. 'Yes, he did. That was just prior to my own trip across the Atlantic. I was staying at Lambton Castle, and I was eager to go down a coal pit to see conditions for myself. Lord Durham arranged it, and he joked that we must hope I did not meet the famous worm below ground!'

'An' did ye?'

'What I did meet was extreme heat and draughts. Those, with the fatigue of an unbroken journey by mail back to London, and the panic of pressing literary work all inflamed my liver terribly. Now it seems that such prostrations may become a thing of the past. I trust it, I believe it.'

Jane nodded. 'The mesmerizin's workin' wonders for ye.' Her eyes felt sore, so she rubbed them with her sleeve.

'Ah, if only I could have commenced mesmerism while Lord and Lady Durham were still alive to press me to make the little trip from here to Lambton! I hardly thought as I lay couchbound, that I should never see them again.'

'We shouldn't cry over spilt milk,' muttered Jane, whose own milk certainly seemed to have spilt, in the matter of Harry.

'True enough.' Harriet eyed the girl. 'I'm increasingly convinced that you too, Jane, would benefit from mesmerism!'

The whole business had seemed a miracle. Formerly Thomas Greenhow was such a figurehead of family opposition. Three months earlier, out of mere curiosity, he had attended a demonstration lecture by Mr Spencer Hall in Newcastle. Being a prominent local medical man, Dr Greenhow was requested to chair the meeting – to which he agreed, purely to ensure fair play. His own scepticism about somnambulism was as intense as ever.

What he witnessed deeply impressed and perplexed him. By 22 June he had arranged for Mr Spencer Hall to visit Tynemouth to mesmerize Harriet.

The results were immediate. Harriet's condition was improving by leaps and bounds. Mr Spencer Hall had easily taught Mrs Hartley, wife of the Vicar of Holy Saviour's, how to induce a soothing trance in Harriet so that her treatment could be continued. He had also taught Harriet the same simple technique, since he was eager to broadcast the benefits. If an authoress as influential as Miss Martineau should be cured and should speak out in favour . . . yet Mr Spencer Hall promised absolute discretion until Harriet herself should choose the moment. Discretion was important. Certain members of Harriet's family would cry foul.

'A course of mesmerism should indeed improve your

eyesight, Jane. It could also heal the hurt caused you by Harry's . . . change of character.'

'When yor magnetized, ye divvent blab yor heart oot, dee ye?' Jane feared that her own tender feelings for Harry, now so disappointed, might be nakedly exposed.

'I myself have not undergone the full mesmeric sleep, Jane. I should not aim to induce that state in yourself – but only to ameliorate your symptoms by suggestion. I believe that the sleep itself is not essential, and is best avoided. Mr Spencer Hall advised me of the extreme susceptibility of persons in that state. True experience and dream may intermix. Hectic delusions can arise – even what seems to be actual clairvoyance. The person can become convinced of the existence of a spirit world.'

'Ye mean that a haunted person could be helped by bein' magnetized?'

'I did not say that, exactly!' Harriet smiled. 'What haunts *you* is this severe weakness of the eyes – together with a certain element of sorrow. I feel we should begin your cure without delay. Why not today, why not now? I am greatly heartened by the successful dedication of that foundation stone. Let us lay the foundation stone of your health.'

Jane panicked. 'Like at Pensher Hill, aye! What the worm coiled itself roond, as came from Lambton. So that's why they chose the place for the Lord o' Lambton's monument.'

'That worm has as much reality as the so-called spirit world and its table-rapping inhabitants. I believe you are prevaricating!' teased Harriet.

Harry Bell had certainly become a changed person, and Jane could date that change to the visit of the menagerie the year before.

Since then, Elwes and Mrs Blagdon had stopped poking

their noses into Miss Martineau's affairs. The Testimonial had proceeded without any foul publicity. By October of 1843 the sum of £1,400 had been raised by subscribers, whose identity remained unknown to Miss Martineau, and this money had been invested in long annuities.

Jane was sure that Harry had triumphed. Yet at awful cost – the awfulness being somehow connected with the Pen Bal Crag and Jingling Geordie's Hole. According to gossip at the farthing pant, Harry was now a victim of nightmares. Anyone seeing him could spot immediately how careless of his appearance he had become, how deprived of purpose, like a madman. He shunned Jane. He would simply rush away without speaking as if she was a disease.

Hard words had been exchanged between Mrs Bell, in her distress, and Jane's aunt. Mrs Bell seemed to imagine that Jane had focused an evil eye upon her ruined boy. Lord knows, Jane's eyes were trouble enough already. Apparently Harry could not, or would not, correct this backyard opinion. Unlike his apparel, which was now as disorderly as Jane's, his lips were buttoned tight. Mrs Halliday treated her niece as if she was guilty of some indefinable sin.

Captain Bell, for his part, now despaired of any decent apprenticeship for Harry. Yet he had also noted a strange, stubborn, crazy courage about his son. It was as if the boy had sworn to keep some terrible secret which he must never divulge; as if Harry was waging a war against a hidden enemy whose identity could never be revealed. This might simply be a symptom of lunacy – unless there was some naturalistic explanation.

Accordingly the Captain sought for one. He had begged an interview with Mrs Halliday and Jane, and been rebuffed. Although Harry would respond to no searching questions when he was awake, from nocturnal babblings of his son Captain Bell gleaned a connexion with the cave below the Castle. So in company with some seafaring friends the Captain had set out to explore the Hole properly. Maybe he might find a gruesome corpse; though this should hardly have shaken Harry's composure and decency so severely.

At the pant there was talk of the cave. Mrs Jackson insisted that Coalwulf, an ancient King of Northumberland, abdicated his throne to take up residence as a hermit in that hole soon after the Venerable Bede died. ('Mebbe he was huntin' for coal, an' he thowt it was a pit!')

Widow woman Hulme stated that the Witch of Tynemouth had lived there, a hag who sneaked out on foggy nights to

> Writhe children's wrists and suck their breath in sleep,
> Get vials of their blood, and where the sea
> Casts up its slimy ooze search for a weed
> To open locks with, and to rivet charms –

'Na, it wasn't a witch,' said another woman, 'it was a wizard.'

Penetrating deeply into the cave, the Captain's party reportedly had found two arched apartments with all the appearance of dungeons. Beyond, they came upon a pit like a well-shaft about twelve feet deep. Captain Bell and a companion were lowered by rope – into a square apartment. A cramped passage led from this to a similar chamber. From there, a tight tunnel led deeper into the bowels of the rock. But here a fallen slab blocked the way; and to remove it might have brought the roof down. The roof looked desperately insecure. Obviously no human being could have crawled any deeper into these excavations for decades – or even centuries.

So the party had returned to the daylight, having found no bones, no signs, no portents, no knowledge.

Jane suspected that Harry might be haunted by the spirit of that long-dead Wizard of Tynemouth. The spirit may not have shown itself to a band of bluff mariners; Harry was more vulnerable, and suggestible.

'Aa'd like to be magnetized by ye,' she told Harriet. 'Yes, Aa'd be grateful. Wey, Aa'd like to learn hoo to dee mesmerism mesel!'

16

Tony spoke in the voice of Harry Bell, who had ended a ruined life so wretchedly in the 'Spital.

'Wey, Aa was very disturbed. But Aa knaa'd Aa mustn't say owt aboot the worm, or Aa'd be locked up as a lunatic. An' Aa mustn't gan near Jane, either, or else Aa might dee somethin' aaful to hor.

'Aa'd heard me Mam talkin' aboot the power o' good as mesmerizin' seemed to be deein' to Jane. Hor eyes weren't nearly as clarty. She could see things clearly. Everyone said as she was much improved. Nay thanks to Missus Halliday's obstructions! Hooever, Missus Halliday couldn't exacly gan against hor payin' guests, not noo that Miss Martineau was so much perkier.

'One day Aa was gannin' for a trudge up to the Spanish Battery, when Jane managed to corner me. Aa couldn't get away. She wouldn't take na for an answer. Hor eyes was aalmost gleamin'. She telt me aboot events at Number Fifty-seven. She said she could magnetize me an' get rid o' what was hauntin' me. Like a feul Aa was tempted. Aa didn't feel too sick in the heed that day. Aa didn't feel like lurin' hor to the cave an' tossin' hor doon an' turnin' hor over an' rippin' hor rags off.

'So she started mesmerizin' me – '

'Pause!'

Mesmerism within mesmerism: what kind of cage of mirrors would this be?

'Play,' I told Tony cautiously.

To my surprise, instead of talking he began to sing.

'One Sunday mornin' Lambton went a-fishin'
   in the Wear;
An' catched a fish upon he's heuk,
He thowt leuk't varry queer,
But whatt'n a kind ov fish it was
Young Lambton cuddent tell.
He waddn't fash te carry'd hyem,
So he hoyed it in a well.

   Whisht! lads, haad yor gobs,
   An' Aa'll tell ye aall an aaful story,
   Whisht! lads, haad yor gobs,
   An' Aa'll tell ye 'boot the worm.

Noo Lambton felt inclined te gan
An' fight i' foreign wars.
He joined a troop o' Knights that cared
For nowther woonds nor scars,
An' off he went to Palestine
Where queer things him befel,
An' varry seun forgat aboot
The queer worm i' the well.

But the worm got fat an' growed an' growed,
An' growed an aaful size;
He'd greet big teeth, a greet big gob,
An' greet big goggle eyes.
An' when at neets he craaled aboot
Te pick up bits o' news,
If he felt dry upon the road,
He milked a dozen coos.

This feorful worm wad often feed
On caalves an' lambs an' sheep,
An' swally little bairns alive
When they laid doon te sleep.
An' when he'd eaten aall he cud
An' he had had he's fill,
He craaled away an' lapped he's tail
Seven times roond Pensher Hill.

The news of this myest aaful worm
An' his queer gannins on
Seun crossed the seas, gat te the ears
Ov brave an' bowld Sor John.
So hyem he cam an' catched the beast
An' cut 'im in twe haalves,
An' that seun stopped he's eatin' bairns,
An' sheep an' lambs and caalves.

So noo ye knaa hoo all the foaks
On byeth sides ov the Wear
Lost lots o' sheep an' lots o' sleep
An' leeved i' mortal feor.
So let's hev one te brave Sor John
That kept the bairns frae harm,
Saved coos an' caalves by myekin' haalves
O' the famis Lambton Worm.

Noo lads, Aa'll haad me gob,
That's aall Aa knaa aboot the story
Ov Sor John's clivvor job
Wi' the aaful Lambton Worm.

'Everyone was singin' that after the panto at the Tyne
Theatre.'

'What year was that?' I asked.

'1867, it would be.'

'You're supposed to be in 1844, Harry. You're being
mesmerized by Jane in the cow shed.'

'When there's a worm in yor heed ye get yor years
mixed up.'

'So tell me about the worm, Harry.'

John was the spoiled and wayward laddie of the Lambton
household. One Easter Sunday, when all the rest of the
family and all the loyal yeomen dressed in their homespun
were in chapel celebrating the Resurrection, John was
sitting by the River Wear with rod and line, trying to
catch a trout or a salmon.

141

He was swearing foully because no stupid fish would bite. He was cussing the fish, cussing the water, cussing his luck. Well, they say that curses come home to roost like chickens.

He felt a fierce jerk on the line – and what a fight he had on his hands now! It took all of his strength and skill to land the catch. But what came out of the water on his hook was a fiendish slimy sort of newt; or a worm, with a gaping greedy gob. Hard to tell exactly what shape it was.

In his fury John hurled this nasty catch into a nearby well.

The creature thrived in the sweet water. Within a few years it was sneaking far from the well to steal milk from cows' udders. Within a few more years it was catching and devouring lambs. Ultimately the foul worm grew to a prodigious size. It was covered with scales as hard as brass, its eyes were bright as glass, and it glowed golden in the sun. At night it would crawl to Pensher Hill and coil itself around the summit. By day it ravaged the land.

Four of ageing Squire Lambton's sons had perished of illness or affray by this date, and the reprobate John had long since turned over a new leaf. He had gone off to the Holy Land to fight the Saracens. When at last the worm advanced upon Lambton Castle, there was nobody young and strong at home to oppose it.

The old steward advised buying the monster off by filling the great trough in the courtyard brimful of sweet fresh milk. Well, the worm drained the trough dry, and retreated satisfied. Yet it returned and returned. Still it wreaked havoc in the neighbourhood, particularly if there wasn't quite enough milk for it.

Many brave knights travelled to Lambton to try to put paid to the notorious worm. Even though they were armoured from head to foot, it easily crushed them in its coils. It crushed their horses likewise. Suppose some powerful, lucky sword blow managed to sever part of its body, the pieces just flowed back together again; so the knight was doomed.

John eventually returned from the Crusade, to discover this appalling situation; whereupon he realized that *he* had brought this ghastly curse upon his home. He was willing to sacrifice himself, but there was no point in simply tossing away his life – he must kill the creature, destroy it.

So he nerved himself to visit a fearful hag who lived alone in the woods. She was an awful witch and necromancer, with tangled hair and wild eyes. Her breath stank of the pit, and her voice was shrill and vicious. To start with, she lambasted young Lambton for causing so much death and misery. He accepted all her harsh words. So then she looked right into him, and saw that he was sincere.

'You *can* get rid of the worm,' she told him, 'but there'll be a price to pay for victory. You must vow to Heaven that when you succeed you'll kill the first living creature that greets you on your return to Lambton. If you break the promise, nine successive lords of Lambton will die agonizingly, by accident or in battle.'

John immediately saw how to fulfil this vow without dire consequences; so he agreed.

'You must visit the castle armourer,' the hag explained, 'and have him stud your metal suit with razor-sharp spearheads till it looks like a hedgehog.'

John did as she recommended. Also, he warned everyone he could think of not to come near him after the fight. He would blow a victory blast on his horn if he won. Hearing this, his father should release John's favourite hound. The dog would run to John; and John would kill it.

When the worm was next sighted rolling hungrily

through the meadows towards Lambton, John was already kitted out in his hedgehog armour. He rushed to intercept the worm on the river bank.

The golden worm seized John – it wrapped itself around him. As soon as it started to crush him, the spears pierced it in a hundred places. In rage the worm writhed around him, tightening its grip vigorously. The blades sliced through its body, cutting it into lots of separate pieces. These flopped into the river. Before they could rejoin, they were washed away – away downstream, never to be seen again.

John hurried home through the woods and blew the victory signal as he came in sight of the castle. But his father was too full of joy to remember the warning. Instead of loosing the hound, the old man himself ran out to meet John. Horror gripped young Lambton's heart.

'How can I possibly kill the poor old man?' he asked himself. 'Yet if I don't . . . nine generations of ghastly death? Well then, so be it! I cannot stab my father.'

John embraced his Dad – then slew the hound anyway. Thus John brought about the second curse of the Lambtons; which perhaps even reached its finger as far as John George Lambton, Earl of Durham, who died broken-hearted after such a fine beginning.

'Harry, are you telling me it was the Lambton Worm – or what's left of it – that was skulking in Jingling Geordie's Hole?'

'Aa felt the worm risin' in me, there in the coo shed, so Aa screamed at Jane to get away. Aa pulled oot me jacky-legs, snapped it open, and stabbed the blade into me hand – to gee us somethin' else to think aboot! It was the worm aal reet!'

'*Pause!*'

Harry Bell had met a creature which had given rise to a

144

legend centuries before? A creature which could live in solid stone like some sort of encapsulated toad? An ectoplasmic creature which grabbed people mentally – and could drag them inside the rock with it?

And Gavin Percy had met the very same 'worm' in the 1950s? A worm which could still be lurking in its hole in Tynemouth – accompanied by Ted Appleby?

'Tommy-rot, tommy-rot,' I said to myself with a shake of the head.

And Jack jeered at me, 'What if it isn't, old son? What if it's all bloody true?'

'Shut up, will you!' Jack had never interrupted one of my therapy sessions before. I didn't usually let him out until the evening. He was taking advantage.

17

The story of Harry Bell and Jane wasn't yet complete. I had to range to and fro, a while longer . . .

Within months of commencing mesmerism, Harriet was perfectly well; while, thanks to Miss Martineau's mesmerism of Jane, the girl's eyes were pure and clear. Jane's heart was also calm – for a while.

By January of 1845 Harriet was hiking through the Lake District hunting for a new home. The Wordsworths consulted her about the possible value of mesmerism to help their mortally ill daughter-in-law. Harriet lodged for six months at the head of Lake Windermere near to the Wordsworths, and by June 1845 she was having a house built for herself at Ambleside. By the end of the following year, she would be off on a working holiday to Egypt, Palestine, and Syria, researching a book on the origin of the Egyptian, Hebrew, Christian, and Mohammedan faiths.

This ambitious project echoed her early essay triumphs. However, she now approached the topic from a secular viewpoint. In her view, the world's major faiths were all *necessary* – at a certain stage of historical evolution. Yet Christianity or Islam were no more (and no less) necessary than fetishism had been 'necessary' in early primitive times. The witch doctor was grandfather to the bishop or the mullah; and they were grandfathers to the positive, logical scientist.

Back home in Ambleside she became even better acquainted with the Wordsworths. William had been the idol of her youth. Now on his winter walks (in cloak, Scotch bonnet, and green goggles) he was pursued by cottagers' children till he cut ash switches from the hedges for them. In summer he was pursued by invading tourists, anxious that he should pronounce his opinions. Alas, these were often those of an old half-witted sheep who

> . . . indicates that two and one are three,
> That grass is green, lakes damp, and mountains steep.

To Harriet, William would confide his *extremely valooable thoughts*. This was hard on her hearing when his false teeth were out. Harriet rather preferred Mrs Wordsworth, shrunken with sorrow as she was by her daughter's death. William boomed and bleated out this sorrow, unaware that a grief was shared.

However, prior to all this Harriet would feel obliged to write an account of her own successful mesmerism, and Jane's. She wrote it for no payment, only for the public good; and thus was treated like John George Lambton. The *Athenaeum* gladly rushed her free, and fascinating, contribution into print in several instalments; then the same journal devoted months to utterly insulting editorials blackguarding all mesmerists and branding Harriet Martineau and her familiar, Jane, as lying rogues.

Oh yes, the shit hit the fan; and Shanky Elwes enjoyed himself hugely and profitably.

For it was he who spearheaded the slander that 'Jane of Tynemouth' was actually a girl of notorious loose character, all too well known amongst the officers of the garrison. Elwes neatly hybridized Mrs Halliday's niece with a different Jane – who had indeed been seduced at sixteen, but who was now a repentant Methodist. It was true that Harriet had also mesmerized this other Jane for epilepsy, upon express request and only after discreetly searching enquiries into her present moral character.

147

Harry (Tony) moaned and beat his fists together.

'Be calm,' I told him. 'You are feeling calm. Calm, do you hear me? Calm. Now carry on, calmly.'

It was Elwes who fed the *Journal* with these slanderous titbits. It was he who stirred up the Shields physician, Dr Forbes – a man easily enraged against mesmerism – to denounce Jane in a newsworthy style.

Not only that, but Forbes and two medical colleagues and several gentlemen of the press even called at Mrs Halliday's to demand that Jane should sign a paper confessing that she was guilty of imposture. If she refused to sign, these worthies promised that she would be sent to gaol as a perjurer. What's more, they would ensure that her aunt never housed another lodger ever again to eke out her widowhood.

'The bloody bastard!' cried Tony. 'Aa could ring his neck. Aa could rive his tripes oot!'

'You are *calm*, do you hear me? Calm. You will be calm.'

'Yes . . .'

By now, of course, Captain and Mrs Bell pretty much concurred with the bad opinion of Jane. Hadn't the young hag bewitched – perhaps *mesmerized* – their boy, and sent him mad? Harry must have been mesmerized, to pay attention to her!

Thanks to all the vile publicity, Jane's health had relapsed disastrously. It was an almost blind girl whom Forbes and company threatened with incarceration. Yet Jane resisted her persecutors in brave silence.

At this juncture, an Ambleside friend of Harriet's visited Number Fifty-seven, Front Street, and discovered the depths of Jane's suffering. Immediately arrangements were made for a friendly South Shields druggist and mesmerist to hurry over to Tynemouth. When he arrived

Mrs Halliday refused him admission. He had to mesmerize Jane at the bottom of the back garden.

'Beside the coo shed!' Tony was shaking and shivering,
though his voice was calmer, as I had instructed.

After this outdoor séance Jane began to see light again.
Her appetite revived. Harriet wrote to Mrs Halliday from
her Ambleside lodgings offering to take over full responsibility for the girl, if only she could be made fit enough to
travel to the Lakes. Out of self-interest, and a pinch of
benevolence, the aunt agreed.

So finally Jane arrived at Harriet's door – in tears, a
bundle of nerves, half-blind, exhausted, and in rags. Mrs
Halliday had let the girl's garments degenerate shamefully
during the time Jane was too blind to sew. Since the coach
bound from Keswick had been full, in her anxiety Jane
had walked the sixteen miles to Ambleside.

'She would have been in worse rags an' tears if Aa'd
taken hor to the cave!'

'Easy, Harry. It doesn't distress you now.'

'No . . .'

Some years previously, Harriet had nearly become the
adoptive mother – of a black American slave child. On
her visit to New Orleans, Harriet had been introduced to
a grieving Irish widower who lived there. The Irishman's
wife had recently died, leaving beautiful little Ailsie as an
embarrassing co-occupant of the house.

Harriet wrote about the man's moral dilemma in her
American travel book. As a result, the Irishman wrote in
turn offering to send Ailsie to England, into Harriet's
care. Harriet conceived a plan to train Ailsie as her own
little maid, until she could decide on a future for her.

All was agreed; yet Ailsie never arrived. Finally a
heartbroken letter came from the honest Irishman,
explaining that Ailsie originally had been a wedding gift
from his dead wife's mother. Now that the girl's beauty

had blossomed, the mother-in-law – who still technically owned Ailsie – demanded that the girl be returned to the plantation. As a sexual resource, she was too valuable to give away.

That was before Harriet's illness. Now that the illness had come and gone, Harriet was faced with a different 'adoptive daughter' – in the person of Jane.

Thanks to renewed mesmerism, Jane flourished. She became Harriet's maid and served her diligently for seven years. At the end of that time . . .

'Wey, thank God – !'

. . . Jane emigrated to Australia, where she became for the rest of her life family cook to the High Sheriff of Melbourne.

Meanwhile, Harry slid from bad to worse.

Not for him an eventual captaincy and even ownership, his father's dream, and maybe a home in tree-shaded Dockwray Square with its well-clipped grass, its tall, dignified, greystone houses, their windows immaculately painted, their steps scrubbed daily, brass knockers polished every morning, and smart carriages waiting outside.

'Aa did have occasional jobs in the valley o' smoke alang the river bank. In the brewhoose at the Low Lights, in Richardson's tannery, a chain manufactory, the clay pipe factory at the bottom o' Wooden Bridge Bank, in one o' them roperies as stretched oot as lang an' narrow as their ropes, interruptin' easy traffic.

'Aa also carted entrails an' blood from Bakers the Pork and Beef Purveyor in Prudhoe Street to the Chirton an' Preston farms to feed the barley as made the malt as brewed the beer. Wey man, Aa *stank* – '

But he lost every job. He mingled with riff-raff – there was still plenty of riff-raff in Shields to mingle with. Not for nothing had the lads of Shields been known as the rudest in all of England, what with their vicious drunken gang battles along the dockside, rolling empty tar barrels ablaze with chips and pine knots at each other along the dark, tortuous lanes, and down the precipices of stairs.

Police had been established to put a stop to such capers; and the constables were always carefully paraded both before and after duty to check that they were sober. Yet the lodging houses along the riverside remained dens of thieves, filled with rogues supplying filched goods to certain bent chandlers, and equipped with escape trapdoors.

'Aa was mostly a petty thief, when Aa wasn't drunk an' disorderly. Aa'd steal the brass taps off rain tubs, the screws off water cocks, pigeons from someone's back garden. Once Aa stole the muzzle off a dog – '

The North Shields and Tynemouth Association for Prosecuting Felons was eager to post rewards and punish such as he.

'Aa saw the inside of aal four lock-ups, in Clive Street, Duke Street, Liddell Street, an' at the Bull Ring. Aa inhabited the Correction Hoose over from Tanner's Bank, next to the laundry – '

In the end he became a despised daft beggar.

'Pause.'

This tidied up the life of Harry Bell, but it answered nothing fundamental. Obviously the *source* of Tony's neurosis wasn't located in his 'past life' as Harry. To uncover that source I would need to send Tony back to some even earlier 'life' – peeling away the psychic layer symbolized by Harry, in search of some ultimate bedrock beneath.

And be damned to the Lambton Worm.

18

'You won't forget about tonight?' said Brenda. 'The Star of Bengal?' Her lipstick was the brightest yet. Maybe I was more conscious of it.

'I'm looking forward,' I said heartily, without specifying what I was looking forward to.

'I booked a table, to be on the safe side.'

'Wise move.'

Jack was licking his lips at the prospect of a King Prawn Madras. To date he hadn't even thought about any revision of *The Gaze*. There was too much Tony Smith on his plate, and Jack was clamouring that his wonderful material just had to be *used*, not locked away in my filing cabinet. I was refusing staunchly.

Already, he had had me delving a bit into the nineteenth century in the Central Library and down at the Lit and Phil Library too. Just checking up, he assured me. But in fact he was fleshing out and supplementing the story of Harry Bell and Jane and Harriet Martineau on his own account in a way which struck me as illegitimate.

Now there were two parallel accounts: the raw material from Tony's lips, which he could have read about when he was a kid in something like those 'Lore and Legend' books which Gavin Percy said he'd had at home – and Jack's improved version. I was sometimes on the verge of getting the two confused, and I feared that Jack might surface during one of my mesmeric séances – *no*, damn it, one of my therapy sessions – and might somehow start revising Tony, transforming him, programming him with fresh material.

On Jack's behalf I'd managed to locate the probable originals of those books of Gavin's, at the Lit and Phil. Correct title: *The Monthly Chronicle of North-Country Lore and Legend*, published annually in 1887, 1888, and 1889 on behalf of the proprietors of Miss Martineau's favourite local newspaper, the *Chronicle*, by Walter Scott of Newcastle upon Tyne and Paternoster Row, London.

Had Tony once read pages of those books on boring rainy days long ago? Or during boring holiday visits to ageing relatives? He didn't recall. Tony was one of those people so irksome to Jack who'll sometimes tell you, 'I read a fascinating book last year.' 'What was it called?' you'll ask. 'I can't remember.' 'Who wrote it?' 'Sorry.'

Of course, if he *did* recall that he'd looked through those volumes once upon a time twenty years ago, why then, there was the source of his 'past life' – dramatized by the imagination. And so much for my therapy. I couldn't press the matter too strenuously.

A new patient, a Terence Adams who was an estate agent, was due at two-thirty.

Scarcely had Brenda returned to her office – it was just ten past two – than I heard a door bang open, voices raised, and Tony came barging into my consulting room. He was brandishing a folded newspaper, which he thrust at me.

It was the *Journal*. Open at a photo of a dark-haired man with black moustache and dark-framed glasses, with a smaller picture inset of the cover of *The Nail*. That was the photo of Jack which Sally had snapped in the House of Mr Chan. Headline: LOCAL HORROR AUTHOR HAMMERS OUT NEW ONE.

'Well?' demanded Tony. 'That's you, isn't it? It says here that *Jack Cannon* lives on Tyneside somewhere. Lots of authors write under pen names, don't they? And you were looking at the horror books in Fenwick's. Specially

153

this one.' He pulled a copy of *The Goblin* out of his jacket pocket. 'Soon as I saw the paper, I went to the book department and bought this. There were still a couple of copies left. It's the book you were interested in, isn't it? It's by Jack Cannon. I remember the cover.' Not the title, but the cover.

'All those horror covers look the same, Tony.'

'How do you know?'

'And that photo isn't *me*. Can't you see that? Do I have a moustache? Do I wear glasses?'

He laughed. 'Old photo, taken when you were younger. It's *your face*. I've stared at it enough. And in Fenwick's you were looking at this book by Jack Cannon.'

'I was looking at a book, that's true. Really, this is just a silly coincidence.'

'I'd call it a connexion.' He tapped the photo. 'This is *you*. Said you could be a writer, didn't I? The way you wrote up my life as Gavin?' He laughed again, jerkily. 'And it's true.'

I took the paper. 'It might mention where he lives. Probably out in Northumberland, like Catherine Cookson.'

'Oh no, it doesn't. And he lives right here. Do you publish everything people tell you when they're hypnotized? Is that where you get your ideas?'

With what I hoped was a patient sigh I pointed to the framed certificate on the wall.

'Tony, I do belong to the British Society of Medical and Dental Hypnosis.'

'So?'

'That's a respected professional body. It has a code of ethics. A code of behaviour.'

('If they boot you out,' commented Jack, 'I'll be able to write full-time. Don't let's panic.')

'What would Mother think? The shock!'

'Blah. She's tough. Give her a bit of excitement.')

'Tony,' I said carefully, 'I think that you're *subconsciously* trying to sabotage our therapy. The subconscious mind is a strange and subtle beast. Sometimes it'll defend a neurosis – a complicated knot in the mind – as fiercely as a cat its kittens. You're resisting the possibility of locating the source of your problem, and fixing it. Sometimes people prefer to be ill – like Harriet Martineau, hmm? Though they mightn't believe it. If you can discover a fantastic reason for not trusting me, then there's your excuse – to break off a process which is obviously doing you some good. I say that it's doing you good, because otherwise your subconscious wouldn't be panicking, right? It wouldn't be trying to prevent us both getting down to the next layer, where the truth is. Believe me, that's how the mind works. Subconsciously – I'll be frank – you may be scared of having the knot untied because it's a sexual knot connected with your performance with your wife.'

'Hang *about*! Why should I *want* not to be able to make love to Carol?'

'Because for some reason sex worries you.'

'You a marriage guidance counsellor now?'

'In your case, yes. Of course. And your wife didn't want to visit the marriage guidance people, remember? That's how you got referred to me. The reason is hidden in a previous life. Find the root of your neurosis, and we find the cure. I'm going to tell you something, Tony. I oughtn't to, really, as this might colour your reactions. But since you have accused me so absurdly – well, *symbolism* is involved. I realize that Freudian therapy failed you in the past, nevertheless a good Freudian analyst would tell you right away – that the cave is a vagina, and the worm is a penis. If you can come to terms with your worm in the cave, then you'll be untied,

155

unknotted. The way we do that is by finding how that knot was tied in an earlier life.'

('Bravo!' jeered Jack.)

I looked expectantly at Tony, ignoring the *Journal* and the copy of *The Goblin* in his hand.

'It's your own choice,' I added. 'But I really believe we're about to make a breakthrough. It's the final hurdle. Such a shame to quit.'

Brenda buzzed me.

'Mr Adams is here.'

'I have to see someone else, Tony. Think it over, will you?'

'Well,' he said, turning away.

'Oh, don't forget your paper.' Show no more interest in it.

('Hey,' said Jack. 'Publicity pic. I'm curious.'

'*I'm* furious,' I retorted. 'You'll phone Sally and protest about this.')

'Read that book if you feel like it, Tony. But as I said, right now I'd honestly advise you to steer clear of horror stories.'

'Yes,' he said, and left. Who could say what his 'yes' meant?

Since Terence Adams was visiting me for the first time I had to interview him – which was fairly dull – before we took a shot at hypnosis. His problem was nightmares of drowning. In his previous life he'd been a merchant seaman whose boat was torpedoed, trapping him below decks. QED. Banal.

When I'd seen my final patient of the afternoon I was heading out through Brenda's office, and she said to me, 'If only I didn't have to go home to change! I could spend the time with your mother. Play some cards. Read to her.'

('Feel free. Move into the house full-time.')

'Change?' I said. Yes, Jack needed some change. Lots of tenpence pieces, to call Sally from a phone box. Obviously, a phone box. Not just round the corner, either.

'Why, John, aren't *you* going to change?'

('Into what? A false moustache and glasses? But let's not deter her from going away for a couple of hours.')

I patted my sober suit. 'I thought I was changed already.'

'I mean into something casual, silly! A splash of curry could stain a nice suit like that.'

('Take charge of the wardrobe! And don't forget the bib.')

'Oh yes, I'll be changing,' I assured her. Dr Jekyll would change into Mr Jack Cannon. 'I'm popping out for a walk first, to stretch my legs. See you here around seven-thirty, right?'

It oughtn't to be too late to get hold of Sally. In spite of grumbles by publishers at Birmingham about being reduced to their local London sandwich bar, authors' gossip suggested that editors were still often out of the office till about four. Then they might put in a couple more hours at the grindstone.

Now it was after five, so there'd be no one on the Mandarin switchboard. However, Jack had the number of a direct office line for Sally – not that he had ever used it before. The phone box he went to smelled of piss and fish and chips. Not really fish and chips. Stale vinegar. Well, not really vinegar. Acetic acid. The piss was kosher.

'Sally Butterworth here.'

'This is Jack Cannon.'

'Jack! Wonderful! I was hoping you'd be in touch about

The Gaze. The revisions, you know? Then we can send the contract out.'

'Mmm, well I'll have to read *Gorgon Gaze* through again. See what I can do.'

'Oh, it's a horrible title. You do have to change it.'

'Reason I phoned you, Sally, is the photo you took of me at Birmingham. That was in the local newspaper here.'

'Really? Oh that's good. I supppose Anne in publicity sent it out with the press copies of *The Nail*. You did receive your own copies?'

'Why should anyone want to review a reissued paperback?'

'Obviously they do, if that was in your local paper.'

'I don't want my photo published, Sally. Mystery local author: where does he live? Who is he? Next thing, the *Journal* will be offering ten quid reward to the first reader who spots me in the street and tracks me to my lair and phones them! Then some bloody reporter will start in on me the way the same damn rabid Tory rag persecuted Harriet Martineau.'

'Who? Are you all right?'

'She was a nineteenth-century . . . never mind.'

'Oh, are you using her in a new book? That sounds a bit of a departure.'

('You are not using her,' I told Jack.)

Jack laughed and fed in a couple more tenpence pieces.

'You're in a call box, aren't you, Jack? Give me your number and I'll phone you back.'

'Not likely!'

'You don't *live* in the call box, by any chance? Oh I get it, you have a pay phone fitted at home. People do! Philippa and Paul, eh?'

'Who?'

'Your adolescents!'

'Oh them. Listen, I really don't want photos of me spread all over. I value my privacy.'

'I think you're overrating the effect, Jack. Anyway, would that newspaper have printed a piece about *The Nail* without the photo to hang it on? That's why Anne sent them out.'

And what if Tony took it into his head to contact the *Journal*, with a fascinating yarn? DOUBLE LIFE OF LOCAL HYPNOTIST! DOCTOR – AND HORROR SCRIBE. By our ace investigative reporter, the reincarnated Shanky Elwes.

The current incarnation of the *Journal* and the *Journal* of the 1840s were not quite identical. Still, journalism was journalism.

'Are you still there?' asked Sally plaintively.

'Sorry. Must be off. Have to go to a birthday party.'

'Philippa? Or Paul?'

Luckily the phone began bleeping for more coins, so Jack simply put it down.

I'd changed into slacks and a tweed jacket. Brenda wore a long green flouncy cocktail dress with lace sleeves and a polo neck of white lace, cameo brooch at the throat. To me she looked positively nineteenth century, only lacking a bonnet. It was unfashionable for women to dress revealingly or provocatively. AIDS, again.

As we sat opposite each other attacking our two volcanoes of curry – slopes of basmati rice, molten crater of giant prawns in lava – and sipping chilled hock and listening to sitar muzak, she said:

'I wonder what lives *I* might have lived before? Where was my home? What was I? Who did I marry? *Did* I marry? Did I have children?'

'You might as easily have been a man,' I said, perhaps none too tactfully.

159

She merely smiled. 'Men get married too, you know.'

'Um.' I tucked in.

'I'd like to *know* who I was. If we're getting to know each other better . . . that's the way to know, isn't it?'

'The rapists don't usually psychoanalyse their fiancées before marrying them,' I replied, most unwisely. Now she radiated tenderness at me.

'Or their secretaries,' I added hurriedly. I was sweating, but that was the curry.

She raised her glass. 'Happy birthday, John.'

'Cheers.'

'I'll still call you Dr Cunningham at work. I do wonder what I *was* before. Of course,' and she giggled, 'you couldn't very well ask me to lie on your couch, not just the two of us together. Maybe your mother could chaperone, if you were to hypnotize me in her room?'

I had an instant ridiculous vision of myself as Mr Spencer Hall, and my mother as the invalid Harriet, and Brenda Jarvis as Jane. And I laughed aloud. This delighted Brenda – till my laugh continued, crazily, longer than a laugh ought to have done. The whole day had been a bloody comedy. Of errors.

If only Tony had decided never to keep another appointment. If only he had denounced me to the *Journal*, for that matter! Then I should have had other things on my mind than a worm in a cave – to which I still lacked the fatal clue.

In retrospect I was to look back on that evening in the Star of Bengal, and wish that I could ever laugh again.

19

'I'm very pleased you came today, Tony.'

'Yeah well, I thought over what you said, and I got to
wondering if I was losing my head. I even thought the
worm might be working me up against you, so it could get
me all on my own.'

'Did you discuss this with Carol?'

'Do you mean about worms and holes – or my
suspicions?'

'Either,' I said easily. 'I presume she's interested in
what's going on?'

'She says,' and his voice tightened, 'how nice it is for
me being able to waltz off into other lives visiting circuses
and falling in love with other girls and hunting monsters,
when she only has one life. She backed me to start with,
to clear our problem up. She says she's getting fed up
now. I, er, well, I didn't exactly tell her about *Ted*. I don't
want her to think I'm really a poof. Or bisexual. I mean,
then I might be an AIDS carrier, or she might think so,
and she'd freeze like a block of ice.'

I nodded. 'Though you couldn't inherit AIDS from a
previous life.'

'I'm not daft. There wasn't any AIDS in the 1950s.'

Tony hadn't really answered my question, but I decided
I was in no imminent danger of any revelations in the
newspaper.

'Right. Let's take you back to the life before you were
Harry Bell . . .'

* * *

161

'Who are you now?' I asked.

'Robert de Neville – son of Sir Ranulph. Who else? I'm heir to the lordship of Raby, of Keverstone, Brancepeth, and Middleham!'

'What year is this, Robert?'

'The seventh year of King Edward's reign, the second of that name.'

Edward II. As featured in a play by Christopher Marlowe, which Gavin had showed to Ted to excite him about pederasty.

Would 'Robert' know the anno domini date?

I asked, 'How many years is it after the birth of Christ?'

'How many indeed? A millenium, and three centuries, and more.' His accent as Robert was certainly north country, though not quite Tyneside. Thankfully he wasn't speaking mock early English, full of 'whilom' and 'eftsoons'. Tony had taken quite a giant jump into the past, but there would be an excellent reason for that, so I felt pleased. We must be much closer to bedrock, perhaps in direct contact with the mother lode itself. Touch wood; or touch rock.

'Pause! Just wait and rest yourself. I'll be back in a couple of minutes.'

I left the room and with a wry nod to Brenda I hurried upstairs to Jack's study to consult the *Britannica*. It turned out that Edward II was crowned in 1307, so the year in question must be 1314. I hastened back to Tony, taking with me a map book of the British Isles.

Raby, as in fact I'd vaguely remembered, was down in County Durham, thirty odd miles south of Newcastle.

'Tell me about your life, Robert. Rewind to, oh, the fifth year of Edward's reign. The second of that name, of course . . .'

* * *

162

'Oh, I was so ill. Sick, tired, lackadaisical, abed for days on end. My blood was thin, my humours were corrupt. I ached, I was dizzy. Bilious today, fevered tomorrow.

'A leech had been summoned from amongst the monks at Staindrop' – he meant a *doctor* – 'but my illness baffled him. Even the leech sent by the Lord Balliol from Barnard Castle was foxed. I'd been so comely and vigorous. Now I was transformed into a sallow weakling, worse by the week. My father feared I was declining inexorably towards death . . .'

He talked on and on, with only a little prompting.

From the age of eight till the age of fourteen, Robert de Neville had been sent to serve a neighbouring lord as a page, as was the custom. In his case, his father had despatched the lad from home at Raby Castle to Barnard Castle, scarcely half an hour's ride away.

Sir Ranulph was a close friend of the Lord of Barnard, John de Balliol, whom Edward Longshanks had appointed King of Scotland but had later removed from the throne for insubordination. Edward I preferred to put in a governor, instead, and garrison the rebellious land. John had now returned from 'retirement' in Normandy to spend his last years at Barnard Castle advising his son Edward, whom he had not particularly named in honour of the king.

Longshanks's son, the second Edward, was bored by the pother and turmoil of Scottish politics. The new Edward preferred pleasure and revels and little boys, abetted by his homosexual lover Piers Gaveston. Thus the king neglected to crush the infant army of Robert the Bruce, which now loomed all over the borders campaigning for a free united Scotland. Soon there must be bloody battles.

Edward Longshanks had insisted that his bones should

never be buried until the Scots were subdued; but his son quickly stowed the body away in Westminster Abbey under a heavy slab inscribed 'The Hammer of the Scots'. Now the son's frustrated advisers were demanding that the hammer should be brought out of the cupboard.

Because Balliol had been slapped in the face by the Crown, his friend Ranulph de Neville devoted his own pugnacious energies to contesting the supposed right of the palatinate prince-bishop of Durham – the haughty Antony Bek – to order all local nobles to wage war willy-nilly all over Scotland under the banner of St Cuthbert. Ranulph maintained that Bek only had the right to issue a call to arms if the land of the bishopric itself was invaded.

'My father was also in dispute with the See of Durham about the rental by which he held Raby Castle and the eight neighbouring towns. This amounted to a token four pounds per annum – plus the delivery of a dead stag to the Prior of Durham on each St Cuthbert's Day.

'The four pounds were no problem. The body of a stag, no problem. However, my father rightly insisted that his whole retinue should be feasted in return. Furthermore, that the Prior's servants should be sent packing on that day. Our own servants from Raby should be employed to serve the banquet. Less likelihood of being poisoned, you see?

'The obstinate Prior was positive that only the persons who actually carried the stag into his hall were entitled to be treated – and then only to a simple breakfast. No onus lay on *him* to feast my father – unless he felt so inclined. Which he certainly did not, in view of what he called my father's rude and disobedient attitude to the prince-bishop!

'This stag dispute had been on and off the boil for years. No doubt it would still be simmering when *I* inherited the title! I did not intend to be at the beck and call of Bek and his priests . . .'

During those six years at Barnard Castle, young Robert waited on the elderly John de Balliol, accompanied him, kept his wardrobe in order, helped him to get dressed, and on the odd occasions when Balliol needed a bath, Robert scrubbed him down.

The state rooms thrust high above the crag which itself rose full eighty feet from the River Tees flowing through its deep trench of limestone and marble. The view of countryside in all directions was splendid, only interrupted by the castle's own towers. The great round tower. And Brackenbury's Tower, weighing down the subterranean dungeon into which scraps of food and prisoners were lowered or tossed from the peak of the vault.

In return for his duties as page, Robert was taught by experts how to ride and hawk and fight. Nor did he neglect social skills; he learned to play the mandora lute and the viol, and to sing and dance, at which he proved extremely gracious. Balliol's chaplain catechized him and taught him Latin *inter alia*. The Balliols were strong on education. Some decades previously John de Balliol's father and his mother Devorguilla had founded a college at Oxford.

Robert came home to Raby excellently qualified to graduate to squire. Fourteen years old by now, he continued combat training even more strenuously, mastering the sword, the axe, the lance, the dagger, and the spiked ball on a chain. He drilled in jousting. He memorized all the garbs, tinctures, charges, partitions, augmentations, and crests of heraldry so that he could identify friend or foe, iron-clad in the new-fangled plate armour. He loved the decorative aspects of heraldry.

He helped the seneschal with the castle business, which

he would direct one day. He kept the keys, which he would one day own. He carried the purse. He bedded kitchen maids and peasant girls scattering his seed in soft fleecy nests. At fifteen he wedded slim, oval-faced, golden-locked Isabel, daughter of Lord Percy. This was a double ceremony; on the same day his brother Ralph, three years his junior, was married to eleven-year-old Alice, daughter of Lord Audley, though Ralph and Alice would not consummate this till she reached fourteen summers.

Robert was everything that a knight in the making ought to be. He was bold, strong, and dextrous. He was honourable – he gave purses to the local maids whom he got with child as a result of his deflowering. He was gallantly courteous, and very fashionable in his attire. He sported long pointy red leather shoes, the points of which had to be tied up around his calf so that he didn't trip; slashed tunics-of-many-colours with hugely-hanging scalloped sleeves, belts hung with trinkets, velvet mantles with ermine trimmings, puffed tam-o'shanters and natty furry hats. Often he wore a very brief embroidered tunic, prominently displaying his tight-clad buttocks and codpiece.

And whenever he donned chainmail and breastplate, and the hooped iron skirt and the cuisses and poleyns and greaves, and the plated gauntlets and the heavy stuffy visored helmet, not forgetting the heraldic surcoat which was his badge of identification, so as to take on any band of Bruce's Scots who came a-raiding, he fought them like a junior Hercules, cleaving and battering.

At the age of seventeen, came the onset of his mysterious enfeebling illness . . .

'AIDS strikes paragon?' I scribbled. 'Image of?'

I crossed this out as irrelevant. 'Robert' was a model of

166

primal bodily health and potency. Potency with females, into the bargain. There was no hint of himself having been buggered by old Balliol as a page boy in the bath, an event which might have represented Tony's sexual assault by an uncle or grandfather. No, the only reference to homosexuality was as regards King Edward, who was a long way distant and who genuinely *had* been a homosexual and pederast.

The troublesome, lamentable, tragical title of Marlowe's play on the subject rang a very faint bell with Tony, though he swore he had never 'done' the play at school and certainly couldn't quote from it. So why did it raise any tinkle at all? Obviously the play must have been on the syllabus at his school. Some boy in an 'A' stream might have sniggeringly read out the naughty passages in Tony's hearing; or showed the text around. The subconscious mind had a photographic, and tape recorder, memory.

One of Tony's own brighter peers might have flashed the play when they were both adolescent. An older boy could have done so when Tony was younger, making him feel threatened. Oh, a whole number of possibilities. But though I had toyed with the idea that Tony's fatal experience might have occurred at school, he oughtn't to have forgotten it so completely unless he was suffering selective amnesia.

Though hark . . . might Tony not be Gavin – but *Ted*? Might Gavin stand for someone else? Might that somebody-else have fastened up Tony in his psychic cave?

Really, I doubted it. My money was on the traumatic incident having occurred much earlier, pre-school. I had the highest hopes of a successful diagnosis by tracing the roots and the outcome of Robert de Neville's emasculating ailment. In early fourteenth-century County Durham, at any rate, it seemed unlikely that yet another mesmerist

167

would interfere, to hold up another mirror within a mirror!

'So there I lay in my sad, sickly, stupefied decline, when important news reached my father. Our enemy Bishop Bek had invited a philosopher who was famous throughout Christendom to visit and stay with him in his palace at Durham. This philosopher was already on the road from London.

'My father decided to waylay the man; to haul him to Raby and lock him up in one of our towers. Thus he would poke a thumb in the Bishop's eye; and perhaps gain leverage in the dispute over the stag and the feast. But my father wanted this man for another reason too – a greater reason! The philosopher was known to be an alchemist. He could change base metal into gold. My father's informant reported that the man refused to use his art to enrich himself. He would only create gold for the benefit of those who would wage war in the service of the Cross, to spread the true faith in Christ. Of course, everyone knew the making of gold was a complicated business, costing much time and equipment; so if the man would not enrich himself on a principle, because of a sacred vow, then he needed a sponsor.

'Bek's plan was plain to my father; and our spy confirmed it. The Bishop would argue that if only Scotland could be thoroughly subdued, then this would free the northern English to join a crusade. At present we could not reasonably abandon our homes, with an enemy at our back. A pile of alchemist's gold would finance the subjugation of the Scots.

'What's more, once the national hopes of the Scots were thoroughly dashed, those troublesome Scottish nobles too might be glad to join the crusade! They were, after all, loyal sons of the Church – and here would be an outlet for their violent energies. Thus subjugation would benefit their souls. First crush Bruce – a costly matter – and then unite against the Saracens.

'My father, who refused to be ordered to Scotland by Bek, had no desire for Bek to fill his coffers courtesy of alchemy. On the other hand, a flood of gold could certainly benefit the *Neville* family – if this alchemist could be persuaded to co-operate. And indefinite imprisonment was a fine persuader.

'So therefore, my father and Ralph rode out with a small armed company and intercepted Raymond Lully before he could ever reach the protection of the Bishop. That was the philosopher's name: Raymond Lully.'

20

'So what have we found out about Raymond Lully, Jack?'

'Enough to be sure that Lully was no alchemist! – and that he couldn't possibly have visited the north of England in 1312!'

Ramon Llull was born on the island of Mallorca around about 1233. It was paradise! Blue skies and seas, snowy peaks, olive groves of silver and steel-grey, the scent of orange blossom, snow drifts of almond blooms.

Mallorca had recently been recaptured from the Moors by James the Conqueror, a real fighter and lover, seven foot tall with a mass of ruddy golden hair and flashing eyes. Ramon duly became his squire when he was four-teen – and he took to life at that dashing court as a fish to water. He dressed himself up to the nines, he became a devotee of courtly – and carnal – love, not to mention a fine musical poet in the tradition of the troubadours, the *jongleurs* or jinglers.

'Jinglers? Do you mean to say that he was *Jingling* Raymond Lully?'

'Ah ha! That he was. There are patterns, John, pat-terns. The eye of Jack, like the eye of God, perceives these. We'll see more patterns presently.'

As well as being the Conqueror's squire, Ramon was appointed companion to his two sons, Peter and James. Ten-year-old Peter was an aggressive bully who would cause his brother James much grief when their father died and the kingdom was divided – with much of the mainland going to Peter, and the island to James. Peter would demand allegiance, and carry out an *Anschluss* . . . but not yet. Four-year-old James was a sweet, friendly lad, and as he grew up he and Ramon, now his tutor, became firm friends. The future King James of Mallorca would appoint Ramon his seneschal and major-domo. Ramon would travel much in the royal diplomatic service, visiting Catalonia and Aragon, Castile and France.

In his early twenties Ramon married Blanca Picany, yet his wild womanizing continued unabated. Inflamed by lust for a lady called Ambrosia de Castello, Ramon was said to have spurred his horse into church in pursuit of her, so as to lay at her feet a madrigal he had composed exalting her charms. A minor scandal ensued. Ramon was forever writing luscious love poetry to that lady, with far from courtly aims in mind. Finally, at her wit's end, Ambrosia invited him secretly to her private chamber,

> Upon a gloomy night
> With all his cares to loving ardours flushed.

Ramon rushed there and entered hot with excitement. Ambrosia coolly disrobed, and displayed cancer of the breast. Profound shock ensued for Ramon; and Ambrosia suggested that he might do better to seek bliss everlasting in the bosom of Jesus.

That was one version of the story of how Ramon turned over a new leaf. According to a different version he was sitting in his room at home, tussling with one of his randy love songs, when he glanced up – and saw a vision of Christ crucified upon the wall. Five times over the course of the next few days he struggled to complete the song. Each time the blood and nails and thorn crown and that suffering body interposed, till finally he got the message.

So he resigned as seneschal. He settled sufficient money on Blanca and his children Dominic and Magdalena, sold off everything else, and gave the proceeds to the poor. Then he set off on a pilgrimage to think things over. Returning in sackcloth to Mallorca, he was widely regarded as insane, or simply lazy. Not so! He climbed up stony Mount Randa to live in a cave for several years and undertake a great work.

'That would be Jingling Lully's Hole, I suppose?'

'Ah ha! You're catching on, John. You're getting there. Keep it up.'

Ramon made a triple vow.

One: he would do his best to be martyred as a missionary. Well, you can't say he didn't try. He frequently managed to be beaten up, tossed into prison, stoned by enraged Moslems, banished from North Africa on pain of death, not to mention being shipwrecked and investigated by the Inquisition. Nevertheless he lived to a ripe old age, and died in bed back home.

Two: he would campaign for the founding of schools of oriental languages to prepare missionaries throughout Christendom to convert Moslems and Jews and heathens in their native tongues. Mallorca was still home to a small population of Moslems, so Ramon set out to learn Arabic from a Saracen slave, and he succeeded magnificently. Eventually the slave tried to stab him. The slave had been rude about Christ; Ramon thrashed him; the man retaliated and was tossed into prison. Ramon decided to forgive the man, but doubting Christian charity the Saracen had already hanged himself in his cell.

Three: Ramon would write *the* definitive book proving the truth of Christianity logically for the benefit of Jews, Moslems, and other reasoning heathens. Military crusades had produced nothing but bloodshed and chaos. Let reason have its day!

'Hang on, Jack! Wasn't that what Harriet Martineau started out by doing? Trying to convert the Jews and Moslems by reason?'
　'Yes. But Harriet got over it. He didn't.'

Ramon not only educated himself deeply in Arabic, but also in Latin – a skill which the jingling courtier and lover had neglected. Friends advised him not to bog himself down in the big scholastic University of Paris, where his command of Latin might prove less than adequate.
　His unique do-it-yourself approach in the cave on Mount Randa resulted in the enormous *Compendious Art of Finding the Truth*. In this encyclopaedic volume Ramon codified the way in which the whole universe could be related back analytically to the attributes of the Christian God.
　He devised concentric circles of subjects (Angel, Heaven, the Negative . . .), and qualities (Duration, Virtue, Magnitude), and faculties (Perception, Cogitation . . .), and questions (How large? When? Where? . . .). These circles could be rotated so as to produce all possible permutations. To facilitate these operations Ramon also invented his own symbolic logic of letters. Thus, at several centuries' remove, he inspired Leibniz's dream of a universal algebra, and unbeknownst ploughed the first furrow of computer programming.

'Er, Jack? Didn't Harriet set out to *codify* the Bible?'
　'Right! She was also a friend of Mr Babbage, who built the first primitive computer, the analytical engine. Do you reckon Harriet might be a reincarnation of Ramon? All that travelling she and he both went in for – and all

173

those practical, populist books that poured from their pens! Every branch of human life and wisdom: Ramon related it all to divinity, and Harriet to political economy. Both tried their hand at novels too! Ramon wrote the first utopian romance: *Blanquerna*, 1284. Lots of magical, allegorical forests in it. He founded all that science-fantasy stuff. Maybe Harriet *was* Ramon, reborn.'

'I don't believe in past lives.'

'Why not? Connexions abound! *Patterns*, John.'

'If you try hard enough you can relate anything to anything else.'

'That's exactly what Ramon succeeded in doing. He produced the key to the whole shebang. The Compendious Art. He could apply his method to anything – and he did! Ar-ithmetic, Ge-ometry, Ast-ronomy, Ast-rology! In short in matters vegetable, animal, and mineral – !' Jack was singing, to a tune from *Princess Ida*.

'Please leave Gilbert and Sullivan out of it.'

'And Law and Rhet-oric and Med-icine and Al-chemy!'

'Alchemy? Not likely.'

Ideally a hand-cranked machine ought to have been built, with the *Compendious Art* as blueprint. Medieval technology missed a trick there. You could have had ecclesiastical computers – wheels within wheels – by the Renaissance.

In the absence of mechanical Llull Wheels, books constantly spilled out of Ramon. He also expanded his travel horizons. He lectured and proselytized all over the place. Certainly he toured Italy, Turkey, and Palestine. Probably, Egypt and Ethiopia. Conceivably, Greece, Germany, Russia, and England. Quite the medieval jet-setter.

'Yes, I said England. That would have to have been before 1299. His date-book's full after that.'

* * *

His friend King James founded a college of oriental languages for him at Miramar in Mallorca – and obviously if you speak to an Arab in Arabic, you speak to a Mallorcan in Catalan; so Ramon wrote in Catalan as well as in Arabic and Latin, and thus founded Catalan literature.

Sadly, following James's troubles with his brother, the college at Miramar fell into decay.

Let's fast-forward to 1310. By then Ramon was seventy-seven years old – thin and pale, with a long white beard and long white hair. But he was lecturing on his Art at the University of Paris, and as usual he was writing furiously. As usual, he was campaigning for his colleges of oriental languages. Perhaps because he sensed that time's string was running out, unlike in earlier years he was now calling for a crusade – despite the fact that personally he got on well with Moslems and Jews, and actually liked them.

This new crusade ought to be fought at sea, not on land. That was because Christians owned more galleys than the Saracens. And thus events panned out – to a certain extent. The King of England also favoured a crusade, so a sea-borne venture was launched which succeeded in capturing the island of Rhodes in 1310; and there it stopped, profitably.

To support his own schemes Ramon applied to the King of France, Philip the Fair, for a letter of general commendation, and received one. 'Notum facimus quod nos audito Magistro Raymundo Lullio, exhibito praesenti, ipsum est virum bonum, justum et Catholicum reputamus.' 'Be it known by these presents that we regard Master Ramon Llull as a jolly good and Catholic guy.'

That was the same Philip the Fair who had recently confiscated all the wealth of the Knights Templars and was currently torturing the captive officers of the order excruciatingly to death and madness to wring confessions, so as to justify his seizure of their assets. This process was to culminate in March 1314 in the square in front of Notre Dame de Paris, before a vast crowd of spectators, when Grand Master Jacques de Molay – godfather to the king's own daughter – was finally led out after years of torment, minus fingernails and such, publicly to plead guilty to sodomy and cat-worship and spitting on the Cross, and to be sentenced to life imprisonment. Unexpectedly, the wreck of de Molay declared the total innocence of the Templars; and an enraged Philip ordered him burnt at the stake.

King Philip was called 'the Fair' because he had fair hair; no doubt there were some greasy smuts in it the next day.

Armed with the royal commendation, Ramon took himself off in King Philip's wake to attend the Council of Vienne. This had been organized so as to officially abolish the Templars internationally, and to share their European assets among interested parties. At Vienne Ramon petitioned the Council and the Pope, who was in the chair, begging them to occupy Constantinople and Ceuta in Morocco as forward bases for the faith – and to found a unified military wing of the Church, not like those reprobate Templars. He also appealed to the Council to base Medicine upon experimental science, instead of on incorrect texts 1,000 years old. And yes, to set up colleges of oriental languages.

Jubilate! Pope and Council issued licences for schools of Hebrew, Greek, Arabic, and Chaldee to be founded in Rome, Bologna, Salamanca, Paris, and Oxford.

When the Council wound up in May 1312, Ramon headed back towards Mallorca by way of Montpellier, with its familiar university and its perpetual fair.

Thence to Sicily, then back to Mallorca; then over to Tunis, and back again to die, in 1316.

And all this while books and pamphlets poured from him; such as the *De novo modo demonstrandi*, or new method of demonstrating, in September 1312, in which he demonstrated in passing that 'Alchymia non sit scientia, sed sit figmentum', that alchemy is no science but only eye-wash. Likewise, in the *Liber principiorum medicinae*, he said sternly that 'unum metallum in speciem alterium metalli converti non potest', that you can't change one kind of metal into another.

His wife Blanca, now long deceased, had been forced to ask her male kinsman Galcerán to become legal administrator of the affairs which Ramon had dumped in her lap; and Galcerán had grown all too accustomed to manipulating the family purse. So, on 26 April 1313, before gadding off, Ramon drew up a proper testament in favour of his son and his daughter and his son-in-law Peter de Sentmenat.

Over in Tunis, in December 1315, Ramon dedicated his latest production, the *Liber de majori fine intellectus amoris et honoris*, to the infidel Mufti, proving that there were no ill feelings despite previous episodes of stoning and imprisonment and expulsion, and Ramon's advocacy of a bloody crusade.

'Which leaves us to explain all those alchemy books which poured forth under his name, eh John? Such as, to name but one, the *Epistola accurtationis lapidis philosophorum Raymundi Lullii ad Regem Robertum*, an epistle concerning the philosopher's stone addressed to Roberto Anglorum Regi, King Robert of England.'

'King *who*?'

'You may well ask! England never had a King Robert. Those were very lucid alchemy books, by the way. None

177

of your usual cryptic fog. Lullian method applied logically and rationally. And signed Lully.'

'Though not written by Llull . . .'

'In those days, if you admired somebody you put their name on your book. If you thought Aristotle was the bee's knees you signed your book Aristotle. Besides, people would pay more attention to it. Now, the real Ramon Llull hung around courts and princes a lot, hoping to raise funds for his schemes. So if you *called* yourself Raymond Lully . . .'

'What does your novelist's instinct tell us, Jack?'

'That the Raymond Lully whom Ranulph locked up at Raby in 1312 – was an imposter! He had already conned some men of influence in the London area; hence Bishop Bek's eager invitation. That would be a fairly easy scam in the early thirteenth century, don't you think, passing yourself off as someone else? No passports. No newspapers. The real Llull probably never had visited England.'

'But what sort of imposter was our pseudo-Llull, Jack? Was he just a charlatan? Or was he fully familiar with the work of Llull, and saw himself as an intellectual equal?'

'Even as someone carrying the work of Llull one vital step further – by applying it to the Great Work, alchemy, the key to the secret of creation? Aha!'

'So how does Tony Smith know about Raymond Lully, either real or pseudo? Is it those lore and legend books again?'

'Connexions, John. Patterns. Ramon, and Harriet. An alchemist's quest for gold – and Shanky Elwes scenting the yellow metal inside Jingling Geordie's Hole. The jingle of coins. The cave on Mount Randa. *Patterns*.'

'So what has Llull got to do with worms?'

'Which Llull, John? Which Llull?'

'Oh, I see. The pseudo-Llull. We'd better call him Lully, as distinct from Llull. Maybe Lully wormed Robert de Neville, to cure him.'

178

Raby, fifteen miles to the south-west of Durham City, originally was a monastic shrine to St Cuthbert. When King Canute made a pilgrimage to that shrine, to mark the occasion he gave into the ownership of the monks Raby itself and the village of Staindrop to the south and the shire surrounding.

In 1131 the monks rented out their possessions to the Northumbrian princeling Dolphin, Son of Ughtred, for four pounds per annum plus one dead stag. Some castle building commenced. Dolphin's son was Maldred fitz Dolphin. Maldred's son married Isabel Neville, who was sole heiress of a great Saxon family. *Their* son adopted the Neville name, in preference to Fitzdolphin. Who could blame him?

And now the man who called himself Raymond Lully was riding his palfrey reluctantly towards Raby, in company with chainmail-clad Nevilles and half a dozen lancers.

Fences of close-woven stakes protected what arable fields there were. Much of the land was stony sheep pasture, rising to hilly moors. Few trees were visible. Drizzle fell.

Presently a square, stub-towered church loomed. It stood beyond a collection of low thatched cottages, mostly built from the stones with which the countryside was littered. As they rode by the church, the burly knight who had introduced himself as Ranulph de Neville gazed piercingly at it, prompting Lully to enquire in French,

'Do you have a quarrel with *that* church, as well as with Durham?'

The knight shook his head.

'Staindrop Church is the burial place of our family. At home my eldest son lies mysteriously sick. He may soon be joining his ancestors underneath the church floor.'

'So that is your secondary reason for abducting me, Dominus?'

Ranulph looked blank. 'How do you mean?'

'You have abducted a mediciner. If I can assist your son, may I be allowed to continue my journey?'

The Lord of Raby stared at Lully. 'You have studied leechcraft?'

'Indeed, it is part and parcel of my search into the body of nature.' Lully stroked his long white beard. 'The true philosopher never seeks gold for its own sake, you know. Transmutation of base metal into gold is simply a *test* – to confirm that the philosopher has indeed made the true Stone, which principally functions as the elixir of life. That elixir is the aim – it transforms the mortal mind and body. So before the philosopher even begins, he must understand the *mortality* and *morbidity* of body and mind.'

'And you have achieved this stone? You have this elixir?'

'Ah, it is a lengthy process, costly in both time and material,' Lully replied evasively.

'But do you carry any elixir with you?'

'What I do have at the moment is some of the impure quintessence, known as aqua vitae. Its effect on an ailing body is remarkable.'

Ranulph scrutinized his captive. The philosopher wore a beaver hat in the style of the Flemings – under which he might be as bald as a coot – and a high-collared cloak which was crumpled from sleeping in, and muddy leather boots. His face was lined, and his beard was white.

180

Subtracting the effects of travel, did not Master Lully appear somewhat decrepit and time-worn for a person who had drunk an elixir of life?'

Alternatively, this philosopher might be as old as Methuselah; in which case he was not in bad repair, all things considered.

'You should drink some of that aqua vitae yourself,' said Ranulph, 'before you pour any down my son's throat, eh?'

Lully smiled thinly. 'I should be delighted.'

Ranulph fell silent, and spurred ahead.

Lully was well aware that he resembled the real Ramon Llull. He had attended the marvellous old man's lectures on his Art, and had observed him closely. Lully had long since studied many of Llull's books with admiring attention, memorizing whole passages and mastering the method which was so eminently applicable to the science of alchemy. Llull could have been an intellectual uncle to Lully.

Not an elder brother, though! That position belonged to Lully's alchemical master, Arnold of Villanova, with whom he had studied for years. Arnold had quit France to distance himself from the arm of the Holy Inquisition, which was furious at the man's questioning of papal infallibility.

To heighten a physical resemblance which he aimed to exploit, Lully had grown his own beard almost to the length of Llull's; and had recently bleached it.

The true adept, such as Lully, was well advised to steer clear of powerful men and princes. Princes had a habit of imprisoning you, even of threatening pain in their greed for gold. The temper of princes, if disappointed, was unreliable.

Massive difficulties attended the course of true science!

Disregarding the foibles of princes, there were still explosions to contend with, and accidental fires, impurity of the raw material, failure to maintain the exact furnace heat perfectly for a month and more, the cracking of badly-made glass vessels, a servant nodding off over the bellows, bad stars in the sky: any of these could wreck an experiment which had been years in preparation. This was well known.

Thus hoaxers and puffers could get away with conning gullible patrons out of large sums of money. First they would demonstrate their 'skill'. They would hide some real gold, fixed by wax, inside their apparatus. They would introduce it by sleight of hand, and then go through the motions of transmutation – resulting in the wondrous production of the selfsame gold. Later, they would let accidents abort their work – and call for more and more money.

Yet large sums of money *were* needed. Lully knew that he was very close to his goal. First he must find the funds to buy time, raw material, and equipment. He had decided to travel to England impersonating the excellent Llull who did approach princes, to gain backing for all sorts of missionary work. Crusades were a popular cause, God knows why. To manufacture gold for a crusade: that must seem entirely praiseworthy.

So far as Lully knew, Llull had never visited England; and he would be unlikely to do so in the near future. Llull would be fully occupied in Vienne on the Rhône, lobbying the papal Council. A church council could easily spin out to a year or two years. If any deep philosophical discussion should occur in England, why, Lully could acquit himself as well as Llull.

On the stormy and dangerous journey over to England, he had induced a trance in himself and had become Lully. He put his own boyhood in Languedoc behind him. He

182

submerged his youth spent in Montpellier. He drowned his middle years when he had wandered Europe in search of the true science . . . Why, he had even picked up a smattering of Catalan from a student friend in . . . where was it? His ignorance of Arabic would hardly be challenged by the English.

Now, en route to patronage by a powerful prince-bishop, he had been kidnapped as if by Saracen corsairs.

Ahead rose the walls and towers of Raby Castle. He noted that they weren't crenellated with battlements, yet they still looked unbreachably strong. The moat lay about the castle like a great pool of liquid pewter. Horns hooted as lookouts spotted the approach of the party.

'Master Lully cured me,' said Robert in wonder. 'Right quickly, too!'

'He was lodged high in Bulmer's Tower, the five-sided one. I believe that number appealed to him as an omen. The very next day my father brought him to my chamber. Master Lully turned up my eyelids, and held my wrist. Then he sniffed the urine in my chamber pot, and extracted some in a glass which he took to the embrasure to hold to the daylight. I remember the rustle of his feet in the rushes and alder leaves on the flagstones as he gyrated, agitating my piss, counting the bubbles or motes that rose – and noting the time it took those to rise, by which he could determine the density of my piss and its vivacity.

'"So what did the leeches give him so far by way of medicine?" he asked our seneschal in French. We all spoke French, of course.

'The seneschal answered scrupulously. "The monk from Staindrop took one handful of wormwood, one of horehound, and one of sheep's dung which he boiled in a quart of water till there was only one pint left. This he strained, and boiled in ale, and gave to Master Robert to drink when it cooled."

'"Hmm, that makes sense. Horehound and wormwood are both stimulant tonics. Additionally, horehound purges sluggish piss from the body; while wormwood will stun any worms in the entrails. However, there is no jaundice evident in this young man."

'"Whereas the Lord Balliol's leech ordered snails and earthworms bruised and boiled in milk with hyssop and wood betony."

'"Yes indeed."

'"He also added precious mummy powder."

'"That would most likely be from a bird stuffed with spices and pulverized, in which case it could hardly prove efficacious."

'"That, to be followed by infusions of white poplar bark daily."

'"Highly renovating for debility! But we behold the young man still laid low."

'From his scrip Master Lully produced his bottle of nostrum, a clear thin liquid with a golden hue. He poured some of this into a spoon, careful not to spill a drop, and let my father see him swallow this liquid. Master Lully's skin flushed immediately, and he sighed.

'He refilled the spoon and held it to my lips. The vapour from the nostrum stung my eyes. It was as if I drank fire – delicious fire. My belly glowed. My heart thumped. Warmth perfused my cold limbs.

'"This is the quintessence distilled from wine," explained Master Lully. "The heavenly component of wine. Only this substance will extract the aromatic quintessence of plants, which mere boiling in milk or water cannot achieve. I have only a small supply; but it is at the noble Robert's disposal."

'"I am grateful," my father said gruffly. He did not

184

wish to appear too grateful to a prisoner. "I can witness the effect. And to produce more of this aqua vitae?"

'"Requires good apparatus, Dominus, and some time. I know another secret I can employ at once, which requires no nostrum, only some privacy."

'Thus it was that my chamber was cleared of onlookers, including my father. As soon as Master Lully and I were alone together, he took from his scrip a tiny shining silver mirror on a chain. This, he breathed upon and buffed and polished, then dangled before my eyes . . .'

'Another sodding mesmerist, Jack.'

'Connexions, John!'

22

Within weeks Robert de Neville was his old self again. Glowing and strong, he was working out with sword and axe, and riding at the quintain pole with a lance. Of an evening in the torchlit Barons' Hall, he wore his most peacocky clothes.

Other members of the family and retainers consulted Lully about their ailments, and in most cases he thoroughly banished or at least alleviated assorted agues, colicks, gripes, wind, surfeits, scabs, and headaches. He treated with crushed frogs' eggs an injured man-at-arms whose wound was festering. The wound stopped producing foul pus, and healed.

Soon Lully was not so much a prisoner as an honoured guest. Ranulph gave orders for the fitting up of a room at the top of Bulmer's Tower as a laboratory to Lully's specifications, as well as for the manufacture or purchase of all the necessary apparatus: the alembics for distilling, the special pelican alembics with their beaks tucked back into the glass body, the long-necked matrass flasks, the retorts and lamp-furnaces and stills, and not least the principal athanor-furnace of Lully's own devising. The athanor would require a stone tower to be attached laterally, filled with fuel, thus ensuring a constant supply as new fuel dropped down to fill the space vacated by fuel already consumed.

Masons were busy, and carpenters, and iron-workers. Guarded wagons rolled in, with thick glassware and glazed pottery packed in straw.

186

As to the *fuel* itself . . . here Master Lully appeared to be nursing a secret.

By now Antony Bek had sent a monk with armed escort to deliver a haughty message demanding the surrender of Raymond Lully into his custody. However, Lully had no wish to leave Raby – and said so of his own free will.

The evening after his declaration of full commitment to the Nevilles, Ranulph ordered a special banquet to express *his* commitment to the alchemist; and there the subject of fuel arose – amidst the roast venison and sugared suckling pig, the poached salmon in wine sauce, ducklings, cinnamon pastries and ginger wafers, and the hot spiced hippocras wine which loosened tongues.

'In the past,' said Ranulph, 'we bought some coal from St Andres Akeland. It is just five miles from here. The monks there at Bishop's Akeland dig coal when it suits them. Coal is hotter than wood, and denser.'

'Coal *is* condensed wood,' commented Lully.

'Here's a problem!' said younger brother Ralph. 'Suppose Bishop Bek hears that we want to buy coal, he may guess why. Out of peevishness he'd forbid his monks to trade with us.'

'The best and most reliable source of coal,' Robert chipped in, 'is from the monks at Tynemouth. They used to dig coal only to fuel the salt pans. Now they regularly ship their coal to the London brewers and dyers.'

'Do the salt pans need much heat?' asked Lully, ever interested in stout equipment.

'Oh, they boil the brine in such giant iron pans you can see the billowing steam from a day's ride away! I inspected them after we chased the Scots back into Northumberland.'

'And after boiling? Can you describe the process?'

'Well, while the water's lukewarm they clarify it with white of egg and sheep's blood. Then they boil, boil, boil

187

till no liquid is left. When the pans cool, they rake the crystals out to dry. And start again.'

'So there's a hive of industry at this place Tynemouth?'

Robert laughed. 'Not at all! Except for the monks, that is. Otherwise there's only a wretched huddle of fishermen's shelters, or shiels as they call 'em. The local folk feed on some stinking black seaweed they call *slauk*, which they tear off the rocks. Oh, the place was prosperous formerly. It unloaded and victualled the sea traffic which had no wish to risk seven more miles of winding river and sandy shoals just to berth at Newcastle. But the burgesses and mayor of Newcastle raged against this drain on their monopoly. Fully twenty years ago they petitioned the Crown for exclusive jurisdiction all the way to the river mouth; and gained it. The wharfs of Tynemouth were all torn down. Even Tynemouth coal is carted to Newcastle to be shipped back down the river and out to sea.'

The boys' mother, Lady Euphemia – formerly de Clavering – spoke up. She was a singularly handsome woman with a mass of lustrous natural chestnut hair framing a sensual face enlarged by the plucking of her hair-line to broaden her forehead, and by the plucking of her eyebrows too. Her red-striped gown was embroidered in silver.

'Well then,' she said, 'so the monks at Bishop Akeland must not learn that they are selling coals to us. What if they believe its destination to be elsewhere? Now let me see. Bowes Castle is too tumbledown to be believed as a destination . . . but perhaps *Barnard* Castle? The wagons would have to pass through Staindrop. They simply unload here, wait a decent interval, then return for more. By the time the monks learn the truth and the news reaches Bishop Bek's ears, we ought to have laid in a fine stock.'

'Admirable!' Ranulph raised his hippocras in a toast, and swigged. A server refilled the glass with hot, fumy wine.

Lully chuckled. 'If, I repeat it, I can maintain an intense, constant heat in my athanor for a sufficient length of time, then we shall witness a marvel in the heart of my furnace which will save us from worrying unduly about fuel and heat.'

'Aye, the stone,' muttered Ranulph.

'Aye that; but first we will see the engendering of the worm known as *salamander*! It is a necessary precursor.'

'A salamander? A newt?' asked Lady Euphemia in surprise. 'You will throw a little newt into your furnace?'

'No, Lady, this is not your mundane salamander of the animal kingdom – just as *philosophic* mercury is not common quicksilver . . .'

'So what *is* philosophic quicksilver?' she enquired.

'Why, that is the name for aqua fortis, the volatile solvent. It is concocted from vitriol of Cyprus, saltpetre, and alum of Yemen – to which you should add sal ammoniac if you wish to dissolve gold.' Lully had always prided himself on clarity and openness, unlike the obfuscations of other alchemists.

'Hmm,' she said. 'So your philosophic mercury is a symbol – and your salamander is also a symbol for some other natural substance?'

'No, Lady, the arcane salamander is a *creature* – one begotten of fierce fire, in which it dwells and which it sustains. My furnace's constant flames, together with a certain ritual, will summon the salamander. Compel it, capture it! The salamander has the power to draw the stone from the heavenly sphere into our mundane level of existence. The salamander will be my philosophic stoker.' Lully drained his hot wine, and reached for a pastry.

'And have you yourself ever captured, or even seen, this philosophic salamander before?' asked Euphemia bluntly.

'Ah.' Lully wagged a finger. 'The process is guaranteed. Arnold of Villanova evoked the salamander, though admittedly not in my presence.'

Euphemia pursed her rouged lips.

'Still,' she remarked after a while, 'you did indeed cure Robert, when no one else could.'

'I hate to be awkward,' I said to Jack as we walked away from the Lit and Phil up Collingwood Street towards the Cloth Market, 'but it would appear that when Longshanks sacked John de Balliol as King of Scotland in 1296 for being such a naughty vassal, the king also seized all of Balliol's English estates. That included Barnard Castle.

'That's why Balliol went to live in Normandy, on his family's native turf. Our enemy Bishop Bek immediately claimed Barnard Castle as belonging to the Palatinate – and Edward commandeered the whole Palatinate and presented Barnard Castle to Guy Beauchamp, the Earl of Warwick. So Barnard Castle stayed in the Warwick family for five generations until the Nevilles finally got hold of it at the time when Anne of Warwick married Richard Neville the Kingmaker.

'Thus, brother Jack, Robert de Neville couldn't possibly have been a page to John de Balliol at Barnard!'

'I don't care,' retorted Jack. 'I prefer the first story, and I'm sticking to it. Hell, John, if we're going to be pedantic, there wasn't any piped water supply to *Tynemouth* till 1846 – so there couldn't have been a farthing pant in '43. Tynemouth relied on a few private wells and one public one, right?'

'You're trying to distract me.'

'Even when the town did twist the arm of the water

company and get domestic supplies laid on from Marden Quarry, they were still forced to pump water from the sea for sewer cleansing and street washing, yes? Thus on any windy day there were snow storms of salt in the streets. We'll not dwell on the eels – the flat black *worms* – blocking up people's water pipes. However, Harry met Jane at the *public pant*. There is a higher form of truth, John. I *like* pants. Just like Gavin liked short pants.'

'If only I hadn't involved you with Tony. You're really interfering. You're risking my reputation.'

'Bit late for regrets, old son. We're getting closer to the worm, aren't we? That wasn't any eel. It was an alchemist's salamander.'

'What?'

'Lully said so. I quote: the worm called salamander.'

We cut through High Bridge towards Grey Street and the Theatre Royal.

'You're also doing your damnedest to screw up any relationship that might bloom with Brenda. Because that would screw *you* up, Jack.'

'Changing our tune a bit, aren't we? I wasn't aware you actually wanted to get married!'

'I don't. I don't think so. Well, maybe. There could be advantages. Mother's getting on. Anyway, I'm beginning to realize that Brenda has good qualities. There's a sort of core of . . . innocent goodness.'

'I wouldn't advise you to try to get rid of me! You'd go mad without me, John.'

'In what way, mad?'

'The madness of banality. The madness of a one-track mind. You'd probably start believing in past and future lives.' Jack laughed hectically aloud, and I had to pretend that I had just remembered a wonderful, side-splitting joke.

'Look, nothing's clear about Tony's case. You talk

191

about connexions but I only see contradictions. Barnard Castle. Public pants.'

'Reality's a melty thing, old son. A branchy thing. With branches of branches, forking all over. Worming all over. That's how you get connexions. Ignore those wormings – try to stick to the straight and narrow – and you'll tumble into chaos.'

'I think I'm more likely to tumble into chaos by your route. You're like some sort of demonic familiar who lures a fellow on and on along the golden road until he damns himself to Hell.'

'We aren't talking demons and devilry. We're talking alchemy and salamanders.'

'Maybe they'll cause the same mayhem! You're trying to conjure up something, Jack.'

'Me, conjure? We don't believe in devils, do we?'

'I think *you* do. And you're me. Meanwhile you're melting my therapy.'

'Just a little round the edges. That's so you can stay flexible, John. The centre is true enough, and you know it.'

'I no longer know what I know.'

'Do you want security? Is that what Brenda spells? A world poxed with AIDS craves security. But it can't have it. Nothing's secure. Everything's loose. That's the way the world has always really been. Horror is stuff oozing through the loose joins to remind us of that. So marry Brenda and be a wimp. Or follow me and discover wonderful, awful things. Powers and possibilities. Strange and terrible and golden.'

We passed by the Earl Grey Monument. The Earl stood high on his column, a stone man in the sky like that other fossilized figure of Admiral Lord Collingwood who overlooked the mouth of the Tyne from an even grander column. A pigeon perched on the head of the Earl, whose stone locks were whitened with bird shit.

To be frozen rigid, never to move, to be embodied in stone . . . However, a pigeon was no bird of doom, no raven or vulture. Busy traffic buzzed by. Through the dying city, yes. Where AIDS was loose.

Raymond Lully had sought an elixir of life . . . and maybe he had succeeded? If Gavin's worm was still in Tynemouth, was an elixir also still to be found?

23

Within four months of Lully's arrival at Raby the Bulmer's Tower laboratory was in full operation, though results could hardly be expected for many months more.

By now it was the autumn of 1312, and golden crops were being harvested. It would still be a struggle to feed the increasing number of mouths in the land. Had Lully used his skill in astrology not only to ensure that the best planetary influences should preside over the ignition of the athanor but also, Nostradamus-like, to forecast the future, he could have predicted dire fortunes for England and all Europe within a couple of years.

Seven soaking, flooded summers in succession would produce paltry harvests, when there was a harvest at all. Murrain would plague cattle, sheep would die of rot. The price of corn would soar from three shillings a quarter-ton to sixteen shillings. The poor would steal dogs to eat, or even eat their own children who were starving anyway. The Little Ice Age would have arrived, cramping the growing season.

Not that a minor ice age would impede the business of war, in which Ranulph and Ralph and Robert de Neville would all play their parts . . . Meanwhile Robert was highly intrigued by the prospect of immortality proceeding out of the alchemical laboratory. Besides being a fighting man, Robert was also a dandy; and a dandy hates decay and mortality.

The laboratory was stiflingly hot. Robert shucked off his ermine-trimmed cloak and plucked the feather-plumed turban from his head. Old man Lully wore a plain leather tunic and a grubby apron on which to wipe his hands. Daylight streamed through the narrow stone windows, shafts dancing with particles of smoke which had evaded the chimney of the furnace. Vapours drifted from alembics. Stills bubbled. Pelicans steamed. A crowd of pots and bottles, some of them massive, held sulphur and mercury, alum and yellow arsenic, saltpetre and borax, vitriol and scales of iron, vinegar and oil.

'First,' explained Lully, 'we calcinate our materials by means of acid, and distil till dry. Next, we dissolve the dry residue back into the liquor we have distilled. Do you follow? Then we circulate the liquid seven more times by evaporation and condensation. Repeated circulation is very important. Next we conjoin – we mix, we close our vessel, and heat it for several months.'

'How many?'

'Maybe four. We require a constant and exact heat all the while.'

'And then?'

'Finally the substance grows dark and thick and bubbly. It putrefies – and a rainbow shimmers in it. Once this rainbow disappears by congelation, we have arrived at the white stone. Lastly, most laboriously, we must repeat the stages which have gone before – '

'Excluding calcination?'

'Yes! Exactly. Excluding that. And ultimately we achieve the *red* stone. If we have succeeded, we only need to project a pinch of the red stone into heated mercury – and the mercury will turn to gold.'

'And the elixir, which restores corrupted matter to purity?'

'That is the merest speck of the stone, taken twice per annum in some convenient liquid. After the first dose you may expect your hair to fall out, and your nails too, and all your teeth. These will all soon grow back flawlessly. Thereafter . . . your wisdom increases.' Lully smiled. 'You, Robert, might readily become a king of England – except that you would no longer care to do so. Instead you would be a secret king, of the cosmos.'

'And the worm called salamander? Is *it* wise?'

'That is the spirit of fire itself, the quintessence vitalizing a body as fluid as flames. *Men* speak and reason. A salamander burns, and shivers. It mediates what is fiery, whereas only Man deploys reason, the gift of God. *Its* wisdom is elemental, not analytical.'

'I see,' said Robert.

I had succumbed to Brenda's suggestions that I should hypnotize her, with Mother acting as chaperone. So this took place upstairs one evening in my mother's room. Brenda lay on the sofa, fluttery with nerves as though this was a bridal evening, a time of ravishment long wished for yet disconcerting. Mother reclined against pillows, smiling encouragement at her.

To me there was something obscene about my mother's complicity. I thought of the old foreign wedding custom whereby the blood-stained sheet was hung out over a balcony the morning following deflowering to demonstrate the virginity of the bride to the public. In this case, I felt as though *I* was being treated thus by Mother. A kind of intimacy was about to occur before her gull-sharp gaze. Brenda was the object of this intimacy, yet I felt it was myself who was really under scrutiny, by two conspirators.

A good thing that I had my own back-up system, in the person of Jack! I could sense my co-conspirator lurking behind the doorway of my mind, keeping watch.

'Well now, Brenda, you understand the process?'

'Oh yes, John.'

'No second thoughts? No qualms?'

'Let's do it. I consent. I want it.'

('Don't let your *mother* put you off,' sneered Jack. 'Don't fluff it.') Not unnaturally he sounded somewhat hostile, though the advice was helpful. This was the first time I had performed in front of Mother. Perhaps her intent gaze was only due to pride and curiosity.

So therefore I hypnotized Brenda. I told her to rewind to her previous life.

Nothing. A blank. Zero. Silence. A void, not even blue. No past life at all. She told me nothing. She had nothing to tell me.

I took her again down the time-line to her birth, and she was a baby once more, lying in her cot beneath a plastic rainbow mobile, gurgling, but articulate.

I took her back from there, but it was like trying to push-start a car on a flat battery. The engine wouldn't fire. Before her birth was emptiness.

I felt impotent. Subdued.

So I woke her; and she already knew. I always instructed my patients that they should be aware of the lives they were relating.

She looked at me soulfully. 'John, I'm so sorry. What does it mean? am I blocking you out . . . unconsciously?'

Dear John, I'm sorry. Yours truly.

Maybe Brenda didn't believe that I believed in past lives? Or perhaps she had no inner life to speak of – no traumas or desires strong enough to generate an imaginary other life, to power the fantasy of one. Maybe she was just herself.

'This happens sometimes,' I said. 'Not everyone is a perfect subject.'

'Does this mean,' interrupted Mother, 'that Brenda didn't live before? That this is her first life now?'

('First life as a person,' suggested Jack maliciously. 'Before, she was a sheep. Or a fish. The universe gave her a break because she was a good sheep.'

'Shut up, Jack. I'm thinking.')

I said aloud, 'It doesn't necessarily mean that. Maybe she worked through all her karma and decided to wipe the slate clean.'

'Is karma that Indian meal you two ate at the Star of Bengal?' Mother asked. 'Didn't you enjoy it?'

(Jack giggled. 'No. It's soul food.')

'What I mean,' I said, 'is that Brenda may have no unresolved tensions left over.'

Now Brenda looked pleased, though still puzzled.

I said to her, 'Your soul took a decision to start out clean and clear, without ties to the past – because nothing tied you. Nothing needed working through once again.'

'Then shouldn't I have gone straight to Heaven? Whatever Heaven is. Shouldn't I have been united with a bright pure light?'

('Like moths,' whispered Jack. 'They get united with bright lights. *Zap*. Sizzle.')

'She's an angel,' said Mother. 'I always thought so.'

Damn my cowardly urge to propitiate people!

'In Buddhist terms,' I went on, 'she might be a Bodhisattva. That's someone who *could* have united with the light, but who chose not to. Chose, instead, to stay on Earth.'

'To help people.' Mother nodded. 'That's right. I don't know about Buddhism but I understand what you mean.'

Ought I to propose to Brenda then and there? Brenda, be my Bodhisattva, be my guide to the light. She looked expectant enough. She could help me with her blank goodness. And I could become bland. A wimp. A weakly interacting mediocre person. I felt a sort of whiplash

198

inside me, in protest. That was my parasite, Jack, expressing his feelings. My tapeworm; and my serpent of power,
of wild secret strength.

'We could try again,' I offered Brenda.

She shook her head. 'I'm satisfied, John. Oh yes. Fully.
In fact this is more wonderful than if I had discovered any
number of exciting lives. Thank you! Now I suppose I had
better be going home . . .'

('*Yes*,' agreed Jack.)

Who knew? Maybe Brenda *was* a Bodhisattva? Though
she could only be that if reincarnation existed.

'I'll drive you home,' I suggested.

A gull could smile with eager joy; Mother did so.

Next morning I walked out, and Jack phoned Mandarin
from the call box that still smelled of piss and acetic acid.

'Sally, this is Jack Cannon. Did I tell you I'm working
on a new book?'

'I thought you said you *weren't*?'

'Well, I am. I am now. Fact is, I'm a good way through
it. This is giving me a spot of bother about revising *The
Gaze* – yes, you can change the wretched title if you like.
Because, you see, I'm in the swing of this other book.'

'That's exciting. What's it called?'

'I don't know. I don't know the ending yet.' Jack fed in
more money.

'If you get the revisions to us within two months,' said
Sally, 'that's okay. I assume they'll be fine. We do need
to have them with us by then, to stick to schedule.'

'Yes, yes. You'll get them. What I was wanting to say
is that this new book might cause a bit of a sizzle,
especially with my photo being on general release. I might
be forced to go full-time.'

'But at Birmingham you said you were retired. You
told everyone you'd taken early retirement.'

'I still do some consulting work.'

'For a shipping office? Why did they retire you, then?'

'I do other consulting. The point is, I'd like to delete the next-book option clause in the contract for *The Gaze*. I could need bigger money for this next one, so it would help you to argue the case with Mandarin if there was some initial element of competition, wouldn't it? A bit of an auction situation.'

Sally laughed hilariously. A publisher's laugh, indicating that alas you knew nothing about reality. She calmed.

'You aren't trying to change publishers because I asked for some itsy-bitsy changes, surely? You'd find other publishers have similar viewpoints, and costings, to Mandarin. Of course you might be lucky, and I'd wish you well, but it would be a real leap into the blue. Mandarin and yourself have built up a good relationship, I'd say, wouldn't you?'

'Yes, of course. This has nothing to do with the revisions. I might be *relying* on my income from writing.'

'Write well, then, Jack. That's how.' Obscurely we sensed that it wasn't how. How it actually was, ah, that evaded us.

'You sound to me as though you're going through a life crisis,' Sally went on. 'Hell, the whole world is – that of course includes the publishing industry. Why don't you come down to the metrop for lunch? Talk things over? We'll fix you up some radio spots, even one of the book programmes on TV. Make it worth your while. Be more prominent, be seen, talk to people: that's the way. The Birmingham Fayre was a good start. I think you're feeling out of touch, Jack. No need! Mandarin will look after you. And you look after us too, okay? But I have to convince people, as you say yourself. How do I convince anyone when you're the invisible man? At least *I've* met you – if only once. You don't even let us know your real address. That slows communications. I think you ought to showbiz yourself a bit; which connects with what you're saying about going full-time. Hiding under a stone is no way to push yourself – which I take it is what you want. I think you're looking at the situation the wrong way round. You mustn't expect a spontaneous miracle simply by shifting to another publisher. Why don't you let us try to set up some real publicity, hmm? Not every publisher even offers to do as much. Let's try it out, see how it flows, take it from there.'

We were being run rings round. What's more, here was yet another attempt on our life; an attempt at organizing it.

'I'll think about it,' said Jack. He pocketed the remaining tenpences and let Telecom cut him off.

'What the *hell*,' I asked as we walked back, 'do you mean about us going full-time?'

'*Me*, going full-time,' was the reply. 'Obviously we can't keep up this Jekyll and Hyde routine any longer. It takes *me* to deal with Brenda and your mother. And with Tony Smith. He's potential trouble, because I'm using his material, right? Once we have the conclusion, I'd say it's time for a major post-hypnotic block. I'd say it'll soon be time to scrub his brain a bit, seal off his past lives in a nice old stone cave; after we've opened and emptied it. Give him the Gaze.'

'You sound as though you want to murder him! Psychically, I mean. Steal, and kill. Jack, this is crazy. You aren't the same Jack. You're shifting. Something's taking over. What do you mean, "deal with" Brenda and my mother?'

Jack fell silent.

'Jack? Where are you?'

'Down a deep hole, a hole inside you,' his voice came hollowly in my head.

I heard jingling. That was the loose change in my trouser pocket, which my hand was playing with.

I felt an urge to visit Tynemouth. Yes, the Pen Bal Crag – where the Castle stood. Overlooking Percy Bay, which was now named King Edward's Bay, commemorating the landing there by the exotic dilettante dandy king who had loved Piers Gaveston, page boys, wanton poets and pleasant wits . . . and who'd had a white-hot poker jammed up his bum.

Jack felt a flood of anger at Sally and Brenda and Mother. Those spear-bearers in a bigger play, a golden drama, were littering it. Tripping him up. Sally was far away in London, and Mother – well . . . perhaps there were limits. But Brenda. Ah, Brenda.

Of course he knew the ending of the book. And its title too. Obviously: *The Fire Worm*.

But first, Tony . . . and Robert.

24

Robert and Lord Ranulph and Ranulph's friend, the Prior of Coverham, all stood together staring at the salamander writhing in the heart of the furnace.

The Prior was a portly, ruddy, elderly man of a philosophic turn of mind, with a mulberry birthmark on his neck. He had ridden the twenty-five miles from Coverham, close by Ranulph's Yorkshire seat of Middleham Castle, specially to witness this prodigy. Here was an elemental creature which lived in flames and was not consumed but rather was nourished, and nourished the fire in turn, regulating the heat exactly.

The white creature was curiously amorphous. It appeared to change shape as it moved: now a fat coiling worm on squat legs, now a thing of tentacles. The eye could not pin it down. But always it remained; it never vanished.

'You have set a seal on it, Master Lully?' asked the old Prior. His breath smelled foul in spite of the fennel which he chewed to veil this.

Lully shrugged equivocally. 'I have summoned it from the elemental world into our sublunar region. Here there's only one place where it can exist contentedly – namely in my athanor.'

'What do you suppose it feels?' enquired the Prior. 'Heat? Torment and pain? I should feel pain, in its place.'

'No, heat is its native element. Does a fish feel pain in water? What would torment it would be the coolness which we find comfortable.'

'Does it merely *exist*, Master Lully? Or can it also think, can it reason?'

Robert looked smug.

Lully replied, 'Its reason is not our reason, since its world is not our world. Yet *we* can pose basic questions of any existent object – Utrum? Quid? De quo? Quare? Quantum? Quale? Quando? Ubi? Quomodo, and cum quo? – and thus encompass that object comprehensively. As I have written in my *Ars Compendiosa de Inveniendi Veritatem*, my Comprehensive Art of Arriving at the Truth.'

The Prior looked slightly bemused, but nodded.

'My categories are rusty,' he admitted . . .

Another hearse silently passed the window, but that was nothing new or even untoward. Tony sat alertly on the sofa. He nibbled at a finger, tearing some skin loose.

'So then a few months later there was a disaster. A sort of medieval Chernobyl. The worm burst out. It expanded in size. It wrecked the lab. It could pass through the walls as if they were water.'

'A medieval Chernobyl?' Jack relished the phrase, and decided to use it. 'I like that, Tony. The worm burst its containment vessel.'

'But not before Master Lully had succeeded, eh Doctor? Not before we all saw him transmute a pint of mercury and a lump of lead into ingots of pure gold. I saw it. My father saw it. So did the Prior of Coverham – he returned for that demonstration, and the Prior was no fool. Lully did create the philosopher's stone, and he almost had the elixir! But then the worm broke out and gulped the stone.'

'Robert *believes* he saw Lully use the stone. He believes he saw the salamander swell up huge. Yet none of you

204

was injured by the wreckage. I must remind you that Lully was a mesmerist.'

'It was no hoax! He was no puffer.' How readily the old term sprang to Tony's lips. How willingly he defended what he had experienced. 'Oh no, Robert knows what he saw. He knows what touched him. What grasped him, and let him go – but never really let him go. And the worm swallowed the stone before it escaped.'

Jack smiled, and rubbed his finger across the stubble of the moustache he had started growing.

'Yes?' he encouraged.

'Then the worm, still huge, made its way to Lambton. Somehow it got chopped down to size – or maybe it was just contracting in the cold. So it gave rise to the legend of the Lambton Worm. Afterwards, it made its way to Tynemouth, and holed up there. Raby, Lambton, Tynemouth: they're all in a straight line on the map, aren't they? The worm couldn't go any further than Tynemouth – because there's only the cold quenching sea beyond.'

'It probably felt at home under Pen Bal Crag,' suggested Jack. 'As much as it could feel at home anywhere. Because of the geology. That crag's magnesian limestone but there's an igneous dyke running underneath. Molten lava once flowed through a fault and hardened. Frozen lava: that's what attracted the worm. The memory of the igneous, fiery depths.'

'The worm's still at Tynemouth, isn't it, Doctor? With the stone, that makes the elixir of health, inside it.'

'Yes, Tony,' Jack said gently. 'It's still there. The most terrible, and wonderful creature in the world.'

'It's aware of us.'

'It's aware of you, Tony. We have to confront it, don't we? We have to wrest the treasure from it. The stone elixir. Only then can the monster sink back down into the central fires where it came from. Only then, can you be

205

free. Free from it, and free from Ted – and free from death also.' Jack spoke with quiet authority, and Tony nodded.

'We must tell no one about this, of course,' Jack added. 'Not ever. This must be a secret, even after we succeed.'

'Yes, I promise.'

'That's good to know. Yes, that's very good.'

'What about the book you're writing?' I butted in. I was still able to get a word in edgeways, though Tony could no longer hear me. He remained hypnotized, though he didn't realize. A net of suggestions held him. A chain of commands.

'I rather think a book pales into insignificance, don't you, old son? The elixir is the universal nostrum, right? So it's a cure for AIDS as well. It's medicine for the scourge. Once I have that, I'll decide what to do about it. I'm thinking that a cult of benevolent initiates mightn't be such a bad idea. A hidden society. I'll have to be careful, of course. This country mightn't be the best place to start our mission. It's too repressive here, since the oil money ran out.'

'It's repressive all over the globe. You can thank the scourge for that.'

'Repression can be manipulated. There'll be suitable places, John. Maybe a Greek island. Maybe a tropical one. Somewhere out of sight, where I can found the new society of immortals; controlling doses of the elixir, distributing those like a new sacrament.'

'A whole island?'

'There'll be money in this. Sure, we could manufacture our own gold; but there'll be money too. Bound to be. Beats flogging horror novels to Mandarin any old time. First, there's the horror to confront. That mightn't be a pushover.' A note of doubt intruded.

I was extremely worried. Jack had become one of his

own characters. There was little I felt I could do to influence him or deter him.

Throughout our minutes of silent communion, Tony had been staring with puzzled expectancy.

'We ought to tidy up some loose ends,' Jack said to him. 'Just for the record.'

A distant bell tinkled faintly, and I heard the sound of Brenda's door shutting as she headed upstairs to see to Mother. A ministering Bodhisattva, ha!

Edward II's counsellors finally insisted that he should tear himself away from masques and poetry and partying and pederasty, and deal definitively with Robert the Bruce and those Scots.

So in 1314 Edward rode north at the head of a great army. Ranulph – as duty bound – rendezvoused with his liege at York, accompanied by both of his sons and by a hundred lancers he had raised and equipped, plus men-at-arms and archers and retainers.

The Nevilles left Lully safely at Raby Castle, brooding amidst the ruins of his laboratory over the escape of the salamander. Ranulph's participation in the Scottish war was costing big money. For the time being there was no way to repair and restock the workshop at the top of Bulmer's Tower. Thus Lully spent his surplus hours educating the rest of the establishment. He instructed the resident pages in Llull's *Order of Chivalry*, which he remembered well, and which a descendant of one of those pages – the future Sir Gilbert Hay – would translate into Scots in 1455 as the *Buke of the Order of Knychthede*. He indoctrinated the daughters, and future mothers, of the household in Llull's child-rearing treatise, the *Doctrine for Boys*, about which Lully personally nursed mixed feelings. Avoiding molly-coddling was all very well, but should growing infants really be confined to a diet of milk until they could run? And kept mainly on bread there-after, with only morsels of meat, and sweet fruit hardly ever? However, he wished to remain in character.

It wasn't long before King Edward, eager for some novelty and just as eager for lots of gold to pay for this war and for future adventures, had heard about Master Lully's successful (if aborted) transmutation; and he made a mental note.

The English army headed over the Borders on a proud march during which the doughty dandy Robert de Neville won himself the sobriquet Peacock of the North. Arriving at Bannockburn, Edward's army engaged the Scottish army. Though the English spitted many a Scot on their deadly arrows from a distance, somehow the Scots held their position. So the English cavalry advanced, into concealed pits and bogs, stumbling and tumbling just as the Bruce had hoped. Mistakenly assuming that the battle was over, all the Scottish camp followers flooded down out of hiding to pillage. The English mistakenly assumed that a second Scottish army had arrived, and ran away, hotly pursued. Another military farce. Or triumph, depending on one's viewpoint.

During the retreat, King Edward stopped over in County Durham long enough to impound the Nevilles' resident alchemist and carry him off to the capital. Lully was housed in the Tower of London, honourably and luxuriously, with instructions to make gold.

Try as Lully might, he couldn't quite recreate the conditions at Raby. Maybe he had used up his available quota of salamanders. So he suggested humbly to the king that a tax on wool might raise just as much money. Edward was much taken by this idea – and the false Lully slipped thankfully out of the country.

He spent the remaining years of his life in sensible anonymity in the Low Countries, writing such treatises as the *Clavicula*, or Little Key, the *De Transmutione animae metallorum*, the *Experiments of Raymond Lully of Majorca the most learned philosopher, wherein the operations of the true Chymicall Philosophy are plainly delivered*, and not least the *Epistle to Robert, King of the English*, who never did become a secret, philosophic king.

No indeed. The land starved. Rain lashed down. Wastrel-bread, potagium, and soaked salted dead sheep were a luxury. War surged to and fro across the Borders. In 1319 at the Battle of Berwick, the Peacock of the North was killed by the Black Douglas. The Douglas also captured brother Ralph. Ralph was ransomed, inherited the Lordship of Raby, and himself took the Scottish King David prisoner at the Battle of Neville's Cross. Lavishly generous to the Church, Ralph was the first layman ever to be buried in Durham Cathedral, thus finally concluding the quarrel of the stag.

However, Robert the Peacock was dead, dead, dead. To be reincarnated five hundred years later as Harry Bell of Front Street, Tynemouth, who was reborn a hundred years afterwards as Gavin Percy, who was reborn almost immediately after his death as Tony Smith. All touched in turn by the worm.

Except Tony Smith, perhaps . . . but now Tony had remembered, hadn't he? Now he knew.

He knew that the worm did guard a treasure – guard it hideously, along with its petrified victims – inside Jingling Geordie's Hole. That was certain.

Epilogue

Brenda's Tale or *Ecstasy*

Brenda felt that she had been waiting all her life. Perhaps she ought to have been a waitress rather than a secretary. Or a nurse. But a secretary was similar. She waited for other things to come from outside, and deflected these in the appropriate direction – into John's office, or into diary or ledger or filing cabinet. Also she waited on John's mother.

Yet until quite recently she hadn't realized that her life had been a wait. Her life had simply been a succession of days reproducing and copying themselves as if on a Xerox machine. Not leading anywhere else. But it had been her life – and who questions the act of living? By comparison with what do you question it?

As life extends, so it develops a momentum, an inertia which is quite difficult to overcome or change, unless the entire world wobbles and alters course. A war might cause this. Or a plague.

Even then, even then! You still carry on much the same as ever – at least you struggle to do so – unless the train goes right off the rails, unless your personal world collapses into meaninglessness.

Or suddenly collapses into meaning. Into radiant significance. A significance you never guessed.

'Familiar acts are beautiful through love!' she quoted to herself as she walked for the thousandth time and more (and yet for the first time ever) along Jesmond Road beside the cemetery towards the Cunninghams'.

The words were by Shelley. They had been printed on an inspirational greeting card she sent to her parents on their latest wedding anniversary. Brenda hadn't totally understood the words till now; they had simply seemed nice and fitting.

Now, as the paving stones shone with recent rain, she understood them. Dirty-bottomed cumulus was still breaking up and drifting off towards the north-west, bergs of wool afloat in an increasingly blue sea. She understood as the elms in the cemetery glowed emerald; as the grains of quartz in the granite gravestones sparkled.

Death, here was death. Rotting flowers lay in humps of soil, and even now a line of black cars and their chauffeurs (smoking cigarettes) stood outside the crematorium chapel. Even now in the hospices of the city people were dying of the new slow scourge. Lovers, children, anyone.

Yet she had come to life.

Was she really in love with John? she wondered. Had a curtain actually lifted upon the stage of her life, to reveal herself and him embracing in true harmony?

Perhaps she was in love with love itself? That feeling of love had quickened irrationally and overpoweringly during the past few weeks. It coincided with John's treatment of Tony Armstrong, whom John referred to guardedly as Tony Smith.

During the same period, John also had begun to change. Now he was growing a moustache. He had resumed wearing those heavy spectacles which he had abandoned years ago in favour of contact lenses. And his personality was altering – which begged the question: with whom was she in love? Was something amorous rising up inside John likewise, with regard to herself, transforming him into a new man?

During the seven years of their acquaintance she had grown comfortably fond of John Cunningham. She felt safe with him; secure, even affectionate. And of course Mrs Cunningham increasingly had made Brenda feel a

211

part of the family. Or the non-family. It seemed as if
Brenda was the missing, necessary component. Over the
past few weeks, however, something new had entered
their relationship; a well-spring of rapture, of joy, had
opened up.

'Familiar acts are beautiful through love,' she repeated
to the sky above.

Somehow it didn't matter if John was drifting away into
some strange distance. Of course she must do her utmost
to pursue, and meet with him again at his psychic destination. If he was undergoing some transmutation which
she hardly understood, well, she too was experiencing a
transforming vigour which welled in her – which had been
there all along, but which the last few weeks had liberated, so that she now saw herself as another person. Yet
the same person. The same person, radiant, all dullness
gone.

When she found out, that evening up in Mrs Cunningham's room, that she, Brenda, had no past life at all,
perhaps this was the key to her change. So far her own
life had been ordinary, oh indeed. This ordinariness had
become a habit, was on the verge of becoming her entire
self forever till she died. She hardly realized that she *had*
a life. Oh yes, she lived, and was happy enough. Yet she
had not been enraptured by existing.

The certainty that she had no previous life to remember, and perhaps no future one, had shone a spotlight,
sunlight, magic moonlight on to her present existence.
Here she was, now and forever. And John too, in a hook
of time, no matter whatever strangeness was happening
to him. Without a past, without a future, she was free.

'Familiar acts are beautiful through love!'

She strolled along that pavement as cars hummed by.
Glossy, raggy black rooks circled the elms where stick-
nests bulged like cancers of the twigs within parasols of

212

leaves. Higher up, snowy gulls beat inland, so many scraps of paper in a wind, so many flecks of mirror. Her heartbeat quickened. Did she flush?

When she arrived at the house, the door to the consulting room stood wide open. John was poised as if about to set out for town. Beyond sat Tony Armstrong on the sofa, worrying at his thumb, looking anxious, recalcitrant, but feeble. Wondering why the fellow was here so early and unscheduled, whether John was trying to turf him out, Brenda advanced to help.

'Ah, Brenda! I thought we'd be gone by now. I left a note.'

She saw John's note on her desk. Before she could pick the message up, he stepped over and retrieved it, crumpling the sheet of paper into his jacket pocket.

'I'm taking Tony down to Tynemouth. Be back by lunch. Postpone Mrs Purdue's session, will you?'

'I don't like the coast,' whined Tony Armstrong. 'The cold sea. You know why.'

Even from several yards' distance John addressed Tony softly. 'It's only for a look around, isn't it? Lovely sunny day. You'll feel happy. Nothing will worry you.'

'No,' agreed Armstrong, in a lacklustre tone.

Why should John be wanting to take him down to the coast? To confront some memory, perhaps. That was why Tony was resisting. Faintly.

'Of course you'll come,' John said soothingly. He turned, and now he really noticed Brenda. He darted a peculiar look, and laughed. 'You're different. No lipstick today.'

'Pink lipstick,' she corrected. 'It's called satin coral.' She had taken an aversion to her habitual red lipstick which now seemed garish – designed for the attention of those who were half-alive, with half-blind eyes which only

213

saw what was shouted at them. A bloody, waxen gash of lips like the backside of some obscene monkey.

'Coral isn't satin,' John said quirkily. 'It's sharp. It rips the skin. There's no coral in the North Sea, none at Tynemouth.'

What did he mean? Was she somehow banished? Uninvited; yet outcast even so?

'It's too cold for that,' muttered Tony.

'Come, come.' John's voice was a caress. The cruel caress of coral, not of satin.

Obediently Tony rose, and went with John.

Brenda phoned Mrs Purdue to reschedule her past-life therapy. Next, she sorted through the mail, then went upstairs to say good morning to John's mother. But the old lady was still snoozing; the bedroom was dark, and Brenda left it that way.

A rush of joy propelled Brenda along to the door of John's study – a sense of exaltation that amazed her, a welling knowledge that she must embrace him somehow . . . in his absence. She must touch, if not him, at least something of his existence. Something of existence itself. A light glowed in her.

The study door wasn't locked. Why should it be? She glanced round the room once, then looked at everything again more slowly. An old desk with drawers, and a modern swivel chair. An adjustable spotlamp. An electric typewriter of the same model as she herself used downstairs, a half-used ream of paper beside it. Net-curtained windows looking over unkept shrubby back gardens. A glass-fronted walnut bookcase crammed with dictionaries, reference books, medical and psychological texts. For a filing cabinet, a huge mahogany cupboard with a dozen doors and drawers, all with keyholes. Over the mantelpiece, a calendar: an old engraving of some dreadful sea monster (a giant squid?) wrestling with a sailing vessel in

214

stormy seas, mariners tumbling terrified, shrieking, into the waves. Somebody's past life would have involved a briny doom. Or perhaps that was a monster of the unconscious arising from the typhoon-tossed black sea; she knew enough to imagine the connexion.

Seating herself in his chair, she swivelled, then rested her fingertips on the familiar keyboard.

In the desk, most likely, would be the manuscript of the psychology book which he was always working on, every evening. John was always typing, Mrs Cunningham had told her. The book had taken him years. One day John might be as famous as Freud or Jung. Brenda could surely help out with the rewriting, the retyping and reorganization. If not with the rethinking.

She slid a drawer open to her right and found a bunch of little keys. Of course she would find keys. She jingled these like some quiet bell to attract John's attention wherever he was. Silence enveloped the room when she stopped. A thrill ran electrifyingly through her being, a shiver rose up her spine, and soon she found the key which fitted the locked middle drawer of the desk.

In which, a pile of typescript lay.

She lifted this out and began reading: *The Fire Worm* . . .

Half an hour later, Brenda sat stunned. After the first page she had speeded up, scanning, dipping deeper here and there.

She felt in touch now, not with existence, but with non-existence – with a malevolent void which would gladly swallow her. The view outside the window (gardens, house-backs) shimmered with the moiré pattern of net, threatening to dissolve, to flow into a different scene, to drift back into the past.

And then it did so.

It was the nineteenth century, the fourteenth century. It was two hundred million years earlier. Dense, swampy, tropical forest grew outside the window. A sluggish river far huger than the Tyne drained its vast estuary through tree-ferns, club mosses, and horse-tails into a shallow inland sea. Through the net and the glass she saw that river. She saw dry, baked, wind-swept desert – the grains of which still lay upon the beach at Tynemouth, Cullercoats, Whitley Bay where the holiday makers plodged and paddled. Sea rolled over the land, drowning it. Sea withdrew. Volcanoes blasted out fire and lava, staining the sky with smoke and ashes.

A hideous roller-coaster continuity swept her hindwards, backwards. The present had been but a fleck of dust, a tiny bright speckle of quartz set in a tombstone of granite a billion years deep and more.

She arrived at the much deeper past, when the young world boiled hotly and amorphously – yet there was life-power, elemental life unakin to any later cool animal life. A hell-world, with hot devil life. The first proprietors of the planet. She stared at them through a window of time, unable to focus. Yet she knew that here was the basis, the origin, the core of existence.

Past-life therapy only scraped at the very skin, only plucked loose a few superficial cells. Yawning far beneath all human lives was an awful elemental force. Oh, it had weakened enormously! Yet only because miles of rock separated it from ourselves. The world was still a soft-boiled egg – fragile shell, some rubbery flesh, then a huge potent molten yolk where the Originals circulated.

Dazed by this vision of another reality, she gripped the desk, shaking her head from side to side. She had no knowledge of drugs, yet she felt as if she must have been drugged; as if the desk drawer or the manuscript had released a wraith of stunning fumes.

It occurred to her that her own brain might be drugging her, to cope with overpowering shock. To save her, yes. To stop her from being destroyed by what she had discovered about John's other self. His *main* self, even. About what that other self was involved in – something which swept away all ordinary meaning.

Yet just then she discovered that the joy was still inside her, like a growing child, alive. The radiance remained undiminished. The love, which had brought her to life.

What had John – Jack – written? 'Without ecstasy and passion-fire there is no world.' That was true. Perhaps not as regards *fire*, not the fire which he now sought. But as regards ecstasy. Yes, that.

The frozen fire-creature – salamander, worm – would burn him. Freeze him. Both. Ice could burn as well as flames. It would encase him, coil around his mind, lock him like a toad in stone. She had to stop that from happening.

But first, she went to the mahogany cupboard and unlocked doors. Duplicate paperback books were shelved and stacked inside. *The Goblin* by Jack Cannon. *The Nail* . . .

Nodding to herself in simple confirmation, she shut the books away, then locked the typescript back in its desk drawer.

John was someone else, was he? Well, that was remarkable. That knowledge did not depress her now. No, it exalted her.

A bell was jingling insistently. Brenda closed John's door behind her and went along to his mother's room.

'Good morning, Mrs Cunningham!' The tasselled bedside lamp now shone.

'Good morning, Brenda. Is John working upstairs this morning? I thought I heard his study door.'

217

Brenda shook her head. 'No, he's taken one of his patients down to Tynemouth.'

'Oh. Can't whoever-it-is use the bus or the Metro? Are they an invalid like me?'

'The idea's to revisit old scenes. Very old scenes.'

'Ah, from a previous life, I see. John should have taken you along. You could use a breath of sea air.'

'Why? Do I look peaky?'

Brenda was used to this sort of thing. (The local curse-greeting: 'My, you're looking ill!')

Mrs Cunningham peered. 'Quite the opposite! You look a changed girl, Brenda. Fresher.'

By comparison with what? In the typescript Brenda had discovered helpful, honest, dowdy Jane. The old lady couldn't help her little drips of impertinence. And she *was* Brenda's ally, wasn't she?

'I changed my lipstick, Mrs Cunningham.'

'I *knew* there was something different!' John's mother cocked her head critically. 'I like it. It's more natural. Subtler.'

Compliments with stings attached; it was second nature.

'Did John admire it?' the old lady asked.

'He thought I wasn't wearing any.'

'Oh, how imperceptive men can be. But my John always has a lot on his mind. He works so hard. Did you have to tell him?'

Brenda flushed. 'I may have done.'

'There's colour in your cheeks today, Brenda. I'm happy to see that.'

Brenda shook her head. Normality, banality. The strange joy in her contrasted so sharply with the flavour of existence hitherto. Would she have wished 'hitherto' to continue? No, for now the sun had risen in her. The landscape which its rays revealed was a fearful one, which

218

she must tread, and where she must triumph, guided by her ecstasy. Otherwise John would be burnt and frozen, set in stone.

'I'll open your curtains then, Mrs Cunningham.' Sounding cheerful, Brenda revealed busy Jesmond Road and the cemetery. 'And I'll fetch some tea and toast.'

'Please.'

Brenda thought about her own parents, at home just a couple of miles away. Both in their mid-sixties now, and quite able to care for themselves as yet. Her Dad had retired from the MNI at Longbenton five years before, the Ministry of National Insurance. Now her Mam and Dad fitted in a couple of continental holidays each year. Saga Tours for the elderly. They'd been all over the Common Market, carrying their AIDS-free health certificates. In another five years would they still be so spry for travel and housekeeping?

Her older brother Alan – the solicitor – was married. His wife Rachel was a breathless, up-to-her-eyes, always-too-busy sort of woman. Three daughters, three nieces for Aunt Brenda: Patricia, Justine, and Annabelle. They lived in Kent, a long way off. Alan and Rachel wouldn't be much help. Brenda would have to care for Mrs Cunningham until the old lady eventually died; and presently she would care for her own parents too. She would, she thought, be a very caring person. Her life would be filled with cheerful, busy usefulness.

She would even have a reward: a noted local medical man as husband, who would no doubt give her a child to look after too. Almost in her forties, she would be in the high-risk category, but she was healthy.

That had *been* the future, the path of preference. Until she had sat down at John's desk – no, *Jack's* – and opened the locked drawer. Now all was changed. Or was it? It was as if the joy had entered her *in anticipation* of what she would discover about John. If she rescued him from

219

that terrible supernatural worm, she could put Jack back in his proper place and recover the balance which had existed beforehand. She could even co-operate in his hidden life. Why shouldn't he write horror novels in private? He simply needed one confidante, to stop the strain from splitting him in half. She could help; she could type. An accommodation could be reached. If only she applied the force of her ecstasy.

Her ecstasy couldn't create a different world for her, where she lived another sort of life, a more glamorous globe-trotting life. She knew from the hypnotic séance in this very room that she had no other life. Her ecstasy could not apply its strength to the actual world which existed, consisting of John, his mother, her parents.

She hurried downstairs to the kitchen to assemble a simple breakfast on a tray. Cooker and fridge and units might have been up to date in the early Seventies; but no longer. The only improvement was a microwave oven, so that John could heat ready-made meals for himself and his mother quickly. Brenda would need a new kitchen. As a wedding present. If. If she could win him from the worm.

To her mild surprise she found that she did truly believe in the worm. Yes, she didn't find that too difficult. Not after the vision which her joy had granted her in John's room.

Ought she not to have felt more surprised? At accepting the existence of a supernatural creature inside the crag at Tynemouth? Oh no. Not when ecstasy had already raptured her. She put any puzzlement from her mind.

As she waited for the kettle to boil, she thought of the child whom she and John might give life to, a child whose ghost almost seemed to pre-exist inside her in the shape of joy. She also thought about sex.

When Brenda was thirteen and her periods had recently

220

started, she had let a boy called Peter Turpin touch her
. . . there. And she had touched him in turn, amazed at
how his thing swelled and stuck out, unable to understand
how anyone could fit such a thing inside the slit she bled
from, or how that could possibly bring her pleasure. She
and Peter had hidden under a huge rhododendron bush
in Jesmond Dene, well away from the nearest path. She
had squeezed his thing to see if it would deflate, and it
had suddenly become a fleshy fountain, foaming and
spurting white sticky smelly stuff all over her hand and
bare thighs. When she had got home she washed herself a
lot, and she was frightened for weeks. She wouldn't speak
to Peter, and he seemed equally reluctant to come near
her, as though she would cause him trouble.

The kettle boiled. Steam jetted. She poured the water
into the teapot, and slipped an old knitted cosy over the
pot.

So little to have happened – and yet, to her, so much!
She had stayed a virgin. She didn't regard virginity as a
condition, peculiar or laudable, any more than she
regarded the possession of breasts or legs or a nose as
being worthy of note.

Lips, perhaps. She felt possessive about her lips, and
both hid them with lipstick and at the same time drew
attention to them, enjoying a mild sensual thrill at applying the greasy stick. One day other lips, strong unpainted
lips, might kiss her lips. She put that other thing from her
mind. Only once had she ever closely examined those
secret, private duplicate lips between her legs. That was
after a girlfriend, Joyce, whispered that *she* knew of a girl
who put lipstick *on those lips* as well for her boyfriend to
kiss. Yes, there was a mouth between Brenda's legs; but
it said nothing, ate nothing. Once a month it was sick,
dribbling blood as though it had visited the dentist's to
have something pulled out.

221

She buttered two slices of toast.

John himself might never have touched a woman that way before. He might never have put his *Jack* inside the secret lips of a woman. 'Jacking off,' Joyce had said, was the name for what boys like Gavin Percy did with their things by hand. Unlike women, they needed to. Otherwise their jack grew big and stiff of its own accord; they spurted in bed at night.

John's jack had grown so big that it had become a separate individual, full of wild thoughts, to judge from those paperback covers. A cannon was a tube which shot stuff out. Yes, that was where Jack came from – from between the legs of John. She would have to come to grips with Jack, to speak to him with her inner lips. Then John would be all right again.

If she could overcome the worm. The worm of old that made the gold, and ached with cold – which she must hold, if she was bold. She shivered convulsively, but then her ecstasy burned bright and she carried the breakfast tray upstairs.

'You're quite right, Mrs Cunningham,' she said as she set the tray down. 'I really must go down to Tynemouth soon. I do wish John would ask me along the next time he goes, patient or no patient! In fact I ought to be there as chaperone, oughtn't I? If I'm suppose to do that here when he hypnotizes people in the next room. I might be able to help.'

John's mother smiled conspiratorially.

'I'll suggest it to him. I think he'll listen to his mother. He's taking you a bit for granted, and he shouldn't . . . not when you're both on the verge of . . . you know what.'

As Brenda went back down to her office she glowed with anticipation.

* * *

When the brown Volvo pulled into the gravelled front drive shortly before one, Brenda went out to meet it. How would Tony Armstrong seem after *his* trip to the coast? She was curious, and thought that John might send him packing while still outside. This was also her first sight of Jack in full knowledge. Joy buoyed her up.

'Hullo, Doctor, hullo, Mr Armstrong. How was the sea today?'

The young man seemed confused by the question.

'I hardly noticed it.' He remained seated.

John said to him, 'I was telling you how Harriet Martineau couldn't even *see* the sea the first time she stood where we were standing.'

Armstrong laughed. 'That's right. There was nothing much there. Just a sort of moving light.'

John said to Brenda, 'Harriet Martineau was a nineteenth-century authoress who lived at Tynemouth for a while.'

'Oh, I've heard of her.' Brenda had indeed. That very morning.

'She's part of Tony's previous life,' John added affably.

'We had coffee and home-made shortbreads in the house where she lived,' volunteered the young man. 'It's a guesthouse with a coffee room. The house did seem vaguely familiar, though I suppose they've altered it a lot since then.'

'I love home-made shortbreads,' Brenda said. 'Fancy eating them in a house where a famous author lived! How nice to have a coffee there.'

'Yes, it was a pleasant outing,' said John. 'Wasn't it, Tony?'

'Pleasant,' the young man agreed. 'Could go there again.'

'Of course.' John beamed. As he stepped out of the car, Brenda spotted yellow sand in the grooves of the black rubber mat in front of the driver's seat. John's Hush Puppies were blotched with dampness which was drying a salty white.

He walked round and liberated the young man – whose trainers also looked wet. Tony Armstrong had hardly noticed the sea but he had been walking in its margin, on sand, on rocks, through weed, getting his feet licked.

'We should take the next trip at night,' John said, directly at odds with the possibility of morning coffee and shortbread biscuits. 'For contrast, hmm? How about next Tuesday evening? We could have a pint and a bag of chips. The pubs oughtn't to be too busy on a Tuesday. The moon'll be nearing full. We can see what Harriet saw by night from her window. The moonlit Priory ruins, a century and a half ago. Same ruins, same moon. There's continuity for you! Things change, but are the same. In another century you might be seeing the same scene, reborn, when the scourge has run its course.'

Tony smiled. 'I'd like that.' He shuffled the gravel, surprised, as though he had recently been shuffling other pebbles elsewhere.

'You'll be cured,' said John. 'Your problem will be overcome. Life will be transformed.' Glancing charmingly at Brenda, he added, 'Love conquers all. Ultimately love is the basis of therapy.'

Any suspicion on her part evaporated.

'*Joy* is the basis,' she suggested.

'Yes, joy,' he agreed. 'That's what we aim at. We must enjoy the world and ourselves.' Firmly he said to Tony, 'Come round here on Tuesday night at eight. Tell Carol that you're going out for a drink with the boys. Not to wait up.'

'Okay.'

John dismissed Tony, locked the car, and walked inside with Brenda.

In the past he always used to eat lunch in company with his mother. Perhaps then they would play a quick game of Scrabble, while John checked through case notes prior to his afternoon appointments.

Brenda herself brought sandwiches, which she either ate in the office or if the weather was pleasant she would cross over to the cemetery to sit on a bench and lunch there. Rarely, she might walk as far as Jesmond Dene, though she never ventured into the Dene itself.

Since Jack emerged, there had been far fewer lunches with Mother. John might deliver a snack on a tray, plead work, and take his own tray along into Jack's study, from which the percussion of typing would emerge.

'It's Mrs Nicholls at two o'clock,' Brenda reminded.

'Right,' said John. 'I think I'll micro some tagliatelle for Mother and me. She likes Marks and Sparks' tagliatelle.'

'Well, *I* could – ' began Brenda.

'No, that's too kind. I'll do it, and I'll sit with her too.'

He had not waited to see what she was going to suggest. As though he already knew.

Pleasure warmed her.

The next Tuesday dawned rainy but cleared in the afternoon. By evening when Brenda returned to the Cunninghams' the dimming sky was almost cloudless and a warm breeze blew from the south-west. The Moon had yet to rise.

Mrs Cunningham must have persuaded John and met no resistance at all, since his invitation to Brenda to come along on the outing to Tynemouth had been made charmingly.

Brenda had wondered what to wear. They would be visiting a pub, and those Front Street pubs were popular watering holes for the lads and lasses. John had also

225

mentioned admiring the Priory ruins; from what vantage point? Last time he and Tony had returned with wet feet. In the end, Brenda had settled on her green tartan skirt and boots, accompanied by a high-necked, long-sleeved, Chinese-style blouse in white silk, with a white woollen shawl in case of chills.

John seemed to approve of her outfit. He had just admitted Tony to the Volvo. Scanning Brenda up and down, he nodded.

'You look quite elegant, my dear.'

Quite? Perhaps he was using the word in some old-fashioned sense. Absolutely elegant. Her own parents had thought so. And he *had* said 'my dear'.

'Ravishing,' said Tony from the front seat, where he was now strapped in. That was the wrong word. No one these days set out to look sexy; sex spelled danger of death. In a way, horrid as such danger was, this came as a relief to Brenda . . . It was as well to be reminded of danger! With an effort Brenda recalled the real reason for this trip to Tynemouth. She had been on the verge of forgetting! Of drifting away in a banal, romantic haze. John – Jack – was going to use Tony to trigger the worm. He was going to try, somehow. Tony didn't seem to understand this. He looked so relaxed, as though drifting in some safe harbour of the soul. Brenda mustn't let either of them know that she knew. Not until the proper moment.

Right now the truth seemed preposterous, an absolute misunderstanding on her part. She must keep watch on how John went about manipulating this evening. Manipulating Tony, too. Surely Tony was acting out – what were they called? – post-hypnotic suggestions, unaware of how he was being influenced, of how he was still hypnotized. You couldn't force someone by hypnosis to do anything which went totally against the grain. No hypnotist could make a subject march into the mouth of a furnace. The mind would take evasive action, find an excuse such as a lame leg. She was sure of that. Joyful conviction flooded her, an exhilarating certainty.

As they drove down the coast road in the gloaming a hundred necklaces of orange lights lay across the slopes of Hebburn and Jarrow, while along the river white lights snaked and towered over the remaining dockland and shipyard. Dimly silhouetted on its hilltop squatted the black hutch of the Pensher Monument.

Soon they were coasting down to the roundabout at Billy Mill. Then they were driving between the black woodland sprawl of Tynemouth Cemetery on the one hand, and architect-designed estates on the other: brick boxes with giant picture windows, many glowing blue with TV light.

At another roundabout shortly before the sea and Long Sands, they turned right along Broadway. Houses, houses. Bank managers, insurance brokers, whoever. At Holy Saviour's, they headed down to Front Street. John nudged the long Volvo into one of the vacant parking spaces in the centre of the street.

Groups of lads and lasses were roaming from side to side, from the lights of the Salutation to those of the Cumberland Arms, onward to the Percy Arms or the Turk's Head. The church with its lopped-off spire was a designer emporium, rechristened The Land of Green Ginger.

Tony pointed to a high, white-painted terrace house.

'That's where she lodged. Miss Martineau.' His accent sounded broader already. 'There used to be a blue plaque, but it fell off.' His finger jerked. 'And that's where I lived. If you could call it living, after – after.' He cast a

227

fearful glance in the direction of the clock tower and the Castle upon Pen Bal Crag jutting into the sea, and his whole body twitched convulsively as if his brain had sent panic motor signals to his legs without consulting him.

John laid a hand on Tony's arm. 'It's all right,' he cooed. 'You'll feel happy. Free. Nothing will worry you. Come, let's try out the – ' he glanced up and down Front Street – ' 'the Gibraltar Arms, hmm?'

That pub and restaurant fronting the bottom of the street, isolated with its back to the Castle, was where Van Amburgh (and Shanky Elwes) had led Harry Bell, slavering and witless, for a brandy.

Ghosts seemed to walk Front Street as they headed towards the sea: spooks of soldiers and fishwives, urchins and ladies in bonnets, fancy girls, men in frock coats and top hats, even an organ-grinder, all weaving amidst the groups of late-twentieth-century youth, themselves haunted by a scourge.

Despite all the parked cars and electric street lighting, despite disco music drifting from the Turk's Head as the door opened, despite the white bright window of the fish-and-chip shop and the pastel-lit Indian restaurant, Brenda felt lost in the past, sucked back a century; she fingered her high collar.

Her feet were walking towards where John said; and towards *when*. Walking joyfully. The joy was a magnet which directed her steps, which pulled her along, relishing her approach, anticipative. She wanted to cry out for help to the modern youths in the street, but somehow couldn't. She could only cry out, she thought dimly, to Harry Bell. To Tony. He too was walking where John said he should, looking blankly content.

It came to Brenda that John – no, that Jack – was controlling her. He was conducting how she acted.

How could that be? And yet he was. She knew it.

228

Somehow, somewhere on the journey down from Newcastle she had crossed a boundary, a borderline – into Jack's world. She was a prisoner of his mind.

'This has nothing to do with hypnosis!' she thought in panic. 'This is something different.'

By now it was dark beyond the corridor of street lamps. Dark, except where silver brightness awoke in the stone windows of the Priory ruins; for as Jack had said it would, the Moon was peering through like some blotched radiant face. A car horn honked nearby, utterly muted.

'I don't think we really need a drink just yet, do we?' asked Jack. 'Nice night for a stroll down to the Haven.'

Soon they were descending the steep road by the side of the Castle moat towards the wedge of pebbles and sand between Pen Bal and the Spanish Battery. Little black shapes of beached boats humped in front of the yacht club; masts were dead trees. The light at the far end of the north pier twitched, twitched. The light of the south pier echoed it from over an oily vagueness of vast water.

They walked the path towards the root of the pier right under the crag and its ruins. The huge crane crouched on the pier like a dingy behemoth, growing larger. She smelled salt-tang and weed. The Moon watched equably. It had nothing to do with this, although its face was utterly cold and coldness was part of what was happening. Coldness and furnace heat.

Sweating, shivering, Brenda pulled the shawl tighter round her shoulders. She flushed. Her ecstasy enfolded her.

Had this powerlessness, this impotence, only occurred on the way to the coast that night? Or had she crossed that strange terrible boundary long before? Such as . . . that day on Jesmond Road when her joy had first awoken? Had she really entered Jack's world then?

She had gone to his study. She had sat in his chair and

229

started reading. She had entered into Jingling Geordie's Hole – and the hole *had entered into her*.

She couldn't understand how, but she realized that it was so. Inside herself, she could still think her own thoughts. Were they really her own, or someone else's? She could feel fear for herself. And yet inexorably she was approaching closer to . . . To.

If only she could scream; yet she could only scream inside. She mustn't scream; she must trust her joy. Her joy was the key. Sand, blown on to the path some other day, gritted under her boots.

Where did her joy come from? Surely not from . . . Only her joy stood between herself and the worm, like a thin membrane, a hymen. She was Jane, poor Jane, being led by Harry Bell and one other towards Jingling Geordie's Hole only a century and a half late. Knowing, knowing where she was being led.

'As you see, the pier's locked up for the night,' remarked Jack when they arrived at the rust-bobbled iron gate blocking the route out to sea. He mounted the twist of steps cut through the sea-wall to the left. She followed; Tony followed. An open iron wicket gave access to the long steep flight of granite steps plunging down outside the wall to the scree of pebbles which the great black North Sea lapped at, licking and retreating.

'Let's take a walk along the rocks.' Jack descended. He flipped on a small pocket torch. 'A bit slippery here. Don't stumble.'

By the light of that torch and by moonlight he led them over the crunchy pebbles then across the igneous dyke.

Brenda sensed the worm moving, and the frozen lava melting – unblocking the subterranean passages and vents – so that new hot lava boiled out of the depths. And yes . . . ! This vision came to her as powerfully as that other vision in Jack's study: the lava blasted the top off

230

Pen Bal Crag, tossing the ruins of Castle and Priory sky high, creating a small volcano at the bottom of Front Street, wreathed in steam where the sea licked its eastern flanks, the tongues of water boiling and evaporating.

Ancient Earth, restored at the edge of this seaside resort! A furnace in the crucible of the crater. Ships at sea could ignore the granite lighthouse at the end of the pier. They could set their course by the Tynemouth volcano. In the crucible there would swim . . . the worm, flames licking around it. Toss a rusty old hammer into the crater and the head would be spat out golden, transformed.

As they neared the source, the world shifted even more; became almost wholly Jack's world, and the worm's. There were gradients, strata. She was nearing the bottom of those strata, deep inside the artifices of another mind, the subconscious of reality.

But not yet locked into the final depth. Pods of slithery slauk popped beneath her boots, and she staggered sideways into a rock pool, barely regaining her balance. She tried to tear herself away. Where was her ecstasy now? Ahead, ahead. Not far.

'Aaaa – !' she cried at last; only the North Sea could have listened.

'Not far now,' Jack repeated cockily. For an instant his glasses caught and mirrored the moonlight, and were two tiny moons themselves as if his eyes had swollen and phosphoresced, altering into some other kind of eye.

If she could dash those spectacles from his face, maybe she would be able to see another way than his. She raised a hand to do so, but it was the wrong hand. Jack stood on her other side. Confused, her gesture robbed of energy, she let her hand flap back.

Had she ever really touched a boy called Peter?

How could she break that vision when she was part of it, trapped in it?

231

'How . . . ?' she gasped at him.

Jack had swallowed John totally by now, ingesting him from the inside out, emerging to wrap around him like a hungry shawl.

He laughed. 'Whisht, lass, haad yor gob! Aa'm tellin' ye an aaful story.'

'Is that all it is?' she managed to say. 'Am I still really in Jesmond Road?'

The sea hissed like a nest of snakes.

'Oh no, Brenda, it's happening. Now here we are at the cave. We climb up. It's only a little cave these days because our Harry set off that bomb and brought the roof down. But we'll all fit in, as easily as Gavin and Ted. And it has depths beyond depths. It opens up those depths to the bugle note, to the magical deed, to the act of ecstasy. Which dissolves the stone. Then it seals up again. Perhaps.'

Harry and Brenda followed the torch, and Harry assisted her into the dark little cave carpeted by dead black weed. Jack squatted in the mouth between them and the sea.

'Take your pants off, Harry,' Jack purred. 'You're here again. This is what you wanted. This is where you wanted it. It'll cure you. Here's Jane, waiting for it. You're the key, Harry, she's the keyhole. Put your key in and unlock her. Into whichever keyhole you prefer, the back door or the front.'

Paralysis numbed Brenda as Harry – Tony – unzipped his grey suit trousers, so like a schoolboy's long flannel trousers, and let them down. He tore his trainers off, in order to pull the trousers over his feet. Jack played the torch beam helpfully. Harry's striped-blue underpants were bulging. He hauled these off and stepped at a crouch towards her, wagging.

'No,' Brenda murmured. She couldn't move. It seemed

as if Jack's hands gripped her arms, and her legs too, even though he was some distance from her.

Harry fumbled with her skirt. Loosening the tartan, he slid it down, lifting her left foot then her right as she stooped, swaying; and laid the skirt down as a rug. He tugged her cotton knickers off. She had always worn white cotton knickers, in Jack's mind.

Then Harry made her kneel on the skirt. Her limbs obeyed him. He spread her limbs so that she lay out-spread, on her front. Prostrate, her breasts squashed against stone.

A fire burned into her, and she struggled. His weight was on her, jerking.

'Ted!' he hissed into her ear. Not Jane now, but Ted. A big Ted. She squealed and her fists beat the rock, clawing torn weed. Her brain jingled like a pocketful of loose change. Harry began to groan.

The worm was coming. Was coming.

Dull pearly light filled the cave. Light glowed through the wall in front of her face. The stone was dissolving, becoming transparent. She saw a long smooth corridor stretching into the distance. Down that corridor, tumbling over and over, shifting shape, sped a swelling blob of white matter.

When Harry cried out, the worm came. Brenda felt herself drawn inside the stone, away from the burning poker into a cool, solid clasp of eternity inside a whiteness with no detail anywhere, no shape. A photographic negative of blackness.

'Who?' a voice gibbered at her. 'Is it Gav? Don't come near, Gav! After . . . after. . . long. It's long. Only a therm-o-nuclear explosion could melt us out. Turn us to gas, and end us. Could kill the white stone octopus. Climb in the crane and bomb the rock to atoms. Gav, is it you? No, don't come near. Don't touch.'

233

Somehow she reached him and cradled him in her white invisible arms, wrapped him in her white invisible legs, in her soft tough sucking tentacles.

'No, Gav, don't!' he shrieked.

She had to hold something, touch something, feel something struggling. If she clutched him for long enough his senses might return. Hers might.

She went on holding Ted, and remembered hot ecstasy.

I read what Jack had typed, and stood up swaying. I had no memory of any of this, none at all. Surely this was only a story? Yet . . . what if not? The sun shone upon the back gardens of Jesmond Road. Eleven o'clock on a Wednesday morning, by my watch.

Downstairs the telephone started to ring. It went on ringing. Ordinarily Brenda should have answered. Where was she?

Where was *Jack*?

Whoever was calling wouldn't quit, so I hurried down to Brenda's office.

'John Cunningham speaking.'

'Thank God. This is Andrew Jarvis, Brenda's father. Is she there?'

I visualized him: a short, thick-set, balding man with a ruddy face. Brenda couldn't be here, or she would have taken the call.

'No,' I said, 'she isn't.'

'Well, do you know where she *is*?'

'I'm afraid I don't.'

'Look, she didn't come home last night. We thought maybe the two of you might have . . . how do I put this?'

'I understand what you mean.' We might have spent the night together.

'This isn't like Brenda – not coming home, and not calling us by now. Something's wrong. You *did* go down

234

to Tynemouth last night? That wasn't just a story she was telling us?'

Did we? Didn't we?

'Are you still there, Doctor?'

'Yes.'

'Yes, *what*? Did you go to Tynemouth?'

I could only take my cue from Jack's story, so it seemed safest to agree.

'We did.'

'For heaven's sake, did you bring her back to Newcastle afterwards? Whereabouts? To your own house?'

'Well, I dropped her off,' I said. 'She wanted to walk. Clear her head.' Implications of tipsiness. Not my fault.

'What time about?'

'Maybe eleven. This is worrying, Mr Jarvis. I think you ought to contact the police.'

'Was she with that *other* fellow? The disturbed one? Did you drop them both off together?'

What had happened to Tony? Jack had written nothing about that. Tony might be able to contradict me. If only I could break off and call Fenwick's, get Tony on the phone. *If* he was at Fenwick's. Carol Armstrong hadn't phoned me, hunting for him. She had been getting pissed off, hadn't she? Maybe she had walked out. Or no longer cared.

'Yes, I dropped him off too.' Don't say where. Let Jarvis assume.

'Was he behaving disturbed?'

'I wouldn't describe him as disturbed. Anyway, I shouldn't discuss – '

'God almighty, Brenda's missing! She walked off into the night with a nutter! *Where?*'

'Beside Jesmond Dene – that's where she asked to be dropped.'

'The *Dene*? That's no place for a young woman to be

alone. Oh but she wasn't alone, was she? You're trying to protect this nutter of yours! Don't you realize that Brenda might be – ' he hesitated – 'might still be in the Dene? If you follow me. The bloody irresponsibility of it. And we thought that you two – ' Jarvis's voice caught on what might have been a sob. 'You're damn right I'm calling the police.' He rang off.

No, Brenda wasn't in the Dene. Lying murdered under a rhododendron. No body in the Dene.

She was inside Pen Bal Crag, where no search party could ever find her. She was encased along with Ted. The worm had embalmed her alive with the elixir of life, transmuting her to ectoplasm which could exist inside stone. Sensible place to live everlastingly; inside of stone. Better than being inside a tree, or a book. Books fall apart, trees rot. I glanced out of Brenda's window at the cemetery across the way, but those were only dead stones over there. They didn't have souls locked inside them.

Jack's typescript upstairs!

'You've got to burn that, old son.' That wasn't Jack talking; that was me. Talking to myself.

Forget about calling Fenwick's. What did it matter? My word should outweigh Tony's any day. Get rid of the evidence – the utterly mad evidence. That's how Jack's account would seem, if anyone else read it.

Where was Jack?

Gone away, sublimated, evaporated into his own domain of the imagination – where he had triumphed and become a free-ranging elemental, a spook, a ghost, a demon spirit.

On the way back up to the study I remembered to look in on Mother.

She was sitting up in bed, with a book; so she was all right.

'Where's Brenda this morning?' she asked.

I noticed her breakfast tray on the side-table. Plate,

236

cup and saucer, teapot. Someone had brought breakfast earlier on. Me. In a hypnotic trance, induced by Jack.

'Mr Jarvis phoned, Mother. Brenda didn't go home last night. He's worried sick. He's calling the police.'

'Oh John, this is awful. What can have happened?'

'I don't know. You must excuse me. Things are frantic.' I backed out.

'Tell me the moment you know anything!'

'Yes.' I shut the door, and hurried to the study. There was still an open fireplace in the room. Never used – an electric heater stood in front. The fireplace wasn't blocked off, nor the chimney. Never got around to it. Would any neighbour notice a small column of smoke puffing from our chimney? In the desk I found a book of matches from the Midland Hotel, Birmingham. Souvenir of Jack's weekend of glory.

Shift the heater aside. Crumple the pages in the grate. Apply lighted matches. Ten minutes' work at the most.

Like some faith-healer absorbing the essence I rested both hands on the typescript.

I shouldn't have done that. It came to me with total and instant conviction that if I burnt these pages I would be annihilating Brenda. And maybe Ted too. Maybe even Jack, my missing part.

Maybe Brenda would want to be extinguished, rather than being locked in that rock. Maybe not. She had someone to touch.

I was in the story too. Would I extinguish myself in the fire, like some spontaneously combusting person? Would there only be grease in the grate, smuts on the rug, a scorched empty bundle of clothes?

If only I could re-enter the story, take control of it, change it.

Sitting down, I fed a clean sheet of paper into the typewriter.

* * *

Phone ringing again. Or the front door bell. No, just Mother's bell. Still time.

The world's still fluid. Everything's loose. I can alter it. I can sense the worm! Writhing in Tynemouth.

I can escape – into a previous life! There's the place to hide. Never believed in past lives, myself, not until now. It's my speciality, right? My area of expertise. Now I believe in it. Escaping into the future: that's not on. There's no future till it occurs. Can't leap ahead. The past exists, though. Because it existed.

The worm wants me. It's reaching out. Don't I belong with Brenda, inside the rock? In her white invisible tentacles?

Bells ringing. Mother, phone, door. All of them at once. Bells in my brain.

Jack has gone; but I can still be someone else.

> '"Why call us to revoltless doom?"'
> With grief the opening buds reply.'

Mumbling his own lyric words to himself, John Cunningham slouches slowly along Broad Chare, heading away from the quayside, Rialto of Newcastle. In one hand he clutches a torn handkerchief, from which a herring pokes. A cart clatters by, the horse's hooves striking sparks from the road slabs.

A herring for his supper. A fishy, not even on a dishy. What a catch, from that cran barrel while backs were turned. What a treasure. He might as well hoy it down a well, the way the accursed young Lambton tossed the worm down a well in the old story! As he stares at the fish it seems to twist in his hand, and its glossy dead eye mesmerizes him.

He's drawing abreast of an old haunt. It's the High Dykes Tavern. Long, tiny-paned corbelled windows, top-heavy upper storeys with upside-down battlements of beams – and an archway to ale. He's aware that someone is dogging him inquisitively. Someone is passing by and loitering, pencilling away in an open leather-bound book.

John pays scant heed. The eye of the herring has captured him, and he has remembered himself. All his struggles as a poet and an actor are burning away like mist. After forty-five years of life, he has recalled who he is.

He is John Cunningham.

He'll surely die in a few days' time. Almost within hours. He feels like death warmed up.

What matters death? Isn't verse immortal? More to the point, isn't *he*? He'll be reborn, of course. Later in time, or earlier. Why not earlier still? He is, after all, on the run. The worm will eat his mind, and spit it hindwards, back into the past, maybe disgorging him at Lambton Castle.

Meanwhile, must keep body and soul together. Slowly John shambles back towards Mr and Mrs Slack's premises in Union Street, to fry the fish and eat it.

'You wet fart. I'm going to write horrors on your heart. You'll be Ted, and you'll be Gavin. You'll be Harry Bell. Particularly Harry Bell. I have you all taped. You're all recorded in stone. It's just a question of shuffling the tapes around, melting them into each other. You could call me a tapeworm.'

The voice is Jack's. It is also the worm's. And it is his own.

There's an infinite white tunnel. White space, white stone. He's encased in rock under Tynemouth Castle; he's the writing in the seaside rock, and a worm's licking it.

'And when you're hot enough with the horror of it, and

mad enough, maybe I'll free myself. Maybe I'll dive back into the fire I came from.'

It must be that the worm reached out to him from Jingling Geordie's Hole years since. It mesmerized him, wrote Jack into him. Now it has him.

The worm must have Tony too. At last. Tony didn't get away this time.

'Where's Brenda?' he begs; though he already knows the answer.

'Oh, *she's* here. Nearby. But also, far far away. You could try to reach her. Crawl up the tunnel, eh? And she'll crawl away, clutching Ted. But she'll be crawling *after you*, too. Or will that be Tony who's crawling after you? – Gavin mistaking you for Ted? There's so much time, so many possibilities, once death is undone, dear John.'

> Noo lads, Aa'll haad me gob,
> That's aall Aa knaa aboot the story
> Ov Sor John's clivvor job
> Wi' the aaful Lambton Worm.